PRETTY LITTLE LIES

RETRIBUTION SERIES
BOOK 3

MORGAN JAMES

ABOUT THE BOOK

After the mission three years that nearly ended my life, all I want is peace and quiet in my sleepy little town. When I find Jules sleeping in her car on the side of the road, I feel an immediate pull to the green-eyed beauty. The darkness in her eyes tells me she harbors a deep secret, and the bruises covering her body elicit a protectiveness I never knew existed.

There are a thousand reasons why I should stay far, far away, but none of them seem to matter when she looks at me with those wide, innocent eyes. Everything about her is wrong… but so very right. When Jules is drawn into a deadly trap, I'll do everything in my power to protect the woman who's come to mean everything to me.

ONE

GIULIANA

The first footfall made my heart beat double-time, and I inhaled deeply, trying to slow its rapid pace.

Thump-thump. Thump-thump.

Two hours.

Seven thousand, two hundred beats.

Once, I'd counted each and every one. But the higher I counted, the more anxious I became. I clenched my eyes closed tighter and drew in a deep, calming breath, trying to bring the sights and sounds of the beach back into focus. I could feel the heat of the sun on my skin, the shifting of the grains of sand as I pulled my knees more tightly to my chest. A slight breeze blew in over the ocean, whipping strands of hair across my face, and waves lapped gently at the shore, bringing with them the salty scent of the ocean.

The vibration of another footstep against the hard floor ripped me from my reverie, and I tightened my hold on my legs. The footsteps drew closer, and I reluctantly opened my eyes. Darkness pressed in around me, and my heart kicked into overdrive as my chest rose and fell on shallow, uneven breaths. The air inside the tiny closet felt thick and hot, making it hard to breathe.

The door suddenly flew open, and I blinked against the rectangle of light. My uncle's form was outlined in the garish glow, and I forced myself not to flinch away from him. I wished I could physically retreat to my beach as I'd done in my daydreams. It'd become a coping mechanism for me, much like soldiers or agents who used such mental tactics when captured and tortured.

"Get up."

My knees ached as I unfolded myself from the floor. It took a moment for the blood to resume flowing normally after hours of being cramped up, and I felt a bit light-headed as I leaned one shoulder against the wall. The closet was my uncle's favorite form of abuse; he knew how much I hated dark, enclosed spaces. It wasn't the first time he'd punished me this way—but it would be the last. All because I'd asked to leave the house.

Uncle Massimo's face twisted into a sneer, and he spun on a heel as if disgusted by the sight of me. My heart clenched in my chest, knowing that it was probably true, though I was unsure exactly why he felt that way. I tried so hard to blend into the background, to avoid drawing attention to myself, but I never seemed to escape his notice.

I wiped my clammy hands on my skirt before straightening my shoulders and stepping into his office. My uncle sat behind the wide cherry desk, his expression unreadable as I closed the closet door behind me and turned to face him. No one ever spoke without my uncle's permission. We stared at each other for a long moment, and my fingers twitched at my sides. It was a nervous tic I couldn't control, and one that I knew my uncle hated most of all. I'd started picking at my nails soon after my father's death, and it irked my uncle to no end.

I was, at all times, supposed to be a poised, perfect

porcelain doll. Uncle resented me for being the only child of his brother, former capo of the Capaldi family, and I knew his plan was to marry me off. I should've been married nearly two years ago, but thanks to my cousin Matteo's pleading, Uncle agreed to push the wedding back to my twentieth birthday. I had hoped it would be someone in the *famiglia* that I was comfortable with, at least.

Unfortunately, that wasn't the case. My birthday was a little over a week away, and Uncle Massimo had arranged my betrothal to Nikolai, a member of the Russian Bratva. The fighting had escalated after Daddy's death, the death toll climbing each week until Massimo struck a deal with their captain. Nikolai needed a wife; I was to fill that role.

Our marriage was intended to strengthen the bonds between the two families and settle the unrest. That was all fine and good for the others—but what about me? Nikolai was notoriously cruel, and I'd heard stories that made my stomach turn. Matteo said he'd been married twice before. Both women had mysteriously disappeared and, as far as I knew, they'd never been seen or heard from again. I'd pled for my uncle to reconsider, but my efforts were rewarded with two hours spent in the dark, cramped closet I'd just exited.

I barely repressed a shudder. I hated the closet—but I hated the idea of marrying an abusive man more. A white gown hung in my room, just waiting for me to put it on and walk down the aisle for my big day—a day I vowed would never happen.

Uncle met my gaze and lifted a well-manicured dark eyebrow. "Well?"

I swallowed down my unease, once more asking the question I'd dared to bring up more than two hours ago. "I wish to go to the mall today."

Uncle stared at me for a moment. "Weren't you just there

last week? I seem to remember you spending nearly three hundred dollars last time."

Three hundred dollars of my money. Though I had technically inherited everything after my father passed, my uncle had taken it upon himself to act as my advisor. What that truly meant was that he owned me. He kept me confined to the house, not allowing me interaction with anyone, not even my own mother. On the rare occasion that I was allowed to leave the house, it was under the intense scrutiny of at least two guards.

He said it was for my safety; I knew better. He wanted to keep me away from everyone—especially anyone who might be able to overthrow his complete and total power over me. Once he married me off, the money that was rightfully mine would go to my new husband—half of it, at least. It was part of the deal that Massimo had struck with Nikolai. I'd be damned if I would be traded like chattel.

Refusing to back down, I pleaded my case. "It's for my fashion blog," I started, and he let out a stifled noise.

He waved one hand in the air. "Isn't it about time you grow up and give that thing up? No one cares about it anyway."

I bit my tongue at the slight. I actually did have several hundred followers, but he was right about one thing—I didn't care about the blog in the least. It was a front, a necessary evil, and something I had to stick to for the time being. "Please, Uncle," I requested.

"No." He picked up his pen again and began to write, the decisive action signaling the end of our conversation. Desperation crawled up my throat.

"Uncle," I started, then immediately snapped my mouth closed. His cold, dark eyes snapped to mine, and the set of his shoulders told me I'd made a grave mistake. Slowly, he stood from his chair and rounded the desk. His gaze never strayed from mine, and my legs trembled with the urge to run. My heart raced wildly in my chest as each step brought him closer until he was barely a foot away.

"Why must you always learn the hard way, Giuliana?"

I swallowed down the hatred filling me and bit off the response that jumped to the tip of my tongue. Curling my hand into a fist at my side, I dug the nail of my index finger into my thumb. The slight pain helped to ground me.

Unfortunately, my uncle did not miss the movement. With lightning fast speed, he snatched up my wrist and brought it between us. Unfurling my hand, he examined my nails, and a sneer marred his handsome features. "Have you been biting your nails again?"

My hand shook where he held it, and I stumbled over my words. "I… I've been trying not to, Uncle." His grip tightened on my wrist, and I knew I would have bruises from those long fingers pressed against my skin.

"Haven't I told you how much I despise that habit?"

"I'm sorry—" I started, but he cut over me.

"How do you expect a man like Nikolai to marry you when you look so filthy all the time?"

The sharp barb sent a pain through my chest, but I refused to rise to his bait.

"I asked you a question!" In a move that took my breath away, Uncle released my hands and gripped my biceps. With a hard shove, he slammed me against the wall. A spark of pain shot through my head, sending a shower of black spots swirling before my eyes.

Before I could recover and even contemplate formulating a response, he released me, throwing me to the side and off-balance. I stumbled and fell, unable to get my hands in front of me in time. My head struck the sideboard on the way down, and pain shot through me as I crumpled to the floor.

Uncle Massimo pressed a polished Italian loafer to my throat, and I clawed at his leg, trying to get him to release me. My lungs burned and my throat ached as he slowly cut off the oxygen. Finally he stepped away and shook his head. "Worthless."

I scrambled away, clutching my throat and pressing my back to the wall, putting as much distance between us as possible. I didn't know why he hated me so much, but I knew that, despite his tendency to hurt me, he would never kill me. I was worth much more to him alive.

He shoved his hands in the pockets of his trousers and adopted a casual pose before speaking. "You may go. Be sure to get a dress for your engagement party."

My mind muddled, I managed to choke out the words, "Engagement party?"

"That's right." A snake-like smile curved his mouth. "Nikolai will be here for dinner after mass on Sunday. You'll want to make a good impression."

"B-but—"

With one swift move, my uncle closed the distance between us and wrapped a hand around my aching throat. He lifted me to my feet and slammed my back against the wall. "Your sacrifice will unite us with the Russians. There has been much unrest, and your marriage will be seen as a peace offering. We've been at odds too long. You are the key to our success." He released me and stepped away.

Fury burned through me, and I longed to scream at him. Biting my tongue, I dipped my head in a portrait of submission. It would do no good to argue with him. A long moment later, I flinched as his hand moved under my chin and directed my gaze to his.

"Clean yourself up before you go. And get a manicure while you're out. Your nails look disgusting."

I lifted my chin. "I'd planned to..., sir."

His dark eyes flared at the inflection—and complete lack of respect—in that last word. His thumb and forefinger tightened on my chin. "One of these days, Giuliana, you will push too far. Perhaps Nikolai will teach you some manners."

With that last parting shot, he thrust my chin away from him and strode back to his desk. Without another look at me, he settled into his chair and resumed his work.

I used the opportunity to silently slip out of the office before I let any tears fall. I hurt all over, my pride included, but I refused to let him see me cry. I wouldn't show weakness. Head held high, I made my way past the guards stationed at the office door and started toward my room. Matteo stepped out of the shadows and grabbed my wrist, pulling me to a halt. Skin still tender, I yanked my hand out of his grasp and massaged the sore flesh.

My cousin's eyebrows drew together, and he gingerly touched my hand. "What happened?"

The same thing that always happens.

I shook my head. "It's nothing."

Anger replaced his concern. "Did he hurt you?"

"Please don't say anything," I begged. It would just make it worse for both of us if Matteo put himself in the middle.

Matteo let out a hiss. "That bastard. I should kill him."

Neither of us were exempt from my uncle's cruel actions, and I knew Matteo would be punished worse if he stood up in my defense. I placed a hand on his shoulder. "My birthday is next week."

"Like I could forget," my cousin replied bitterly. "Did he say anything about it?"

I nodded. "Y-yes." I shakily drew a shuddering breath. "My engagement party is this Sunday."

Matteo's eyes flared wide before sympathy infused the dark brown deaths. He pulled me into a hug and spoke next to my ear. "Oh, *principessa*. I would stop it if I could."

His hold was too tight, and his sympathy nearly broke me. I eased out of his hold. "Everything will be fine," I promised. At least, I hoped that was the case.

Back in my room, I selected a large handbag and shoved the clothes I'd purchased last week into the very bottom before covering them with a magazine then draping a chic, decorative scarf over the side. I didn't want to stuff it too full and draw any attention to it, so I only selected the most expensive items. A knot had begun to form on my forehead from where I'd struck the sideboard, and I brushed my bangs to one side to cover it.

Johnny and Tommy fell into step beside me as I approached the front door and walked to the car. My leg bounced nervously the whole drive, and I finally let out a small sigh of relief when we reached the small boutique. The owner, Lila, smiled at me as we entered. She was the one person I could count on to always brighten my day, and I returned her heartfelt smile. She greeted me with a hug, and we immediately began to select items from the racks.

Blatantly ignoring the two bodyguards lurking by the front door, Lila and I made small talk as we searched. I spoke loudly and exuberantly about what I'd planned for this week's blog, hoping the men would tune me out.

Lila tossed a couple new items over her arm. "Let's try these first and see what you think."

Casting a look out of the corner of my eye at Tommy, I followed her to a dressing room in the back of the store. Lila entered first and hung up the clothes then turned to me as I entered. Her lips pressed into a firm line as she glanced at my forehead. She gave a slight shake of her head but didn't say a word; she just held out her hand and waited for me to retrieve the clothes I'd shoved into the bottom of my bag.

"Thank you for doing this," I whispered to her.

With an abrupt nod, she exited the dressing room and moved behind the counter, taking the items with her. I let out a deep breath as I closed the curtain behind her. *One step closer.*

I took my time trying on the clothes, not wanting to draw any attention to myself. Lila spoke to me through the curtain as I changed, and I stepped out to view myself in the three-way mirror when I was done. We examined the outfit for a moment, and I let Lila take a few pictures for my blog before deciding it was time for the next ensemble.

"Can you help unzip me?" I asked, just loudly enough for the men to hear.

"Of course," she replied, stepping into the dressing room behind me and closing the curtain. Lila unzipped the dress, and I turned around to face her. She held out several bills and I smiled gratefully as I slipped them from her fingers.

"You have no idea how much I appreciate this."

"There's a bag of clothes in the back hallway," she whispered. "Nothing fancy, just the basics to get you through," she said.

Impulsively, I pulled her into a tight hug. "Thank you so much."

"I'll miss you," she said, her eyes shiny with tears.

"Someday, I promise I'll repay you," I said.

She waved off my concern. "Just be safe."

With one last quick hug, she was gone, and I knew it was the last time I would ever see her. I listened for a moment as Lila kicked up a conversation with Tommy. I quickly changed into the nondescript yoga pants and long-sleeved shirt she'd left for me and grabbed my bag. Leaving my heels behind, I slipped into the ballet flats I'd stowed in my purse.

Sliding the curtain to one side, I peeked out. Johnny was staring at his cell phone, one foot crossed over the other as he leaned against the wall near the entrance of the store. Tommy was turned slightly away from me as he flirted with Lila.

Taking a deep breath, I slunk out of the dressing room and angled toward the back door. The knob turned easily under my fingertips, and I pushed it open just far enough for me to slide through, then closed it quietly behind me. The door exited into a dimly lit service hallway used for deliveries and for Lila to come and go each day.

Trying not to rustle the bag, I scooped up the clothes that

Lila had left for me and sent up one more silent thank you. Moving silently but quickly down the hallway, I exited into the back parking lot, keeping my head low.

I glanced around and found the car I was looking for. Lila's boyfriend had arranged the purchase of the small blue Cavalier and had left it in the back of the parking lot for me. I forced myself not to run even though my heart beat wildly, sure that I would be caught at any moment. I opened the rear door and tossed the clothes inside, along with my purse, before climbing into the driver seat.

I closed and locked the door, then fished around under the floor mat for the key. Shoving it into the ignition, I waited a heart-stopping second for the engine to turn over. As soon as it caught, I shifted into gear and pulled slowly out of the parking lot. Knuckles white, I curled my fingers around the steering wheel and turned onto the main drag.

Two hundred miles later, I finally stopped glancing in the rearview mirror. I had no idea where I was going, but it didn't matter. I was free.

TWO

ERIC

The woman screamed obscenities at me from the back seat, and I rolled my eyes at her lack of creativity. People were always doing dumb shit, but as sheriff I tried to treat them with common courtesy. More often than not, I let the person off with a warning and they were more than happy to get their head out of their ass and not do it again.

I'd been sheriff of Pine Ridge for just shy of two years, and the slow pace was a welcome change from the constant hustle and bustle and high crime rate back in Chicago. I enjoyed what I did, and I genuinely liked most of the people. Just like any other small town, we had our share of troublemakers, but even the bad apples here weren't that bad. Except maybe this one.

"You're despicable!" she spat.

Ironic, coming from a woman who was potentially an accessory to attempted murder. Best case, what she'd done was obstruction of justice.

Hands cuffed behind her, she leaned forward to close the distance between us. Like I couldn't hear her obnoxious voice well enough. "By the time I'm finished with you, you'll never work in law enforcement again!"

I clenched my jaw. I was sorely tempted to hit the brakes and throw her face-first into the cage dividing the cab of the cruiser. Unfortunately, I'd taken an oath to protect and serve, even for the worst of society, like the woman currently blistering my ears from the back seat. Plus, I'd just have to listen to her bitch even more if she ended up with a broken nose because of it.

I'd hoped that she would tire herself out, but her vile, senseless chatter as I navigated down the mountain toward Kalispell told me she'd only gotten started. The more I ignored her, the more fired up she got. I breathed a sigh of relief when the jail came into view.

I'd kept her in lockup overnight to let her cool her heels, but all she'd done was make a nuisance of herself. The small sheriff's office in Pine Ridge had only two holding cells, since we didn't see much in the way of crime. Or we hadn't until recently. The first murder the town had ever seen was more than a hundred years ago during the Gold Rush, when Harrison Leeds killed his partner out of greed. As of yesterday, we could add one more to that tally.

Jack Prescott had moved up to Pine Ridge several months ago and was in the process of building Briarleigh Lodge and Resort up on Mount Chineroot. He'd been having some trouble recently, mostly missing or damaged supplies—but when someone had hurt his fiancée, Mia, shit hit the fan. I didn't think I'd ever forget the sight that'd greeted me when I'd stepped into that clearing in the woods yesterday morning. I never would've forgiven myself if something had happened to Mia.

I couldn't say the same for the man who'd held her at gunpoint, though. He'd caught a bullet and probably died a better death than he deserved. Though cause of death was obvious, EMS had taken the body down to the funeral parlor yesterday so the town mortician, Dick Chancellor, could perform the official autopsy. After everything Jack and Mia had been through recently, I felt obligated to bring the woman in myself.

I pulled into the garage attached to the jail and watched as the large bay door slid shut behind me. I'd radioed ahead to let dispatch know I was transporting the prisoner this morning, so they were ready for me by the time I climbed out of my cruiser. I unclipped my taser and duty carry from my belt and placed both in a lockbox, then slipped the key into my pocket.

The woman fought my hold as I helped her from the back seat. "Get your filthy hands off me!"

She stumbled, and I clamped one hand around her elbow to keep her from taking a header straight into the concrete floor. With a shake of my head, I tapped a button to open the first set of steel doors to enter the jail. A loud clanking noise filled the air as the lock disengaged and the door swung open. A corrections officer stood just inside, a tiny smirk on her face. "Sheriff."

Lips pressed into a firm line, I gave a tight nod as I practically dragged my prisoner along. "Hey, Russo."

As soon as the door closed, securing us inside, I released the woman into Russo's care. I couldn't wait to wash my hands of her completely. While Russo searched my prisoner and stripped her of her belongings, I filled out an inmate form with the woman's information. All the while, she raged on, screaming at the top of her lungs that we were violating her rights and that her lawyer would be there soon. With the waist-deep shit she was in, I welcomed the opportunity.

As soon as Russo was finished, she opened the second set of doors to lead the prisoner, now clad in a bright orange jumpsuit, inside. "Coming, Sheriff?"

"Yes, ma'am. I'd like to speak with Rooney if he's around."

"Down by dispatch," she tossed over her shoulder. "You know the way."

Though she couldn't see me, I nodded in acknowledgement. I trailed along as Russo led the woman to another steel door and waited for it to be buzzed open. As soon as we crossed into the next section of the jail, I turned to the right while Russo led the woman off to the side. Rooney stepped out of an office and greeted me with a tip of the chin. "Donahue."

I stuck out a hand and shook. "Sheriff."

Together, we watched Russo settle the woman in front of a screen to have her mugshot taken. She looked like she'd been on a weeklong bender, her hair mussed and makeup smudged. All the while, she shot me hateful glares.

"She's a pleasant one," Rooney commented from the side of his mouth.

"No shit," I huffed under my breath. I was sure this wasn't the last I'd see of her; if not physically, I'd at least get a call from her lawyer as she'd threatened. Thank God for body cams. A tiny smile lifted my mouth. I couldn't wait for them to review the footage for themselves and watch her crazy ass unleash hell.

Turning my attention to a more important matter, I spoke up. "I got statements from the victims this morning. Report's been uploaded for you."

Rooney nodded. "Appreciate it. See what we can do."

I wasn't sure how involved the woman was in the events that had transpired. The jury would have to determine whether justice would be served. I prayed they would get the full story out of her, because we wouldn't be getting any details from the body in the morgue.

"Ready for vacation?"

Rooney was taking his wife of twenty-five years on a weeklong cruise down around Mexico. They'd never gotten around to having kids, so instead they spent their spare time traveling and enjoying each other.

He grinned. "Deanna is already packed and ready to go."

"When do you fly out?"

"Not 'til the beginning of next week."

I laughed and shook my head. "Nothing wrong with being prepared."

"Just grateful I won't have to deal with this shit for a whole week." Rooney jerked his chin toward the prisoner, and I nodded in commiseration.

"Amen." I touched the brim of my hat. "Thanks again, and safe travels."

I took my leave and wound my way back through the maze of corridors and steel doors. I nodded at the corrections officer, then grabbed my taser and pistol from the lockbox and hopped into the cruiser.

As I headed back toward Pine Ridge, I felt a weight lift off my shoulders. I prayed that, now that this was over, the quiet peacefulness would descend again and we could all get back to normal. As I merged onto I-93, my phone rang, and I groaned when I recognized the number.

Reluctantly, I tapped the button to answer and lifted the phone to my ear. "Hey, Cynthia."

"Oh, God, Eric... I think he's back."

I briefly closed my eyes and drew in a steadying breath. The worry in her voice was real, though unfounded. We'd had the same conversation several times over the past few months. "Just take a deep breath, Cynthia. Everything's fine."

Cynthia's ex-husband, Josh Drummond, had worked under me for several months by the time I'd found out what was happening. Josh had kept Cynthia sequestered at home away from prying eyes, but things had grown increasingly worse. She'd finally come to me in confidence after being treated for several broken ribs in the hospital, and I'd encouraged her to press charges and file for divorce.

With Josh in jail and Cynthia now working as a waitress at Rosie's Diner in Pine Ridge, she'd been forced to sell their house. The meager profits had been split between her and Josh, and Cynthia had moved in with her mother on the outskirts of town. My former deputy had definitely fallen from grace, but he'd brought it on himself the moment he chose to raise a hand to his wife.

"But I heard—"

"Cynthia." I kept my tone friendly but firm. "He's still serving his term, and he's aware of the restraining order that will go into effect once he's released. Sheriff Rooney will let me know if anything happens."

On the other end, Cynthia drew in a shuddering breath. "Thank you for everything. I don't know how to repay you."

Wisely, I didn't respond. I had a feeling I knew exactly what form of payment she would prefer. Ever since she'd pressed charges for assault and Josh had been placed in jail, Cynthia had started reaching out to me. The initial innocent, friendly phone calls had gradually become more frequent and insistent. I always tried to maintain a professional demeanor, hoping that, in time, she would turn her attention elsewhere.

After a long, awkward silence, she finally spoke again. "Well, I'm sure you're busy. I'll let you go."

"Take care, Cynthia."

I hung up before she could come up with something else and shoved down the guilt for doing so. I genuinely felt bad for the woman, but I refused to cross that line with her.

The hairs on the back of my arms lifted, and I glanced around, checking the rearview mirror, taking in my surroundings. Nothing seemed out of place. Still, I couldn't disregard the chill that had settled over my skin. It was that little instinct that'd saved my ass more than once, and I refused to disregard it. Forty peaceful miles later, I began to think I was losing my edge.

The prickle in my spine never went away, and as I crossed the line into Pine Ridge, my radio crackled to life.

THREE

GIULIANA

I bit my lip as I eyed my gas gauge, the needle of which had been dipping perilously close to empty for the past half-hour. If I drove any farther, I'd be running on fumes. I was quickly learning just how often I had to fill up the gas tank.

When Daddy taught me to drive, I hadn't really understood the concept. The tank was always full. Now, hundreds of miles—and dollars—later, I was beginning to realize that I needed money if I planned to keep going.

I eased up on the accelerator and coasted down a little knoll. As if fate had directed it, a billboard came into view on the right side of the road. The once-red words, now faded almost completely to pink, read "The Fox Hole, five miles."

I drummed my fingers on the wheel and bit my lip. It was the first place I'd seen in the past forty minutes, each mile of road growing more desolate than the last. I mentally cursed myself for not grabbing a map at the last gas station I'd stopped at a few hours ago. I'd decided to just keep driving until I found someplace that looked, well... safe.

I wasn't very good with geography, so I'd spent a lot of

time over the past week driving aimlessly. I'd wanted to get away from the city as quickly as possible, but I didn't want my uncle to find me so easily. Instead of setting out with a destination in mind, I'd headed south.

A few hours later, I'd turned west and ended up circling back up to the north. A couple hours ago, I crossed the Montana border. Though I'd had this idea in my mind that it was the Wild West, in a lot of ways most of the towns looked normal. It was almost disappointing. I didn't want to be in a city though, surrounded by tons of people. So I'd kept driving. Which had led me here—to the Fox Hole.

I'd heard of places like these. What were they called? Sportsman's clubs? A few minutes later, another sign came into view: "The Fox Hole, next right." *Keep driving or take my chances here?* My heart leaped in my chest as I flicked on my turn signal and steered onto the next road, following the arrow.

A few moments later, a small building came into sight. Dilapidated and made of rusted gray steel, the Fox Hole looked a little worse for wear. Still, I was in no position to be picky. Plus, it kind of made sense. Out here in the wilderness was the perfect place for a sportsman's club—if that's what this was. A faded Molson sign listed precariously over the door, but I saw nothing else on the exterior to give me any clue of what I might find inside.

Hopefully, I could at least get something to eat, maybe ask for a job. Worst case, if they weren't hiring, maybe they could tell me who was. I climbed from the car, inspecting the outside of the building as I did so. Other than an eagle on the side of the building and a flashing Open sign over the front door, there was nothing else. The windows appeared dark and dingy, and a slight shiver ran down my spine.

This wasn't ideal, but it wasn't long-term. I needed food in my belly and gas in my tank. God willing, maybe I could make some money to spend on a hotel room. Last night I'd forgone a room completely to save money. It had been cold and miserable, and I had no desire to do it again.

Besides, this couldn't be the worst thing in the world. I figured that rugged, bearded outdoorsmen were infinitely better than what I'd come from. Up here in the mountains, I wouldn't have to worry about anyone recognizing me or hanging around too long.

I stepped into the building—and froze as the door slammed shut behind me. My eyes slowly began to adjust to the dim light, and I scrunched up my nose as the smell of alcohol mingling with disinfectant and... something else hung in the air. It took me a moment to process exactly what I was seeing before my mind made the connection. *Oh, God....*

Several pairs of eyes turned to me, and I was tempted to turn around and flee back out the door. Swallowing hard and steeling my spine, I pushed through the fog-like scents and made my way deeper into the room. Music pulsed through the speakers, and a few grizzled men sat next to a narrow but empty stage. Music switched up, and my heart returned to its normal pace as the next performer stepped out and their attention swung back to something more interesting than a newcomer.

It was still fairly early, just before dinnertime, so I wasn't surprised that the place was mostly empty. A quick scan of the room showed a middle-aged man behind the bar rearranging bottles and glasses. He lifted a brow at me as I moved closer and he spoke around the toothpick sticking out between his lips. "Need some help?"

"Hi. Um..." My gaze darted around the room once more. I'd yet to see any cocktail waitresses milling around, and it filled me with hope. "I'm looking for a job. Maybe waiting tables or something?"

His dark gaze slid down my body before meeting my eyes again. "Talk to Shirlene. Down that hallway"—he pointed to the back of the bar—"last door on the left."

"Thank you." Giving a quick nod of acknowledgement, I followed the man's directions and found myself in front of a dingy white steel door that had seen better days. Rusting along the bottom and showing a myriad of greasy fingerprints and other marks, I grimaced and used two fingers to turn the handle.

I stepped into the locker room, my senses immediately assaulted by the aroma of multiple perfumes competing with one another as they wafted on the stale air. Several chairs were set up in front of a mirror, the counter cluttered with makeup, hair accessories, and other beauty paraphernalia. Scantily clad women occupied most of the chairs, and others milled around at the end of the room, clothes flying through the air in the makeshift closet area.

Venturing further into the room, I shot the woman closest to me a tentative smile. "Um, hi. I'm looking for Shirlene."

The woman looked me up and down before raising a brow and returning to her makeup. Clearly they weren't receptive to new hires. Dropping my eyes from her, I walked toward the closet. Aerosol hairspray and glitter formed a cloud in the air, and I choked on the foul material, batting it away.

A bleach-blonde and a redhead stood in the middle of the dressing area, arguing heatedly.

"You know that's mine!" The blonde grabbed at something in the redhead's hands, but she held it high over her head, using her extra four inches of height to her advantage.

"It's mine! I get compliments on this one all the time!"

"Shirl!" the blonde yelled over her shoulder without taking her gaze off the redhead. "Ginny stole my gold G-string!"

I stopped in my tracks.

"Did not!" the redhead—Ginny—retorted. "Sabrina is a

lying cunt!" Her palm whipped out and caught the blonde across the cheek.

"Oh!" Sabrina clutched her face, eyes round with surprise. "You fucking Amazon bitch! I'm going to kill you!"

"Ladies!" An older woman came around the corner, her raspy, pack-a-day smoker's voice cutting through the argument. "We have plenty of outfits to go around."

I examined the small woman in the too-tight clothes. Her skin was several shades too dark, as if she spent twenty minutes a day in a tanning bed. Wrinkles bracketed her eyes and mouth, caked with a layer of makeup. Smoky eyeshadow and black eyeliner paired with her wine-colored lipstick made her look like the Alice Cooper of house mothers.

Shirlene pushed between the two younger women and held out her hand expectantly. With a roll of her eyes, Ginny dropped the G-string into the woman's hand. "Sabrina brought in more money last night, so she gets to wear it tonight. You can have it tomorrow."

"What the hell—"

"That's not fair!"

Outraged at the apparent injustice, Sabrina and Ginny spoke at the same time, but the older woman ignored them, turning to me instead. Her gaze, surprisingly shrewd, swept over me. "Honey, you lost or looking to dance?"

I froze like a deer in the headlights, eyes darting frantically around the room. Maybe they didn't have servers here. I hadn't seen a single waitress on the way in. Maybe the women here did both jobs. Could I do that—take my clothes off in front of dozens of strangers?

My empty gas tank told me I had to do something. I was getting desperate for money, and I was willing to do whatever I had to—within reason. I'd never been naked in front of another person, and I wasn't sure I could start now. "Um… no. Just looking for the bathroom. Sorry to bother you."

Turning on a heel, I strode out of the room and headed back down the hall the way I'd come. A wiry little man stepped out of a doorway to my left, and I reared back to avoid slamming into him. "Oh! I'm sorry, excuse me."

I started to duck around him, but he threw a look over my shoulder in the direction I'd just come. His gaze narrowed, and he held up a hand. "What're you doin' back here?"

"Um…" I wrung my hands together, eager to get out of there. "I was just leaving. Sorry to bother you."

"Hold up," he said when I started to step away.

I took a tiny step back and met his eyes.

He studied me for a long second. "You lookin' to dance?"

I shook my head. "No, I… I'd hoped to find the owner and ask about waiting tables or something, but…"

I trailed off, and the man waited a moment. "Well, ya found me." He extended an arm toward the office he'd just vacated. "Come in for a sec."

I bit my lip. If he was willing to let me wait tables, I should at least hear him out. Dragging my feet, I skirted him and stepped into the office, then took a seat on the edge of a grungy blue plastic chair.

The man rounded the desk and took a seat. "Name's Jimmy."

"Giul—" I halted midword and swallowed. "Jules. My name is Jules."

His eyes narrowed for a second, and he steepled his hands together. "Yer looking for a job?"

I nodded and folded my hands in my lap. "Yes, please. I'm… new here."

"Uh-huh." His gaze slid over me again, sending a little shiver of unease down my spine. I felt dirty just sitting here, but I forced myself to stay still. "How old are ya?"

"Twenty," I lied. It was close enough.

"Gotta be twenty-one to serve," he stated. "Plus, I don't really need a waitress. Most of the girls rotate."

Apparently one year made a hell of a difference in this industry. "I promise I'll do my best if you just give me a chance."

I didn't bother to mention that my birthday actually was only a few days from now. But I would be twenty, not twenty-one. I swallowed hard and prayed that he wouldn't see through my ruse.

He leaned forward and pressed his palms flat on the desk. I shifted uncomfortably as his eyes moved to where I'd swept my bangs over my temple, shielding the bruise that was still an ugly shade of purple. His gaze dropped to my long sleeves, then skated up my arms and over my neck before meeting mine again. "Do I need to worry about him showing up?"

I flushed, hot all over, humiliated that he'd so accurately summed up the situation. He probably thought I was running from a boyfriend or husband, but his assumption was close enough. I shook my head. "N-no. He doesn't know where I am."

He sighed heavily through his nose, then lifted a hand to point one finger at me. "This is my business. If he shows up and starts shit, yer out on yer ass, ya hear me?"

I nodded shakily. "Yes, sir."

He leaned back and crossed his arms over his chest. "Ya got anything else to wear?"

I eyed the long black sleeves and black yoga pants I'd changed into in a gas station bathroom this morning. I didn't want to expose the marks still evident on my wrists and upper arms. "Not yet."

He ran his tongue over his teeth. "Fine. But I'm doin' ya a favor, don't forget it."

"Yes, sir."

"Mickey will show ya the ropes. The bartender," he clarified at my look of confusion. "Talk to him. First, though"

—he held up a finger and pointed at my head—"go get some makeup to cover that up. No need to advertise it."

"Thank you." I scurried out of the room before he could change his mind. It occurred to me that we hadn't discussed hours or pay, but at that moment, I didn't even care. I was just happy to have a position that didn't involve taking my clothes off or sharing underwear with another woman.

I hesitantly made my way back into the dressing room area and found Shirlene. I explained what I needed, and she directed me to a vanity in the corner. She quickly—and heavily—lined and shadowed my eyes and expertly applied coverup over the bruise on my temple.

"Son of a bitch," she rasped out sotto voce.

"What?" I darted a look around her to the mirror.

"The good-for-nothin' asshole who put this here." She stood back and surveyed me, hands on her hips. "Good as it's gonna get. Men," she sneered, shaking her head. "Can't live with 'em. Can't shoot 'em."

Her snarky dose of wisdom nearly caused me to choke. I thanked her and scooted out before I was subjected to any more fighting over thongs.

During the past forty-five minutes, another handful of patrons had trickled in, and they tossed curious glances my way as I cut across the room to the bar.

I introduced myself to Mickey, and he gave me a crash course in waiting. He would pour all the drinks; all I had to do was deliver them. The next hour slipped away, more men gathering around the bar and the stage.

"Ah, shit."

My gaze jumped to Mick, who had turned toward the front door. "What's wrong?"

Pausing in the act of drying a glass, he tipped his head toward a long-legged man who'd just entered the club. "Darren Murphy. Sabrina's ex. He's a real piece of work." He put the glass on the rack. "Asshole better not start any shit tonight."

I glanced at the man, who was currently striding toward the stage, a lilting wobble to his step. My jaw dropped open in disbelief. "Is he… drunk?"

Mick snorted. "Better question is, when isn't he?"

I watched as Darren took a seat at the very front of the stage, wedging himself between two larger men.

I made a mental note to avoid the man as much as possible as I loaded up the drinks and carried them over to the stage. I dodged grabby hands and kept a healthy distance between myself and the drunk man seated at the corner of the stage. The music faded as one dancer finished up and strolled off the stage, hips rolling. How she managed to walk like that in the five-inch heels, I had no idea, but I'd developed a deeper level of respect for these girls over the past hour.

The first strains of "Hot For Teacher" blared from the speakers, and a new girl came out. Heavily made up, I couldn't tell who it was. I placed a few more drinks in front of the men as the woman started her set. A man to my left whistled, and Darren jumped to his feet. "You looking at my girlfriend, asshole?"

My head swung back and forth between the two men. I was pretty sure everyone in here was watching Sabrina, but I assumed common sense wasn't the man's best friend. I could see from the expression in his eyes that he was itching for a fight.

Not one to be intimidated, the man to my left shoved his chair back and stood. "More than lookin'. I fucked the slut last night."

Oh, shit.

My eyes widened and I took a step backward as they exploded into motion. Shouts broke out as the men rushed each other. The rest of the men joined in, and a chair went sailing across the room.

I darted toward the bar. "Mick! What do we do?"

"I'll handle it. I warned that stupid shit," Mickey muttered as he pulled himself up and over the bar and threw himself into the fray. Taking advantage of Mick's absence, the few men at the bar reached across, grabbing bottles of liquor and pouring themselves beer from the taps.

"Hey! Stop!" I yelled as one clambered over the bar.

On stage, Sabrina was screaming, but the men showed no signs of calming down. For a long moment I stood helplessly. I'd never experienced anything like this before. I shook off the fog. Jimmy would know what to do. I sprinted out from behind the bar toward the back offices. The mass of men had spread out, and I dodged them as I ran.

I ducked behind a table to avoid flying fists and broken wood from smashed tables and chairs. The table moved as a couple of men crashed into it, splintering the wood, and I jumped out of the way. A small scream suspended itself in my throat as a pair of strong arms caught me around the waist, lifting me off my feet and stopping my heart in my chest.

FOUR

ERIC

"Code 24 in progress at the Fox Hole."

I touched the button on my radio. "On it, Central. I'm about a mile out."

Lucy from dispatch recognized my voice. "10-4, Sheriff. All available units report for backup."

A road came into sight just up ahead on my right, and I whipped the SUV in that direction, pressing down on the pedal. Gravel flew as I slid to a stop and flung open the door. Stepping inside the club, I quickly assessed the melee. Across the room, a small woman cowered behind a table, and I bolted forward.

I caught the tiny brunette around her waist just in time and yanked her against my chest. I quickly turned to shield her as part of a table landed where she'd been standing just seconds ago. She fought like a wildcat against my hold, and I bent my head to speak next to her ear so she could hear me over the din.

"I'm not going to hurt you."

She felt light as I scooped her into my arms, already striding away from the dangerous group of men. Her long brown hair brushed the back of my hand where it tumbled down her back. I swiftly carried her toward the back of the club and dropped her onto her feet. I kept a hand on her shoulder to steady her, and her beauty hit me like a ton of bricks as she turned to face me. Jesus. She was even more gorgeous up close. Giant green eyes stared up at me, and I forced myself to let go of her. "You good?"

She looked scared out of her mind, vulnerable as hell, but she managed a shaky nod. I wanted to reassure her that everything would be okay, but there would be time for that later. "Good. Stay here out of the way."

With that, I rushed back into the sea of bodies, ducking swinging arms and flying objects as I shoved between two men. I heard the front doors fly open, and two of my deputies joined in, pulling the men apart and slapping cuffs on. Pain exploded in my cheekbone as an elbow came out of nowhere. Whirling around, I reached for the asshole who'd gotten the drop on me and planted my fist in his face. He got one cheap shot in before I laid his ass out on the floor of the bar.

Less than five minutes later, the dust had settled, and all the men were lined up on the floor beside the stage wearing identical sulky expressions. There was no way I could haul all of them to jail. I didn't have enough cruisers or patience to deal with this shit tonight.

I gestured to my deputies. "Start interviewing and see who initiated it, then take him in. Let the rest go."

They nodded and split up, working their way down the line. I turned away and caught sight of myself in the mirror running behind the bar. A trickle of blood ran down from my lower lip, and I brushed it away as I scanned the room, looking for the girl.

Gone.

Disappointment hit me that I wouldn't see her again before I left. She was probably tucked away in the back, somewhere she would be safe.

I rested my hands on my duty belt and lifted my chin at Riley as he approached.

"Story's the same across the board. They all say Murphy started it."

I barely refrained from rolling my eyes. Would that asshole never learn? "Have Hawkins take him in."

Riley strode away, and I caught the owner's squirrely gaze. "Keep your clients under control, Jimmy."

He nodded. "Squeaky clean around here, Donahue."

I seriously doubted that. Exhaustion tugging at me, I strode out the door and climbed into the cruiser. Murphy glared out the rear window as Hawkins pulled out of the parking lot, and I followed suit. At the intersection, he turned left to head south, and I turned right, heading toward Pine Ridge.

My turn signal clicked in the background as I turned into the gas station parking lot and pulled up next to the gas pump. Shutting off the engine, I ran my hands over my face and winced at the pain when I grazed my cheek. I started the pump and rubbed my hands together in the brisk air as I glanced around.

A small, light blue car parked just behind the convenience store gave me pause. It was backed in, partially obscured by the building and the trees of the forest behind it. The owner's car was parked along the opposite side of the store, where he always parked. The hairs on the back of my neck lifted, and I replaced the nozzle as the gas pump kicked off.

Pulling the flashlight from my duty belt, I slowly approached the car, sticking close to the building for safety. Though it was mostly dark on this side of the building, all the artificial light obscured from view, a shaft of moonlight fell from the sky and penetrated the windshield. I took in the tiny form curled up on the driver seat. Knees pulled up to her chest, arms tucked in close to her body, long brown locks tumbling around her head. My heart hit the dirt at my feet. I didn't have to see her face—I knew.

Electric green eyes wide with fear snapped to mine as I gently rapped on the window. Her hands fumbled with the keys in the ignition and she turned it over a click so she could roll down the window a couple inches.

"Did I do something wrong, Officer?"

I didn't miss the bags of clothing in the back seat or the toothbrush and cup in her cup holder. I returned my gaze to hers. "Can I see your registration?"

Her face crumpled and she bit her lip as she gave a little shake of her head. I arched a brow. "License?"

She stared me dead in the eye before quietly shaking her head. "Get your things and come with me."

Her gaze dropped to the nameplate on my chest. "Officer Donahue—"

"Sheriff," I corrected, unsure exactly why I needed to distinguish the difference.

She bit her lip. "Sheriff Donahue. Have I done something wrong?"

I stared at her for a moment, dumbfounded by her ridiculous question. The girl obviously had nowhere to go, no driver's license, and I seriously doubted the car was legally registered. I didn't know the whole story, but I didn't need to. She was safer with me than anywhere else. "It's already below freezing. I can't let you stay out here by yourself." She started to protest, but I cut her off. "We can do this the easy way or the hard way."

Her face fell, but she rolled the window up, and I barely bit back my sigh of relief as she turned the car off and pushed the door open. I helped her gather her things, and we carried them back to my SUV. I opened the door to toss her things in the back, and she started to slide in after them.

She flinched as I touched her arm, and I quickly released her. "Ride up front."

She shot me a questioning glance but didn't argue. Moving off to the side, she watched as I closed the back door, then held the passenger door open for her. With a murmured thanks, she climbed inside.

FIVE

GIULIANA

Shit. Shit. Shit.

My pulse pounded as I clicked the seat belt into place. Was he going to take me to jail? Oh, God. "Are you arresting me?"

He paused, his hand resting on the gear shift. "Should I?"

Considering he'd just found me in a vehicle without a valid license or registration and I'd fled from a fight?

I shook my head. "No, sir."

He studied me for a long moment. "Okay."

Okay? What the hell did that mean? Anxiety warred with relief, twisting my stomach into knots. I wanted to push, ask what he meant by that, but I wasn't sure I wanted to know. He put the car in gear and pulled away from the gas pump, then steered onto the main drag.

The tree-lined road was dark and empty, and it sent a flurry of butterflies kicking up in my stomach. A layer of snow clung to the thick boughs, and it somehow managed to look both beautiful and ominous at the same time. The desolate stretch of asphalt solidified just how isolated this place really was.

There's no such thing as a good cop. My uncle's words came back to me, and my heart began to hammer away in my chest. I'd been sheltered from my family's business for most of my life, but I knew one thing: cops and members of *la famiglia* did not mix. The phrase he'd actually used still sent a shiver down my spine—*the only good cop is a dead one.*

My stomach roiled at the thought. I knew my family weren't good people, not technically speaking. Though I didn't know all the details, I knew that Daddy had died at the hands of the police officers and agents who had shown up to the raid that awful night three years ago.

Still, I couldn't quite grasp the hatred that my family held for the men and women who upheld the law. They were people too and didn't deserve to die any more than my father had. Why should they be persecuted for doing their jobs? In fact, my family had worked with more than one crooked cop or politician, but, in their eyes, that was perfectly acceptable —because it suited their objectives.

This man, though… I studied him from the corner of my eye. It hadn't really sunk in earlier how big he was. Broad shoulders that filled half the cab of the SUV; his arms and chest looked like those of bodybuilders I'd seen on TV. He was sheriff of the town, that much I knew—but I also knew that men in the highest positions were often the most corrupt.

I promised myself when I left my uncle's house that I would never let a man have that kind of control over me ever again. The sheriff struck me as a man not to be trifled with. I'd yet to see him smile or offer anything other than mild concern. I couldn't read him, and that made him dangerous in more ways than one.

I shifted uncomfortably and turned to face him, pressing my back against the door to put as much distance between us as possible. "Where are we going?"

He flicked a glance my way before returning his eyes to

the road. "Well, you have two choices. You can either sleep in one of the cells at the jail tonight…"

My eyes widened and I shrank back a bit more until the cold glass from the window bit into my neck.

"…or you can stay the night at my place."

Oh, God. Neither option sounded good. Go home with this man or be stuck inside a box of a cell. Just the thought made my heart kick up in my chest, and my hand fluttered to my throat. The edges of my vision began to bleed to black, and a weight pressed on my lungs, constricting them as memories of that closet came back. The darkness pressed inward, and I could practically feel the walls closing in.

The car slowed to a stop, and I forced myself to drag in a breath. I realized my free hand was pressed to the dash of the car, as if to push it away, to keep it from crushing me. My eyes snapped up to find a pair of hazel ones watching me intently. Despite myself, I couldn't tear my gaze away. A full minute passed before he spoke, his voice low and even as he studied me. "Which way?"

I gazed out the windshield and realized we'd come to an intersection, the reflective lines of the stop sign glowing in the headlights. I quickly glanced around for other cars to see if we were holding up traffic. The road remained empty and dark, and I couldn't decide if that was a good thing or bad.

I turned back to the man. No one was around to save me now. I should go to the jail. I should spend the night, then leave first thing in the morning and drive as far from here as possible. But the idea of sleeping in that cell, little more than a box…

My gaze reluctantly moved back to his. "How can I be sure you won't hurt me?"

His eyes looked more brown than green as he tipped his head slightly to one side. "You can't. You'll just have to trust me."

Trust him? I wanted to scoff at his words. Didn't he know

how hard this was? He had to be feeling the same thing. He'd picked up a strange woman off the side of the road.

My hand pressed flat on my chest over my heart, and I prayed I was making the right choice. "Your place."

Deep-set hazel eyes bored into mine, searching, validating. They appeared even darker now, illuminated by only the lights on the dash, but I knew the exact mixture of brown and green and gray. They'd arrested me in the club when he'd set me down and turned me around to make sure I was okay. Something had passed between us in that moment, as if a spark had coursed through his body into mine.

Despite my naivete and the fact that he'd spoken few words, I felt deep down that he was inherently good. I couldn't begin to describe why. It wasn't just that he'd pulled me out of harm's way at the club. Not even the fact that he was doing… whatever this was. Refusing to let me sleep in my car, helping me. He was too big, his voice too deep and rough. I shouldn't trust him, and yet… I knew he wouldn't hurt me.

Whatever he saw in my gaze must have been enough. With a concise nod, he flipped on his blinker and turned left, away from the sign pointing toward Pine Ridge. Less than ten minutes later, we pulled up in front of a small ranch house, and he pressed a button to raise the garage door.

I glanced out the window, drinking in the sight. Even in the near-dark, the home looked clean and well-maintained. A small porch jutted off the front, and a layer of snow covered the roof, making it look like a Kinkade painting. As the garage door lifted, the headlights reflected off another vehicle inside.

"Is that yours?"

Donahue followed my gaze to the red truck as it was revealed to me. He nodded. "My personal vehicle. Not that I drive it much," he murmured with a trace of humor.

Sheriff Donahue pulled into the garage and parked in the

bay to the left of the truck. I cautiously opened my door in the narrow space and squeezed out. By the time I closed the door again, the sheriff had already collected my things from the back seat.

"Follow me." He tapped a button on the wall to close the garage door, and the motor whirred quietly to life.

I followed several feet behind Donahue as he made his way through a small mudroom. He paused just long enough to shrug out of his coat and hang it on a peg, then toe out of his boots, leaving them in a tray to dry.

"Do you want me to leave my shoes here?"

He turned at the sound of my voice and gave a slight shake of his head. "Don't worry about it."

A second door opened into a hallway, and he turned to the right, guiding us out into the main living area. The living room sat on my left, a small but relatively tidy kitchen to my right. Blankets and books and magazines cluttered the space, making it feel lived-in without looking dirty. I felt a little tension lift from my shoulders. The house was small but cozy, and the slight disorder made him seem more human.

He dropped my bags on the couch and tipped his head at me. "Make yourself at home. I'll be back in a minute."

He headed back down the hallway that connected the living area to what I assumed was his bedroom at the very end. Through the doorway, I could see him hastily snatching clothes up off the floor. Carrying them into the hallway, he opened a tiny door in the wall. My brows drew together as I watched him shove them inside. I had no idea where the little door went, but I guessed that was one way to clean.

Despite myself, I felt my mouth turn up in a tiny smile. I didn't know this man from Adam, and I'd only seen the sheriff side of him. Even for a brief moment, it was reassuring to know that he was a normal man, hiding his clothes behind a tiny wall in the door.

I heard more movement as he disappeared from sight, and

less than two minutes later, he came back down the hall toward me. Part of me was ready to turn tail and flee out the door. He stopped several feet away and jerked his thumb over his shoulder. "You can take my room. I'll crash on the couch tonight."

What kind of man offered a perfect stranger their room? Flattered and humbled, I shook my head. "I can't do that. I'll take the couch."

He was already doing too much. I couldn't let him give up the comfort of his bed for me. I'd braved the freezing cold while I slept in my car last night, so anything with four walls and heat was better than that.

"My room is clean. Mostly," he amended with a small grimace. "And it has a lock. You'll be safe in there."

My gaze narrowed at him. Was I that obvious? I had some serious work to do if I was giving off a naïve damsel in distress vibe. Pulling my shoulders back, I stared him down. "Right. Because a lock never stopped anyone."

"It'll stop me."

His calm words sent a shock through me. I glanced away, unable to look into his eyes any longer. He saw too much, knew too much about the part of me I'd tried to keep hidden. I was free of my uncle, free of the life I'd been born into. I'd finally escaped, and I refused to be a victim.

"You don't even know me," I pressed. "What if I try to kill you in the middle of the night?"

Our gazes remained locked, and I swore I could see a hint of a smile deep in the hazel depths. "If you get the drop on me, I would say I deserved it."

We stared at each other for another long moment, a contest of wills. This man had offered me his home, his very own bed to sleep in. I had to believe deep down that he was a decent person. Not every man was like those in my family. The sheriff was dangerous, but he wouldn't hurt me.

"Fine."

"Okay."

Neither of us moved. Silence pressed in on us until he finally spoke. "Bathroom is the second door on the right. I'm going to get a shower, then it's all yours."

"Thanks."

He stared at me. "Since you'll be staying in my house… do I at least get to know your name?"

My cheeks burned with embarrassment and the realization that he was just now asking. Who did that? What kind of man invited a stranger into his home without even knowing the person's name? I met his gaze, unable to read anything in those captivating eyes. Was this some kind of a test, some exercise in trust?

He didn't say a word; he just watched, waited. I licked my lips before responding. "Jules."

With a tight nod, he turned away. The door closed behind him, and seconds later, I heard the water turn on. There was a change in the tempo of the drumming water, and I imagined him stepping under the spray. Releasing a sigh, I made my way down the hall on quiet feet to his room.

His scent hit me even before I crossed the threshold, a mixture of something woodsy and utterly masculine. My curiosity was piqued as I looked around the small room. He didn't have many personal items aside from a few pictures on the dresser. I ventured closer and saw him with another man, both holding long rifles at their sides.

The sight sent a little thrill through me. Every man I knew carried a pistol—more than one, usually—and knives. The wicked-looking rifle at his side made him look that much more dangerous. I studied the lines of his face that stared back at me from the photograph.

He wasn't a pretty man. His forehead was a little too broad, his features a little too coarse. The bridge of his nose listed slightly to one side as if it'd been broken—maybe more than once. Wide mouth, thick lips that would be firm and—

I blinked at my thoughts. My uncle had made sure I was never alone with a man, and I'd never even been kissed. My only knowledge of sex and intimacy came from novels and the occasional cousin who'd let their escapades slip in front of me. My gaze slid down his form to the broad shoulders encased in a tight black tee shirt, his biceps straining the material. I could almost imagine the ridges of his abs where they met his narrow hips. He was rough and rugged, his mouth pressed into a firm line even in the photo. I wondered if he ever relaxed, ever smiled. I seriously doubted it.

Turning away, I examined the rest of the room. The walls were stark white, the floors covered in a light gray carpet. The only color in the room came from the thick blue bedspread tossed over the queen-sized bed. I set my bags at the foot of the bed and pulled out a clean pair of yoga pants and a fresh long-sleeved shirt. Soon I'd need to find a place to do my laundry. I wondered if the sheriff could direct me to someplace tomorrow.

As if my musings conjured his presence, I heard the bathroom door open. I spun around, surprised. He'd only been in there for a few minutes, and I hadn't even heard the water shut off. He must've taken a shower in record time.

He flicked a glance at me through the open doorway of the bedroom. "All yours."

Biting my lip, I nodded. Without another word, he padded quietly down the hall into the living room. I waited a few more seconds before grabbing up my clothes and dashing into the bathroom. I locked the door and glanced around. My eyes lit on a tube of lotion that sat on the counter, and I picked it up, testing the weight in my hand. It was about three-quarters full, and I hoped it would at least retain its shape a little bit.

I bent and wedged the flat end under the door until it refused to go any further, impeded by the rounded cap sticking out on my end. I unlocked the door and gave a little test pull. It moved only a fraction of an inch, then stilled. Good enough. It wouldn't stop someone determined to get in, but hopefully it would hold up long enough to alert me to someone's presence. I didn't really think that the sheriff would try to attack me in the bathroom, but still… better safe than sorry.

Stripping down, I took the fastest shower in history. Though I wanted to linger under the heat of the spray and let it soothe my tired, sore muscles, I forced myself to finish quickly. Peeking around the curtain, I grabbed a fresh, folded towel that he'd left on the vanity. Quickly as I could, I toweled off and dressed. I hung the towel on a hook to dry, then removed the bottle of lotion from beneath the door and replaced it on the vanity. Gathering my clothes, I unlocked the door and peeked out.

The living room was almost completely dark, but light from the bedroom spilled into the hallway, guiding me back to the room. I hustled inside and locked up behind me, storing my dirty clothes in a plastic shopping bag. Exhausted, I crawled onto the bed and curled up on my side, not caring that the lamp on the nightstand was still blazing brightly.

I couldn't bring myself to sleep on his sheets, so I shimmied to one side of the bed and pulled the comforter over me like a sleeping bag. For the first time in days I felt—if not entirely safe—comfortable. I was clean and in a real bed, and I appreciated it more than I could say. Finally giving in to the fatigue tugging at my brain, I closed my eyes and drifted off to sleep.

SIX

ERIC

The smell of coffee permeated the air, and I breathed deeply, anticipating the first hit of the caffeine. I hadn't slept for shit last night, hyperaware of the young woman barely thirty feet away. I hadn't truly been worried for my safety—at least, I wasn't afraid that she would try to hurt me. I was concerned, however, about why she was here and what she was running from.

The hairs on the back of my neck lifted, and I was aware of her presence before I heard her soft footsteps draw closer to the kitchen. Adopting a casual pose, I turned my head just enough to see her from the corner of my eye. She'd frozen in the hallway, as if she wasn't sure whether to flee back to the bedroom or out the front door.

"Would you like some coffee?"

She waited a beat, then: "Yes, please."

I turned and leaned against the cabinets, my hands curled around the edge of the Formica countertop as I met her gaze. Now that it was daylight, the bruising on her temple stood out against her complexion. I'd seen it last night but hadn't wanted to press her. Was that from the fight in the strip club or something else? Anger suffused me, a hot fury boiling through my veins at the thought of whoever had put it there.

She looked even younger this morning, devoid of makeup or any embellishment. Still, the slightly baggy jeans and long-sleeved T-shirt couldn't hide the gorgeous curves of her figure. My mind flashed back to the black pants and black long-sleeved shirt she'd worn last night that had hugged every curve. There was no denying her beauty.

Olive-toned skin stretched over the classic features of her heart-shaped face. Her cheekbones were high, her lips full, but her eyes… They were the first thing I'd noticed about her, and the sight of them even now arrested me. Deep as a river and a hundred shades of green, they threatened to slay me where I stood. They were filled with a pain so acute I could feel her despair deep in my bones. In that moment, I would have gladly shouldered all her burdens just to erase that look of wariness from her beautiful face.

"Looks like I survived the night."

She blushed. "I wouldn't do anything to you. Especially not when you've been so nice."

Her soft response made me feel like an asshole. I'd been trying to tease her, but it had backfired epically. The last thing I wanted was for her to pull away. "Did you sleep okay?"

Her gaze darted over my shoulder, avoiding my gaze. "Yes, thank you."

Liar. I could tell from the dark circles under her eyes that she hadn't slept for shit either. "I didn't expect you up so soon."

She gave a little shrug. "I don't sleep much."

It was the first admission she'd really made, and pleasure flared around my heart. I ruthlessly tamped it down as the coffee pot spat out the last of the brew. There was no reason for me to get excited that she'd chosen to offer up a tiny slice of information about herself.

Busying myself, I pulled down two mugs and divided the coffee between them. Pushing the container of sugar across the island to her, I gestured with my chin toward the fridge. "Milk and creamer in there if you want it."

"No, thank you."

Always with the fucking impeccable manners. My lips pressed into a thin line at her response, and I watched as she spooned a scoop of sugar into the cup. Did she not like creamer, or did she feel like she would be putting me out by using it? I wanted to ask how she actually took her coffee. Suddenly, I felt like I was overanalyzing every damn thing. What she liked or didn't like made no damn difference to me. That's what I told myself—but I didn't believe it.

Frustrated with myself and her, I grabbed up my coffee and stalked into the living room. She followed at a snail's pace, edging around the furniture to keep the most distance between us. Jules gingerly sat on the edge of the couch and set her cup on the coffee table between us. Her hands folded in her lap as her gaze darted around the room. I studied her posture, trying to read her. She looked uncomfortable but not crazy. I didn't know if that was a consolation or not.

"So." I searched for something to say, and my mind went back to the first time I'd seen her at the club. "You're a dancer?"

Her eyes darted to mine. "Not anymore, but I studied ballet when I was young."

I hesitated for a moment, thrown by her response. Was this girl serious? Her wide green eyes, full of innocence and naivety, told me she didn't understand my question. Great, so I was dealing with some little rich girl who'd run away from home.

"How'd you end up at the Fox Hole?"

"Um..." Her eyes darted away. "I needed money, and it was the first place I came to."

"Not quite your style, huh?"

She shook her head. "I thought it was a… what do you call it? Sportsman's club or something."

I fought the urge to shake my head. Had the girl grown up under a fucking rock?

"Why the Fox Hole?"

I turned a surprised gaze on her. "What?"

"Why is it called the Fox Hole?"

I coughed so I wouldn't choke on the coffee that had gone down the wrong pipe. "Well… you know how some men refer to beautiful women as foxes?" She nodded. "And, um…" I grimaced. Knowing some of the women who worked there, "hole" probably had a multitude of innuendos. Jules's eyes widened with a combination of horror and intrigue, and I felt my face flame.

Jesus Christ.

"Anyway." I tugged at the collar of my shirt, desperate to change the subject. "There's not much up this way, but I'm sure we can find you a job somewhere. What skills do you have?"

She bit her lip and dropped her gaze to the ground. After a long moment, a single word left her mouth on a whisper. "None."

The discomfort from a moment ago immediately dissipated, and a strange pain shot through my heart at the sight of her slumped shoulders, insecurity written plainly all over her face. Regardless of where she came from or what she was doing here, I wanted to help her. There was something about her that I just couldn't put my finger on, that I couldn't puzzle out. For now, I had to be content with what she was giving me.

"You open to any kind of work?"

She eyed me warily. "Anything that pays—within reason."

Good enough. I picked up my phone, an idea brewing. Jack Prescott and his soon-to-be-wife, Mia, owned the ski lodge up on the mountain. I knew they were looking for people to help get ready for the grand opening, but I wasn't sure what all they needed. This kind of killed two birds with one stone. I wasn't sure how long Jules planned to hang around, but this might work in both their favor. Jules could make a little money until she decided what to do, and it would help Jack out in the process.

There was another added bonus to the scenario. Jack had done multiple tours with the Army, and he didn't take shit from anyone. He would be able to keep an eye on her and make sure nothing happened. I wasn't really worried that she would try to steal anything, but I did worry for her safety. Pulling up the most recent string of messages, I began to type.

Me: Still looking for some help?

It was early, but I knew Jack would respond as long as he wasn't busy. Three dots popped up almost immediately.

Jack: Who do you have for me?

Me: More like what I have for you

I didn't bother to beat around the bush.

Me: Got a runaway here who I think could use some cash and a safe place to land for a while

I let Jack mull that over for a while, deciding what he wanted to do. It was a lot to take on, but if anyone could do it, it was him. Sure enough, a new message popped up less than a minute later.

Jack: Am I going to regret this?

Probably.

I slanted a look at the young woman across from me. She sat ramrod straight, shoulders perfectly level, feet crossed at the ankles. Her hands lay in her lap, but I noticed the faintest fidgeting as she picked at her nails. She glanced down and, as if realizing what she was doing, pressed her hands flat together and tucked them between her thighs.

Me: Might be a flight risk

Jack: Female?

Of their own volition, my eyes skimmed over her body

once more, and my original assumption solidified in my mind. Jules was the epitome of grace and sophistication, the product of a good upbringing, probably in a wealthy environment.

Me: Yeah. Bet my right hand she's from money. Can't get a thing out of her

Jack: Bring her in

I glanced at the clock as I sipped my coffee. I had about half an hour before I was due on duty, but thankfully I didn't have to head right into the station. Being sheriff gave me a little more leniency. I threw a quick look at Jules, who hadn't moved. "I'm going to go change, and then we can head out, if that's okay."

Her head bobbed in a quick nod. "Of course."

I watched as she nervously wiped her palms on her thighs. Did all men make her uncomfortable, or was it just me? The officer inside me wanted to prod, to question her until she broke and told me everything. The slightly more compassionate man I barely knew even existed anymore told me it was a bad idea to push her.

After studying her mannerisms over the brief period of time she'd been with me last night and this morning, I knew I wouldn't get anywhere with her. If anyone had a chance of getting her to open up, it would be a woman. Maybe Mia could work some magic. I was curious as hell but determined not to let it show.

Leaving my empty cup on the table, I strolled down the hallway to the bedroom. I quickly dressed and retrieved my pistol and duty belt from the safe inside the closet. Five minutes later, I found myself back in the living room. Jules was still on the couch, sitting primly on the edge, and her expectant gaze lifted to mine.

At first glance, it looked like she hadn't moved a muscle. But as my gaze swept over the empty coffee table, I realized she'd cleaned up our coffee cups from earlier. Sure enough, they sat on the counter by the sink.

I turned back to her. "Thanks."

All I got in response was a curt nod. I'd never known a woman who spoke so little, but I really wasn't surprised under the circumstances.

I lifted my chin at her as I examined her plain outfit and bare, fresh face. "Are you ready?"

In my experience, a woman was never ready. My ex-wife had taken an hour or more to do her makeup before she was ready to leave the house. But Jules surprised me.

She popped to her feet and nodded. "I'm ready when you are."

It wasn't lost on me that she kept the coffee table between us. The only time she had let me get within arm's reach of her was when she was in the cruiser next to me and when I unlocked the door to the house. Self-preservation was deeply ingrained in her; I could tell that much. I wasn't sure why, exactly, but the fact that she didn't trust me raised my hackles. Because I was an asshole like that, I wanted to push her.

I tipped my head, indicating that she should precede me toward the garage. Eyes cast low but still vigilant, she skirted me and headed through the mud room the same way we'd come in last night. I couldn't help it. The gentle sway of her hips drew my attention, and I was lost in their hypnotic allure.

There was no hiding the fact that she was downright gorgeous. I could practically feel the softness of her curves under my hands, the sweet taste of her lips. I wanted to take that long, beautiful hair and sink my fingers into it, sift through the soft strands as they lay over my pillow. I wanted…

I halted in my tracks, completely horrified at the turn my thoughts had taken. Jules hesitated next to the cruiser, her hand frozen on the door handle. She threw a questioning glance my way, spurring me into movement once more. There were a hundred reasons why I could never get involved with this woman, not the least of which was the fact that she was too young for me—way too damn young.

Fuck.

Instead of acknowledging Jules's reticence, I opened my door and slid into the seat. Through the window, I watched Jules bite her lip before reluctantly climbing inside. I wished I could tell what was going through her mind. Was she already dreading being in close quarters with me again? Or had my hesitation fueled her discomfort? Once more I wanted to punch myself for my wayward thoughts.

I pushed the button to lift the garage door as she snapped her seat belt into place. We remained quiet, each of us lost in our own reverie as I made my way along the curving, winding road up the mountain to Briarleigh. I parked in the employee lot and led Jules to the side door. I'd been here enough over the past couple of weeks to know exactly where I was going, so Jules stepped aside and allowed me to guide her down the hallway.

The light was already on in Jack's office, and I gave a peremptory knock on the door jamb before stepping inside. He waved us in without bothering to lift his head. I knew he was deliberately being casual. I guaranteed that before we even stepped foot inside his office, he knew it was us. Jack had an uncanny ability to tell from a person's tread and presence who they were before he even saw them.

Emulating Jack's casual demeanor, I stepped inside and took a seat in the chair farthest from the door, knowing instinctively that Jules would want the one nearest the exit. I watched Jules's hands clench tightly in her lap as she settled on the edge of the seat.

I made quick introductions. "Jules, this is Jack Prescott, Briarleigh's owner." His lips quirked up in a tiny smile at my wording. I figured Mia would have something to say about that, considering she owned half the company as well. "Jack, this is Jules."

He turned his dark gaze on Jules. "Nice to meet you."

He didn't stretch a hand out for her to shake; he didn't make any movement at all. He just sat there, unimposing—as much as a man of Jack's size could be—and studied her across the desk.

"You, as well."

Sitting this close to her, I could hear the soft click of her nails as she picked at them. It was only vaguely gratifying to know that I wasn't the only one to have this effect on her. Then, as if she'd been rebuked for it time and again, her hands curled into tight fists, then relaxed. I watched with mild curiosity as she pressed them flat on her thighs, affecting a graceful pose. I wondered if someone had admonished her for the bad habit in the past or if she was just hyperaware of her actions.

Acting as intermediary, I spoke up. "Jules is looking for a job. I thought maybe you could use her around here for a bit."

I tacked on that last bit for both their sakes. She might run well before the lodge opened, or Jack might want rid of her.

He tipped his head in contemplation. "I'm sure we can find something for you. Do—"

The radio at my shoulder crackled to life, and I listened to dispatch rattle off the code for a domestic dispute. Jesus. I tossed an aggravated glance at Jack, who tipped his head imperceptibly at me. Glancing over at Jules, I met her wide green eyes. I was almost glad for the call, because part of me didn't want to leave her side, though I knew I needed to. "I need to get on the road. I'll be back around four to pick you up." I stood and flicked a glance at Jack. "That good with you?"

He nodded. "Of course."

With one more look at Jules, I headed out the door, forcing

my feet to keep moving forward. I needed to push all thoughts of Jules from my mind. I couldn't allow myself to go there—I wouldn't.

I needed to get a handle on my emotions. She stirred something within me that felt like protectiveness but also a lot like possessiveness. And I wasn't sure what to do with that. I wasn't her protector, and I certainly wasn't her boyfriend. Nothing could ever happen between us for a multitude of reasons—none of which I could remember at the moment.

SEVEN

GIULIANA

Suddenly, it was just the two of us. It felt as if the air had been sucked out of the room with Sheriff Donahue's departure, and my pulse kicked up as I stared at the man sitting behind the desk. With dark hair and even darker eyes, he was intimidating though he hadn't moved a muscle since I'd walked through the door.

Maybe that was precisely why he was intimidating—he didn't have to move. He didn't have to tower over me or raise his voice. I knew just by watching his controlled facial expressions that he was dangerous. He was not a friendly person, and I couldn't bring myself to think of him as Jack, as the sheriff had introduced him. I didn't want that kind of familiarity with this man. He reminded me too much of the men I'd left behind in my previous life.

Though I didn't fully trust the sheriff, I'd felt marginally better with him by my side. I steeled my spine and lifted my chin, mustering as much courage as possible. I refused to give him the advantage of seeing my discomfort.

Mr. Prescott pinned me with another intense stare. "How do you know Eric?"

My eyebrows drew together before it finally clicked—Eric was Sheriff Donahue. Oh, Lord. How to answer that one? "We… um… met at the Fox Hole." One eyebrow lifted as Jack stared at me. "I was there last night when a fight broke out. I kind of… left," I finished lamely.

"You don't want to go back?"

I shook my head and mimicked Eric's words from earlier. "It's not really my style."

Mr. Prescott leaned back in his chair and steepled his hands, resting the tips of his fingers against his mouth as he stared intently at me. "Have you ever done anything illegal?"

I shook my head vehemently. "No, sir."

Not personally—not exactly. I figured that Sheriff Donahue would probably disagree, considering I was driving around without a license or valid registration for my car, but he thankfully hadn't raised the issue again. I knew the sheriff saw too much, knew more about me than I'd offered up, yet he was still willing to help me get me this job, and I didn't want to ruin it.

There was no way I would tell Mr. Prescott that I had familial ties to a notorious crime syndicate—that my father, in fact, had been its previous capo. Besides, they weren't really my family anymore. All those years, I'd heard them speak of loyalty, but that was the furthest thing from the truth. The truth was that they wouldn't hesitate to sell out one of their own. Daddy was barely cold in the ground before Uncle Massimo struck the deal with Nikolai.

Mr. Prescott waited a long moment before responding. "Is there anything else I should know?"

I knew what he was asking, but I couldn't bring myself to tell him. I wanted to leave that part of my life far behind me. I shook my head.

He gave me an appraising nod. "Should I assume that you do not have a bank account?"

I nodded but didn't say a word. If there was anything I'd learned from my uncle, it was that everything was traceable. I couldn't afford to put any money in a bank under my name. Opening an account would be like waving a giant red flag under Uncle Massimo's nose.

Mr. Prescott's chest lifted on an inhale, and I fought the urge to squirm. "As you can see, there are still some renovations going on. A lot of last-minute details will need to be taken care of before the soft opening here in a few weeks. Do you want as many hours as possible?" I nodded, and he continued. "Does day shift work for you?"

I clasped my hands in front of me. "Yes, sir. That's perfect." I bit my lip, waiting for him to elaborate. He knew he couldn't deposit a paycheck into my account, and I wondered how he planned to work around that.

As if reading my mind, he spoke up. "You'll be paid at the end of each day in cash. Do you have somewhere to keep it safe?"

I pressed my lips together and thought it over. Right now, all I had to my name was the little Cavalier I'd driven up here. It wasn't worth much, and I doubted anyone would try to steal it. For the time being, I could stash the money away inside. A car had plenty of hiding places if you just knew where to look for them. I met Mr. Prescott's gaze again and lifted my chin. "I can take care of that."

Deep brown eyes pierced mine, but he didn't say anything. "Do you have any work experience?"

Shame welled up, hot and fierce. I had no training in anything to speak of, and I couldn't tell him I got the job at the Fox Hole out of sheer pity. I'd never waited tables like normal teenagers, never really been outside my own home. I hadn't even attended school; Daddy paid tutors to come to the house each day to provide an education in a variety of subjects, including various languages and ballet. Ultimately, I'd been groomed to be the perfect wife and no more.

Humiliation burned my cheeks, but I refused to break eye contact. "I've never had a job before, unless waitressing for two hours at the Fox Hole counts."

He eyed me for a second. "So nothing in retail?"

I shook my head. "No, but I've done my fair share of shopping, so I might be able to help with that."

"I would like to put you in charge of the pro shop, if that's okay?"

I wasn't really sure what that entailed, so I voiced my question. "What needs to be done with it?"

"Everything," he responded. "The room has just been finished, but we haven't installed the counter for the computer system yet. We'll need to stock it and prepare it for customers."

"Sounds good."

He dipped his chin. "Let me show you around."

Mr. Prescott stood and gestured for me to precede him out of the office. I paused in the hallway then followed him into the main area of the lodge. Under a great archway, the building split between the hotel portion and the great room for the ski lodge. Thick logs comprised the walls, and huge wooden beams stretched overhead, giving it a rustic yet elegant look. Mr. Prescott gave a brief tour of the kitchen and employee areas before returning us to the corridor.

Right at the intersection of the lodge and hotel was an open room that appeared to have been recently finished. Windows ran along both sides so the contents would be visible to people coming from either direction. Jack grasped a wrought-iron handle on the heavy wood door, and he held it open for me as we stepped inside. Metal shelving units had been installed along the walls, and circular clothing racks were stuck in the back corners, ready to be dragged out and filled with merchandise.

He propped his hands on his hips and turned to me. "This is the pro shop where we'll have all the retail items. Right now, all of the inventory is out in the warehouse. I'll introduce you to Summer in just a second. She works out in the rental shop and takes care of getting the inventory where it needs to go. Some of the stuff we'll use as rentals, but the higher end stuff we'll put here in the shop to sell."

I nodded. That made sense. Mr. Prescott continued, "Soft open is in about three weeks, right after the first of the year, so you should have plenty of time to get everything set up."

I looked around the space again, mentally calculating. The space was only about six hundred square feet, but the metal rails on the walls would allow for plenty of modifications. I met Mr. Prescott's eyes. "Do you have a specific guideline you'd like me to follow?"

He shook his head. "Just make it look nice."

As I gazed around the room, I contemplated Lila's shop back in Chicago.

Jack eyed me critically. "What do you think?"

"Well," I began slowly, "personally, I think I would place the cash register along the left wall. It allows for good flow, plus you can keep an eye on both the entrance and the fitting rooms."

He nodded approvingly. "That sounds like a plan. I'll get one of the guys in here today to get the cabinets installed, but the computers are still all packed up. What I'd like for you to do is draw up a plan and start getting stuff organized and displayed."

That was easy enough.

"Let me introduce you to Summer."

I followed Jack out of the pro shop and down a short hallway that exited outside. The small flagstone pathway had been cleared off, and we crossed it to enter the rental shop. Counters lined the exterior wall of the space so customers could follow the line through the building as they collected their skis, poles, and boots, which were stored on the huge metal racks in the middle of the room.

Mr. Prescott gave me a brief rundown. "Everyone enters here, then once they have all their equipment, they can head to one of the locker rooms in the back to change." He pointed to two doorways at the back of the building. One was marked Women; the other, Men. "Keys for the lockers are available here as well as in the hotel. People can store their things and change, then head directly out onto the slope."

Our voices drew the attention of a young woman about my age whose blonde hair hung around her face in braids. Jack tipped his head toward her. "Summer, this is Jules. She'll be taking care of the pro shop."

"Cool." Summer held her hand out to me, and I shook it.

"Nice to meet you."

Jack spoke up. "We'll be installing the furniture today, then we'll need to move the saleable inventory inside. Do you have it all separated out?"

Summer nodded. "Almost done."

The metal shelving stood about eight feet high and would eventually be filled with all of the rental equipment, from skis and poles to boots. Everything would be sorted by size, from kids' stuff to adults'. Only about half of the shelving units were full, so it looked like Summer had her work cut out for her.

"What I would like you to do," Mr. Prescott said as he turned to me, "is to get as much inventory on the shelves as possible without it looking cluttered. I'll speak to someone about getting the sales counter installed this afternoon so you can get started."

I nodded, already excited at the prospect. It was the first time in my life that someone actually trusted and encouraged me to do something by myself. Most of my life we had help, and I'd been waited on hand and foot. Things changed once I moved into my uncle's house, and he hadn't let me interact with the staff—probably because he thought I would coerce them into helping me leave.

I couldn't help the tiny smile that flitted over my lips. "I can't wait."

A clattering noise from my right made me jump, and a boy about my age shot me a sheepish smile as he picked up the box he'd dropped. "Sorry."

Mr. Prescott nodded at him. "No problem, Sam. This is Jules. She'll be working in the pro shop."

The young man approached and held out his hand. "Nice to meet you."

"You, too." A tight smile lifted my lips, and I quickly shook his hand before stepping away to put more distance between us.

Mr. Prescott gestured to Sam. "Sam works part-time in our maintenance department, but if you need help with anything, I'm sure he'd be more than happy to help."

Sam turned a smile on me. "Of course."

I gave him a polite smile and turned my focus back to Mr. Prescott, my mind already whirling with possibilities.

EIGHT

ERIC

I wished I could cite someone for stupidity.

I glanced around at the colorful display of clothing covering the pristine layer of fresh white snow. The Johanssons were a thorn in my side—in everyone's sides, really—and we were at their place at least once a week. Today's dispute had called me away from Jack and Jules, and I wasn't in any mood to deal with their bullshit.

Beside me, Earl Johansson blustered his innocence. A few feet away, Riley, one of my deputies, was questioning Earl's wife, Irene, off to the side. Apparently she'd gotten it in her head that Earl had been at the Fox Hole last night and was cheating on her. When he came home reeking of beer and sweat, she had proceeded to toss all of his clothes into the yard. Every article of his clothing littered the snow-covered lawn. And I mean *everything*.

Using the toe of my boot, I kicked aside a pair of dingy briefs. The waistband had separated from the fabric, which appeared almost yellow against the blinding white of the snow. "Looks like you could use some new drawers, Earl," I remarked dryly.

He shot a glare in Irene's direction. "Need a new something," he groused.

Couldn't deny that. Irene was meaner than a cornered snake, and I couldn't really figure out why he'd stayed with her so long. Not that Earl was the cream of the crop, but I was pretty sure I would've saved myself the headache years ago and divorced her. But I wasn't there to offer advice on love.

I turned to the man in question. "I'm done wasting time coming up here. Get your shit together or one of you is going to jail next time."

"But, Sheriff—"

I held my hand up to cut him off. "Final warning." He hung his head, and I motioned to Riley. "Let's go."

He snorted as we headed toward our cruisers. "Should've taken the stupid shits to jail."

I shrugged. "Neither wanted to fess up and throw the other under the bus. Can't do much if no one wants to press charges."

As soon as I got back to the office, I sat down at my computer and logged in, quickly debating the merits of what I was about to do. If Jules wasn't going to tell me anything, then I only had so many options. I didn't think she was dangerous or crazy, but her mannerisms worried me. Not to mention the bruise blossoming across her temple. From the color, it appeared to be at least a week old, but it was hard to tell. None of the options that ran through my head were good, and my gut twisted into a knot.

I felt like an asshole for digging into her past without her knowledge, but it couldn't be helped. If she was going to be staying with me, at least for the interim, I needed to know what I was getting myself into. The closest hotel was nearly an hour away in Kalispell, and last I'd heard, the hotel at Briarleigh wasn't yet finished.

I figured she was at least safer with me then on her own somewhere, which was precisely why I hadn't hesitated to bring her home last night. She hadn't given me her last name, and even if I pressed her, she would probably just lie. So that was a nonstarter.

I could've had Hawkins run her information when he and O'Neill brought the Cavalier in last night, but I wasn't sure what I was dealing with. Now I was glad I hadn't. I didn't really want anyone else knowing that she was here under suspicious circumstances and give them a reason to question her.

The LEDS database popped up as it connected, and I tapped in the plate number. A few moments later, a man's face appeared on the screen, and my brows drew together. Roger Egerton was significantly older than Jules, with a broad forehead and a ruddy face. My eyes dropped down the page to find his birth date. Midforties. I chewed on that for a moment.

I quickly skimmed the rest of the details. There were no outstanding warrants, no moving violations of any kind. The car, I noted, was not reported stolen. So how the hell had Jules gotten a hold of it? Maybe the man had loaned it to her? That didn't quite sit well, though. I could understand allowing someone to drive a car for a few days or months even, as long as you were close to them. But everything I'd picked up on so far said that Jules was on the run.

Maybe the better question was, who was Roger Egerton to her? A relative? A friend? He didn't strike me as any type of relative. The facial features weren't even remotely similar, unless the man was far enough down the family line that the resemblance had changed drastically.

So... Egerton was a friend, then? A boyfriend? He didn't appear to be her type, but that didn't mean he hadn't been manipulated by a pretty face. That didn't sit well in my gut either, though I didn't want to examine the reason for that too closely.

If she'd purchased the car legally, she should have transferred it into her name. Unless, of course, she didn't have the funds—or the desire. As far as traceability went, it was smarter—though much riskier—to not put her name on anything.

I double checked the DMV database, hoping that LEDS was maybe just not updated, but it showed the same information. I leaned back in my chair and contemplated what to do. I didn't want to risk spooking Jules by questioning her. She was already well aware that I knew—or at least had an inkling—that her license and registration weren't valid.

Hell, I didn't know if she had a license at all. She hadn't offered one up last night when I'd walked up to the car. My gut sank. Thank God she hadn't gotten hurt while she was driving.

That thought brought to mind the little Cavalier she'd been driving. It was currently sitting out back, thanks to my deputies on night shift. I snapped on a pair of nitrile gloves, then headed out the back door. A fine layer of snow had settled over the roof and hood, and I brushed it off before pulling it in the back bay. Thankfully we had some extra space, because the Cavalier wasn't moving for a while.

I hated being a dick, but there was no way in hell I was giving Jules the car back until I found some answers. She was much safer here than traipsing all over God's green earth, running from whatever—or whoever—she'd left behind.

I sifted through the glove compartment and console, then checked between the seats. Aside from a few stray crumbs, I didn't see much. Leaving no stone—or fabric—unturned, I checked under all the seats, both front and back before checking out the trunk. Two hours later, I'd found a pen, a straw wrapper, a couple napkins from a fast food restaurant, the car's owner's manual, and a pair of cheap sunglasses. Nothing else. Even the compartment for the spare tire was empty.

Propping my hands on my hips, I pressed my lips together in irritation. Son of a bitch. I didn't know what I'd been hoping to find, but damn. Something—anything—would have been helpful.

I finished out my shift and made my way up to Briarleigh, my mind spinning. Entering through the side, I cut down the hall to Jack's office and silently cursed when I peeked inside. Jules was already here. I'd been hoping to catch Jack alone for a second so we could talk.

I didn't want to give Jules the impression that anything was wrong or let on that I'd been looking into her background, though, so I pasted on an impassive expression. Jules whirled around as I stepped inside. The fear on her face quickly leached away, replaced by a carefully blank expression.

"Are you ready?"

Her eyes darted back to Jack. "Almost."

Jack spoke up. "We were just discussing living arrangements."

"I appreciate the offer, but I'll be fine." Jules smiled inanely at Jack. "Same time tomorrow, right?"

It was her way of ending the conversation, and Jack hesitated for a long moment before responding. "Sounds good."

I shot Jack a quick look that said we'd be in contact, and he dipped his chin in a small nod. I held out one hand and gestured for Jules to precede me. As soon as we were back in the car and headed away from Briarleigh, I asked the question that had been pulling at my mind. "Where are you staying tonight?"

"Mr. Prescott offered to let me stay in one of the guest

cabins, but I declined." I could feel her turn to look at me, but I refused to give in. "I'll figure something out."

She didn't have a plan? "Stay with me."

That way, I could keep an eye on her.

Unfortunately, she was already shaking her head. "I couldn't take advantage of you like that."

"Nearest hotel is down in Kalispell, and you don't have a car," I pointed out. "What exactly was your plan?"

She bristled at my tone. "Why can't I have my car?"

I snorted. Other than the fact that she'd probably pack all of her shit up if I gave it back? Hell, she'd probably leave tire marks on the driveway in her haste to get away. Hell, no. She wasn't going anywhere, not until I knew she would be safe. "It needs a little work."

Not a complete lie. Still, I felt like shit when her face fell. "Like what?"

"I had one of the deputies pick it up last night. Said it was running a little rough, so McBride is gonna replace the spark plugs. Nothing major," I said smoothly. And I really did plan to have the town mechanic look it over—eventually.

She dipped her head. "When can I get it back?"

When I know you won't run. "Soon."

She remained quiet until we pulled up to the house and into the garage. She paused with her hand on the handle. "Where else can I go?"

"Stay here." I turned in my seat to look at her. "Your stuff is here, and you're already comfortable in the bedroom." Hopefully.

"I don't know…" She bit her lip. "I don't want to put you out."

I almost laughed. "You're not holding me up from parties or anything, if that's what you're worried about. I'm hardly ever home anyway. You'll pretty much have the place to yourself."

She thought it over for a second, then countered my offer. "Only if I can pay you rent."

"No." I drew the line at taking money from a woman who so clearly needed it.

She crossed her arms over her chest. "Then I'm not staying."

Damn stubborn woman. "You just started working today. You don't have the money for rent."

If I'd hoped that I could shut down her insistence with my logic, I was wrong. "Jack said he'll pay me each day. I'll pay you a little bit each day. Like paying for a hotel each night."

Goddammit. I bit back a growl. "Fine."

Looking immensely pleased with herself, she climbed from the car. I glared at her back as she moved toward the doorway that connected the garage to the house. She paused with her hand on the knob and threw me a challenging look over her shoulder, the green of her striking eyes glittering like emeralds. Heat raced through my veins, and I fought the urge to adjust myself as my cock pressed against my fly.

Fuck, I was in so much trouble.

NINE

GIULIANA

I stood at the counter that would soon hold the computer system and cash register and stared at the paper in front of me as I chewed on the end of the pen. I'd sketched out a quick design for the way I wanted the shop to look and, so far, I was pretty pleased with the results.

With my plan solidly in place, I dragged the circular clothing racks into temporary spots on the floor. I entered the room from the front door and walked around, trying to get a feel for the flow of the space. It looked good… but empty. I decided I needed to start getting inventory out so I could get a good visual.

Boxes of hangers were stacked along the back wall, just waiting to be filled with merchandise. Using a box cutter, I sliced open the first box and pulled out a thick black parka. A piece of paper fluttered to the ground, and I picked it up. Typed beneath the designer's logo was the name of the coat and a list of sizes. Huh. Well, that was handy.

Skimming the inventory list, I discovered that these were all men's sizes. I made a note on the outside of the box with a thick black marker, then set it off to the side and turned to the next box. I repeated the process with each one, sorting men's, women's, and children's clothing as I went.

Once I had about a dozen boxes open, I began the process of unwrapping everything. Each article of clothing was placed on a plastic hanger, then moved to the metal racks. After they were all hung, I stepped back to contemplate the layout.

I had started with the metal racks first because they had casters so I could roll them from place to place until I was happy with the design. As I pushed the men's parkas further to the front, a sound from the doorway startled me. I whipped around to find Mr. Prescott there.

He hovered just inside the room, his dark eyes on me. "Looking good."

I dipped my chin. "Thank you."

He studied me for another second, then gave a tight little nod. "Yell if you need anything."

For some reason, my heart slammed against my ribs as he stood there staring at me. Did he truly mean what he'd said? "I will."

After he was gone, I went back to unpacking boxes. The next box held a mannequin, and I pulled it out. I gazed speculatively at the clothing I had just placed on the racks, then turned my attention back to the mannequin. I carried the form to the front of the store and set it just inside the display windows so everyone passing could see.

I dressed it in a pair of black snow pants and a trendy zip-up sweatshirt, then finished off the ensemble by draping a thick parka with the furry hood over the mannequin's shoulders. I was so busy adjusting the clothing that I never heard the footsteps approach.

"Ooh, when did we get that?"

I jumped at the woman's voice and spun around. A pretty, petite brunette stood there, blue eyes sparkling as she ran her fingers over the material of the jacket. As she inspected the outfit, I eyed her. She was beautiful—except for the cuts at her lip and forehead and the fading bruises marring her cheeks. What had happened to her? Dread congealed in my gut as the most obvious answer came to me.

"I love this." She stepped back to eye the outfit more critically, then made a circuit around the mannequin before turning her blue gaze on me. "This looks great."

"Thank you." I stood there awkwardly, unsure of what else to say, not wanting to draw attention to her injuries.

The brunette shot me a smile and held out her hand. "I'm Mia. Nice to meet you."

I shook her hand. "Jules."

Mia wandered the racks for a moment, then turned to me. "This is going to look fantastic once it's done. You've done a great job."

Once again, I thanked her. "I haven't decided what to put on the walls yet, but I was planning to do a display of boots over here." I gestured to the wall to my left.

Mia nodded. "I think that's perfect. Close to the dressing room without being in the way."

They were my thoughts exactly. Hopefully people would come out of the dressing room and see them, then decide they needed a new pair to complete their outfit.

"What about accessories?" Mia asked, turning her blue eyes on me.

"I'm not sure what would be best," I admitted. "I was thinking of keeping them close to the counter, because they're small and easy to walk away with."

Mia smiled. "Smart."

I couldn't help but smile back. I was glad she approved of my choices.

"You seem to be pretty good with this"—she waved her hands around to encompass the room—"girly stuff."

"Um…" I froze like a deer in the headlights, and Mia laughed.

"Do you like to decorate?"

I lifted one shoulder. "Sure, I guess."

"Well… I'm getting married soon, and I could use some help."

I turned a surprised gaze on her. "Congratulations. Who's the lucky guy?"

She tipped her head at me. "No one told you?"

"Um… no?"

She let out a little laugh. "Jack and I are getting married at the end of the month."

Jack? Like, Mr. Prescott? I couldn't imagine the two of them together. Mia seemed so sweet and he was so… intense. She must've seen the surprise on my face, because she grinned. "I know what you're thinking. He's really a big teddy bear."

I seriously doubted that, but I kept my mouth shut.

"I know I just met you and it's a little weird, but… would you mind helping? I wanted to go shopping today."

"For what?"

"Wedding things!" Her eyes lit up, her voice rising several octaves with excitement.

I couldn't help but return her infectious smile. "Of course." I followed her out the side door into the parking lot to a little sedan. As I rounded the car, my eyebrows lifted in surprise when I saw the license plate showed that the car was from Alabama.

Mia caught my curious gaze and smiled sheepishly. "It's a rental. I'm just using it until I get something new." After what I had done, I was the last person who would judge her. She must have mistaken my silence for doubt, because she continued almost wearily, "It's a long story."

"Oh, it's okay," I rushed to assure her. "You don't have to tell me. I wasn't fishing for details."

Mia shot me a funny little look as she slid into the driver seat. "I have a feeling you're a good secret keeper."

My cheeks flushed, and I dropped my eyes to my lap as I clicked my seat belt into place, remaining quiet. Weren't we a pair? We made small talk as Mia navigated the car down the winding mountain roads into Pine Ridge. She was bright and bubbly, and she immediately put me at ease. She told me about Briarleigh, and how she herself had just moved up here a little over two weeks ago.

"So where are we headed?" I asked. "Is there anything even around here?"

Mia threw me a guilty look. "I hope so." My eyes widened in astonishment, and I couldn't help but give a little laugh.

"I haven't been down here to Pine Ridge but once or twice," Mia admitted sheepishly. "But I did hear that there's a little boutique in town somewhere."

At the bottom of the mountain, Mia came to a stop sign. She turned left toward Pine Ridge. I knew that Eric's house lay in the opposite direction, just a few miles away. Speaking of intense men who made me uncomfortable...

Last night with Eric hadn't been any easier. I was constantly on edge and had barely slept a wink. I'd be lying though if I said it was entirely fear keeping me awake. He hadn't made a move, hadn't really even acknowledged my presence, but I felt his eyes on me all the time. I was as acutely aware of him as he seemed to be of me.

Mia pulled into an angled parking spot and threw me a smile. "Ready?"

She had told me a little bit of the animosity between some of the townspeople. Not everyone was happy about the new ski resort, especially the man whose family had owned the land for generations. I glanced out the windshield at the town with no small amount of trepidation.

Mia let out a little laugh. "It's safe, I promise."

Pushing my door open, I followed her into the little diner.

According to the hours posted on the door, it closed at two o'clock each day. I listened idly as Mia went about ordering catering from Rosie, the owner. Once we were done, we crossed the street to the florist. I was immediately enveloped by the sweet scent of roses and other unidentifiable flowers as I stepped over the threshold.

A colorful array of poinsettias was set up in the display window, ready for Christmas. A pretty young woman greeted us from behind the counter, partially obscured by a vase full of bright, freshly cut blooms.

Mia ordered flowers, then we headed two doors down to the general store to look for decorations. It was huge inside and looked like nothing I'd ever seen. They had everything. From toys to medicine to animal feed, it seemed the general store was the place to buy whatever odds and ends the residents of Pine Ridge might need.

We passed several rows of groceries, and I slowed. I was still hungry from going to bed without food last night, but it was nothing I wasn't used to. Uncle Massimo had kept me on a strict diet—more so before the wedding—to ensure I stuck to the coveted size two he preferred. The only reason he didn't insist I lose more weight was because of my breasts. He'd said they were my best feature and would draw Nikolai like a moth to light.

I'd been so thin at one point that I'd dropped an entire cup size. Uncle had thrown a fit when my wedding gown gaped open at the bust, and he'd finally given up trying to make me the perfect size zero. The thought alone made me sick. A zero, like I wouldn't even exist. And I barely had. I'd been so hungry sometimes, I thought I would starve to death. Some women were naturally slim—I, to my uncle's consternation, was not one of them.

I eyed the row of canned goods I'd never been allowed to eat. As a child, our chef had always made dinner for us, typical two- or three-course Italian meals fraught with pasta that looked nothing like the label on the can of Chef Boyardee. I eyed it speculatively. It was the same basic ingredients: pasta, sauce, and meat or cheese. I refused to think too much on the meat part of it, but, really, how bad could it be?

I grabbed several cans and shoved them into my basket before moving on down the row. An orange rectangle caught my eye, and I picked up the package of instant noodles.

Beside me, Mia laughed. "I don't think I've had those since college."

I turned to look at her. "Are they good?"

"You've never had them before?" She rolled her lips together in an amused little smile when I shook my head. Reaching out, she grabbed a handful and stuck them in my basket. "They're like a rite of passage for everyone."

We shared a grin, and for the first time in forever, I felt like I'd found a friend.

TEN

ERIC

Things had been slow all morning, and I decided to take the time to check on the one thing that had been weighing on my mind since yesterday. Jules had obviously never registered the vehicle in any state, and I wanted to do some digging. There was a chance that my questions might raise some red flags, but I couldn't help it. I needed to know exactly what I was dealing with if I was going to help her.

Tapping the car's plate number into the database again, I watched as Roger Egerton's information popped up on the screen. I typed his name into the White Pages, and waited for the results to pop up. I wasn't disappointed. There were only two listings, one of which appeared to match the man in question. Picking up the landline on my desk, I punched in the number and waited for the call to connect.

There was a soft click, and a man's wary voice filled the line. "Hello?"

"Hello," I replied smoothly. "Is this Roger Egerton?"

"Who wants to know?" he shot back.

I mentally rolled my eyes but forced myself to keep my

tone level. "Sir, this is Sheriff Donahue from Pine Ridge, Montana. I'm hoping you can help me." I phrased it up as a request so he would hopefully be willing to help me rather than going on the offensive.

"With what?"

I could hear the suspicion in his voice, and it sent a tendril of irritation through me. Was he naturally suspicious, or did he have a reason to withhold information? Being sheriff for nearly the past two years had taught me a lot about politics and people. Sometimes you had to kiss ass to get what you wanted.

Infusing as much friendliness into my tone as possible, I continued. "I believe we found your car broken down on the side of the road. I was just making sure you had a way to remove it."

"Not my car," he replied.

"Oh?" I pretended to think on that for a moment. "Are you sure? I have a blue Cavalier here that was most recently registered to you. Is that not correct?"

"Damn people," he grumbled on the other end of the phone. "Sold that car a month ago. Should've had it switched over by now."

"No problem," I continued placatingly. "I can just reach out to the buyer. Do you remember her name by chance?" My heart leapt at the thought of getting Jules's real name, but I should've known it wouldn't be that easy.

"Her? No, no," the man replied. "It was a guy. Didn't say anything about a wife or a girlfriend, but I guess he could've been buying it for her."

Damn it. I'd been hoping to get more than this small lead, but it was more than I had before. "No problem," I reiterated. "Do you remember the gentleman's name?"

The other end was silent for a moment while I assumed the man drew back a month ago to the purchaser. "Can't say I do. Jake something, maybe? I talked to a lot of people interested in the car back then, so I can't tell you for sure."

I scowled at the phone, unhappy with the answer. Without access to the title, I couldn't even track the new owner down. I made a mental note to check her glove box again. "All right, I replied. "One last thing—can you tell me which notary you used?"

"We went to a notary up in Broadview, off Clay Street. Name's Steve, he's a friend of mine. Everything was legit. Maybe he can help you. I think he keeps records of all that."

They certainly did. I thanked the man and hung up as a lightbulb came on in my head. So Roger had sold the car to a man who'd then turned around and… what? Sold it to Jules? Let her borrow it? My lips pressed together in a firm line. I didn't like either option. More than likely, it meant the person knew she was in trouble and didn't do shit about it. Absolute worst case I could contact the notary and have him pull files of his recent notarizations.

It hit me again that, if Jules came from money, maybe whoever was looking for her had the funds to find her. Maybe she'd specifically requested it this way, risking being picked up without a valid registration—or a license. Thankfully it had only been me. God only knew what would've happened if someone in a larger city had pulled her over. Her ass would probably be in jail, worse off than she'd been before.

I knew Jules would never open up to me, so that was out. Hopefully she would be more comfortable with a woman. Decision made, I pushed out of my chair, ready to head to Briarleigh and enlist Mia's help. First though, I wanted to run everything by Jack. He wasn't at the lodge this morning when I dropped Jules off, so I wanted to catch him before he left for the day.

Things had been slow at the station; no surprise there. At this point during the year, people tended to hunker down and stay inside out of trouble. Christmas was coming up soon, so I would enjoy the last few days of peace before the holidays wreaked havoc on our town.

Seemed like the holidays brought out the worst in some people. Those who didn't have families tended to gather at Murdoch's, the bar in town, or out at the Fox Hole. One thing always led to another, and with an infusion of liquor and negative emotions came fistfights. With a nod and a wave to a couple of my deputies, I strolled out the front door.

Snow had begun to fall over the past hour or so, and I took a few minutes to clear off the SUV before climbing inside. As soon as I turned onto the main drag, I saw that the snowplows had already been out and were working hard to keep the roads clear and safe. Our entire land department consisted of four people. It was a lot of ground to cover, and, especially in this weather, they tended to double up.

They were always dealing with fallen trees or downed electrical wires. Because we were so far away from the big city and most of the electrical plants, they often had to do damage control to minimize issues before the power company could get out here.

Snow clung to the branches of the trees, sparkling in the late afternoon sunlight. Another half an hour and the sun would be gone completely, obscured by the mountain.

Pulling up to Briarleigh, I parked in the side lot along with the employees and climbed out of the SUV. I made my way in the side door and headed straight for Jack's office, praying that Jules was still otherwise occupied. I wanted a few minutes alone to share the information I'd discovered—or lack thereof. He was on the phone, but the office was blessedly empty when he waved me inside. His brows lifted as I closed the door then took a seat in one of the chairs to wait.

A moment later he ended the call and stared across the desk at me. "Sheriff?"

"Everything good so far?" I asked.

He gave a curt nod. "She's quiet, keeps to herself."

I hadn't expected anything else, and I didn't know if it was a relief or not. "Well," I remarked, "I don't really have any news, but I do have a couple updates."

Jack eyed me with interest but remained silent, so I continued. "I ran the plates on her car and found out they're registered to a Roger Egerton in Illinois. It gets a little more interesting. Found out that he sold the car about a month ago…"

He raised an eyebrow as I dragged it out. "…to a man."

"Curious," he remarked.

I nodded. "You see the bruise on her face?"

His expression darkened, and he gave an abrupt nod. "I tried not to make a big deal about it, just asked her if she had anything to worry about."

Jack spread his hands wide. "She said no, so she was either playing dumb or trying to keep it under wraps."

I hated what that meant. My gut twisted into a tight knot at the thought of someone hitting her. No one deserved that, least of all Jules, who was one of the most reserved, mild-mannered women I'd ever met. "What's your take?"

"Same as you," Jack replied.

"Flight risk," I said with no small amount of resignation.

"Flight risk, hell." Jack snorted. "Girl's got one eye over her shoulder and one foot out the door. She never gets within arm's reach. I had to pass her off on Sam because I didn't want to scare her off."

"Sam?" The name didn't ring a bell.

Jack nodded. "Sam Pickett, Gary's son."

I bristled. "That little shit?"

"I thought she'd be more comfortable with someone her age. Something wrong with him?"

Nothing was wrong with him—that was the problem. He'd never been in trouble that I could recall, and he seemed like a good enough kid. If I remembered correctly, he'd graduated five or six years ago with decent grades and an offer to play football at a state school.

He'd come back to Pine Ridge about a year and a half ago, right after I'd been elected sheriff. Now he was working at his dad's hardware store in town, putting the business degree he'd earned to good use. I was sure they'd hit it off. Damn it.

"Nothing at all." Sarcasm leached into my tone, and I sighed. "What else?"

Jack shrugged. "Otherwise she's smart, poised, doesn't miss a thing. I think she's still waiting on the other shoe to drop."

"I know." I gave a little shake of my head. "I don't know what to do about that."

From across the desk, Jack eyed me shrewdly. "What do you want to do about it?"

Hell, I didn't know the answer to that myself. All I knew was that a young woman who appeared to be on the run needed my help. I let out a little growl. "I wanna find the fucker who left those marks on her and make sure it never happens again."

Jack dipped his chin in a nod. "She's safe enough here. Maybe she'll open up a little bit when she feels more comfortable."

"Actually," I admitted, "I really came here to enlist your help in that aspect. Specifically, Mia's help. I think Jules will relate better to a woman."

Jack leaned back in his chair. "They're out together right now doing some shopping. I'll see if Mia can get anything out of her."

"Appreciate it."

Jack's dark gaze darted over my shoulder to the door, and he gestured with his chin. "Open that."

I didn't hesitate to ask why. I just reached behind me and turned the knob, then used my fingertips to fling the door open away from me. Seconds later, feminine voices reached my ears—one I recognized as Mia's; the other, Jules's. I gave a little shake of my head in disbelief. I didn't know how he did it. Fucker had a crazy sixth sense, at least when it came to Mia.

"They're having a crap season," Jack remarked.

I whipped my head toward him, my eyes widening in understanding, and I picked up the thread of conversation as I leaned back casually in my chair. "Offense sucks," I commented. "Wouldn't be so bad if somebody could catch the damn ball."

The women appeared in the doorway just as I finished my sentence, and I glanced over my shoulder at them with a little nod. "Miss Hamilton."

"Please." Mia waved her hand as she entered the office and moved immediately to Jack's side.

I watched as they exchanged a look before turning back to Jules. She remained in the doorway, as if afraid to step inside with all of us. I kept my posture casual in an attempt to put her at ease. "You all done for the day?"

"Um..." She looked over to Mia. "Do you want help carrying the stuff in?"

"No, no," Mia assured her with a smile. "We can tackle that tomorrow."

"If you're sure…"

"What did we buy now?" Jack lifted a brow.

"Wedding stuff."

"Wonderful," he drawled. "Spending my money again, woman."

"*Our* money." Mia grinned cheekily. "And I prefer to think of it as greasing the hands of the locals."

I bit back my grin. Jack sure as fuck had his hands full with Mia. Couldn't say the asshole didn't deserve it, though. I saw the expression on his face change as Jack watched his soon-to-be-wife, and I dropped my gaze away, uncomfortable. I peeked up at Jules, who surveyed them with a strange look on her face, like she didn't know what to make of their interaction.

I couldn't blame her. I always felt like I was intruding on some personal moment any time I was in the same room as them. I could feel the love between them, as if it were a tangible thing that I could reach out and touch. Knowing something like that actually existed made me want to either run like hell or reach out to grab it for myself, I wasn't sure which.

"You ready?" I spoke low, for Jules's ears only, though I was pretty sure Mia and Jack were so absorbed in each other they probably wouldn't know if a fucking tornado touched down outside.

Jules's gaze jumped to me, and she bit her lower lip before nodding. I gestured with my head for her to go first, then I left the office, closing the door behind me.

ELEVEN

GIULIANA

I used the keys Mr. Prescott had given me to unlock the door, then I stepped inside and made my way to the back of the store to turn on the lights. The switches were concealed by a metal panel set in the wall, and the lights flared to life as I flicked each toggle.

I peered around the room, now fully lit. Someone had brought in several more boxes of inventory and stacked them along the back wall by the fitting rooms. While Mia and I were shopping yesterday afternoon, the computer system had been installed. I meandered toward the sales counter and stowed my purse in a drawer before I turned my attention to the new widescreen monitor that took up a good portion of the counter.

My brows drew together when I saw a flash of red peeking from beneath the computer screen. I tipped my head to one side, and my breath caught in my throat as I pulled the rose from its hiding place. Unsettled, I glanced around, expecting whoever had left it to pop out and surprise me.

Who would have left it here? I racked my brain, trying to figure out who had been in and out. The doors had been locked when I'd arrived, so someone must've left it in here last night, then locked up behind them.

I mentally cataloged the changes. It could have been the person who'd installed the computer. Or… maybe the person who'd brought in the inventory currently filling the back wall. I tossed a look over my shoulder, heat flaring in my cheeks. Sam, maybe? He seemed nice enough, but…

I shook the thought away. I couldn't afford to get involved with anyone. Sam was cute in a boyish way. Even if I was interested in dating, he didn't make me feel all fluttery inside. Not like a certain sheriff who'd opened his home to me.

I used my foot to open the bottom drawer and dropped the rose inside, where it landed on top of my purse. I gently kicked the drawer shut again, determined to put it from my mind as I booted up the computer.

"Morning!"

Lifting my head, I gave Mia a bright smile. "Morning."

"Sorry I'm late. Have you been here long?"

"Not at all." I shook my head and picked up a manual someone had left on the countertop. "Looks like they installed some new software, too."

"Awesome." Mia plucked the booklet from my hand and flicked through it before setting it aside.

As soon as the main screen appeared, I double-clicked the new icon. Dozens of indecipherable images popped up.

"Um…" I threw a glance at Mia. "Do you know how to use this thing?"

Her eyes widened briefly. "No way. I don't know anything about retail."

I turned my gaze back to the computer and the elaborate inventory system. All of the merchandise would need to have barcodes applied to the tags, then each would have to be scanned into the system so we could keep track of everything. Mia was here this morning so she could learn about it and understand how to work it too. Unfortunately, neither of us had any experience, so we were both starting from scratch.

"Well," I began slowly, "I guess what we should do first is determine prices."

Thankfully, I hadn't unpacked much of the inventory, only enough to get some on the racks and test out the space. Mia grabbed one of the black parkas from the nearby rack and brought it over. It was marked with a suggested retail price, but I pulled up the internet to check out some of the other competitor's prices as well.

I looked at Mia. "What do you think?"

She glanced at the packing slip to verify what we paid for them. "How about a 20 percent markup?" she asked.

I did some quick math on the calculator, then nodded. "I think that's pretty reasonable. It's comparable to the competitors, but we'll still make a profit. Besides, people coming to a resort would expect it to be a little higher."

For the next hour or so, Mia and I played with the inventory system, learning the ins and outs of how to print and scan barcodes and adjust pricing. The inventory would automatically update after each sale, deducting the amount sold.

"This is pretty cool," Mia said, delight in her eyes.

"I know." I grinned. "I've done plenty of shopping, but it's cool to see this side of it."

Mia glanced at the clock on the computer. "Do you mind if I skip out on you?"

"No problem at all." I waved her away. "I can tackle the rest of this."

With a grateful smile and a little wave, Mia headed out the door. I spent the next several hours printing off barcodes for each new box of items we opened. Mia and I had already taken care of everything currently on the shelves, so the only thing to do now was the incoming stuff. I wondered who was going to manage the shop and how soon they planned to start hiring workers. I knew Mr. Prescott had interviewed several people over the past few days, from what Mia had said.

I broke down the last empty box and set the cardboard aside to be recycled. I stretched my back and looked around the room, pride infusing me. Bit by bit, it was finally starting to come together.

Mr. Prescott hadn't stopped in yet today to check on things, and I was kind of thankful for that. He seemed nice enough, but he still made me uneasy. I hadn't gathered the courage to ask Mia about the cuts and bruises on her face. I prayed they weren't from him, but it was my nature to suspect the worst.

There was an intensity between Jack and Mia that I didn't understand. I hadn't seen them kiss, hadn't even seen them touch each other, but there was a strange tension between them that made me uncomfortable. I didn't want to risk butting in and making things worse for her if that was the case. I knew all too well how someone interfering could jeopardize an already tense situation.

My thoughts immediately turned to my uncle, and goosebumps rose along my arms. Had he tried to track me? Of course he had; I was sure of it. Hopefully, he'd lost me somewhere off I-57 around Champaign where I'd tossed my phone out the window. I remembered each grating ring as my uncle called repeatedly, the angry messages that blistered my ears. Finally, I'd had enough—enough of the fear, enough of the guilt.

I felt horrible for leaving Matteo behind without a word, but he would understand. I didn't have a choice. If I'd stayed, Uncle Massimo would've sold me to Nikolai, and God only knew if I'd have survived that. It was better this way. Maybe someday I could reach out to Matteo and let him know that I was safe. But not yet.

The bridge of my nose burned, and an overwhelming sense of grief at the loss of the one person who'd cared for me tugged at my heart.

TWELVE

ERIC

I pulled up in front of McBride's auto shop and cut the engine of Jules's little Cavalier. Charlie was expecting me, so I bypassed the waiting room and went straight into the shop. I spied an old, scuffed pair of boots sticking out from underneath a Chevy truck, and I nudged one with my foot.

A surly voice filtered up to me. "Whadya want?"

The corners of my mouth twitched. "Is that any way to talk to your sheriff?"

Charlie McBride rolled out from under the vehicle, the wheels of the creeper squeaking loudly, in desperate need of grease. I extended one hand and pulled him to his feet. "Where do you want it?"

Charlie picked up a rag from the nearby workbench and began to wipe his oil-stained hands. He tipped his head and punched a button to lift one of the huge doors. "Middle bay. Pull 'er on in."

I did as he asked, then climbed out of the Cavalier and passed the keys over to him. He looked appraisingly at the car. "What all does it need?"

I snorted. The better question was, what didn't it need? "Everything. Brakes feel a little spongy; might need a tune-up."

Charlie dropped to his haunches and ran his hands over the tread of one tire. "When do you need it back?"

"Whenever."

He nodded. "No problem. Shouldn't be more than a day or two."

"Appreciate it." I leaned against the workbench and rested one ankle over the other, arms crossed over my chest as I watched him inspect the car.

"Not your style," Charlie commented, and I swore I could hear a trace of laughter in his tone.

I rolled my eyes. Meddling old fool. "It belongs to a friend."

"Must be that lady friend I been hearing about."

Fucking small towns. "She's young enough to be my sister."

Charlie grunted. "You sayin' that for your benefit or hers?"

I pressed my lips into a firm line to keep from snapping out a retort. I knew I should've had one of my deputies drop it off, but I wanted to make sure that Jules's car was taken care of properly. Not that Charlie wouldn't do a good job regardless, but I felt an obligation to her. I needed to know that she would be safe when she decided to leave.

I hated the disappointment that filled my chest when I thought about her heading off to someplace new. Though we were only roommates—barely even acquaintances, at that—I liked having her in the house. It didn't feel so empty, so devoid of life. After I left Chicago, I'd put myself in a kind of solitary confinement. Without even trying, Jules had gradually begun to draw me out. I'd forgotten how nice it was to have another person around, especially a woman. We still did our own thing, but I didn't feel so... alone.

"Just fix it up, old man, and quit matchmaking."

He waved me off. "Don't worry, son. I'll make sure to take good care of it for yer woman."

Goddamn it. The last thing I needed was for these interfering idiots in town to think she was mine—regardless of how good that sounded. "She's not my woman."

"Keep tellin' yerself that."

I turned to leave before I exploded, unsure exactly of why it bothered me so much. I didn't lay claim to women. Even though I'd cared for my ex-wife at one point, I'd never felt that head-over-heels, can't-live-without-her emotion that people talked about. The women I'd dated afterward had meant even less. So why was I so worried about Jules?

I shook my head. The older I got, the more my protective instincts flared to life, I decided. I'd seen so much, while Jules was so young. She'd barely started her life, and she was still unaware of all the danger in the world. Protectiveness was in my nature, and I had a soft spot for a young girl on the run. That was all.

A cruiser pulled up in front of McBride's, and I waved over my shoulder to Charlie. "Give me a call when it's ready."

A grunt of acknowledgement came from under the Cavalier, and cold air cut through me as I pushed open the door and stepped outside. Riley lifted an eyebrow from the driver seat as I slid into the cruiser. "All set?"

"Yep." I slammed the door against the biting wind. "Goddamn, I swear it's dropped twenty degrees since this morning."

"Another storm rolling in," Riley commented as he rolled out of the parking lot and back toward the sheriff's office on the outskirts of town.

"Great," I grumbled as I settled into the seat.

For a long moment, Riley was silent. Then— "Mind me asking why you dropped the car at McBride's?"

Goddamn it. "Yes."

"Yes, you mind? Or yes, you're gonna tell me?"

"Fuck off."

Riley laughed. "Come on, boss, just curious."

I turned in my seat to look at him. "Why?"

He lifted a hand from the wheel in a shrugging motion. "Dunno. People are talking." Of course they were. I rolled my eyes as he continued. "Say she's a looker. I just thought—"

"Stop thinking," I cut in, my cold tone slicing through the air.

A tiny smirk lifted his mouth. "You got it, boss."

Motherfucker. My chest lifted on a slow, deep inhale. Was I going to have to kill one of my deputies for checking out Jules? "She's too…" Naïve? Beautiful? Perfect? All of the above? "Young," I finished lamely.

Why did I keep coming back to that, like it was the best excuse I had? *Because it's true. And you need to keep reminding yourself before you do something stupid.*

Riley nodded haltingly like he knew I was full of shit. "If you say so."

"Not you, too," I groaned, letting my head drop back against the seat.

He laughed, undaunted. "You haven't really dated anyone since you moved here. And when you do, you go to Kalispell or somewhere that's an hour or more away."

I lifted my head to look at him. "How do you know that?"

He slid a disbelieving glance at me. "Everyone knows that."

Well, shit. Whatever. It wasn't anyone's business what I did. "Tell everyone to mind their own damn business," I groused. Christ only knew what they'd say if they knew she was staying with me.

He chuckled. "Easier said than done. There are more than a few guys willing to take her off your hands."

I turned a sharp gaze on him. "Choose your next words carefully before I find myself down a deputy."

Riley laughed despite my threat and held up a hand placatingly. "Didn't say one of 'em was me. But you might wanna make up your mind before someone does it for you."

"I might wanna knock your teeth down your throat, too," I shot back.

"Don't shoot the messenger," he countered. "Besides, might be good for you."

I hummed a noncommittal sound and turned my attention out the window. Unease roiled in my gut. Jules was beautiful; men from here to the border—both of them, more likely— would line up to be with a woman like her. I imagined her with a man her own age, dating, laughing… kissing. What bothered me was the irrational yet overpowering urge to break the fictional man's jaw.

I watched the red brick of the sheriff's office roll into view without really seeing it, my attention focused wholly on Jules. It was a waste of effort; it could never be more than what we had right now—a mutual agreement to share the same living space.

Riley pulled to a stop in his designated space and I climbed out. "Thanks, man. See ya in the morning."

I didn't bother to go inside; I had a fuck ton of paperwork to get caught up on, but it could wait until tomorrow. I climbed into my cruiser and rolled down the main street of Pine Ridge, keeping one eye on my surroundings while I considered the woman who took up part of my house—and most of my thoughts.

It bothered me immensely that she had lied to me. Maybe not lied, exactly, but she was definitely holding back the truth —where she'd come from, why she was here, what she planned to do next. I wanted to ask her all of these things and none of them at the same time. I was terrified of pushing her further away.

A frown settled over my lips as I drove toward Briarleigh to pick up the woman in question. I entered the building through the side door and poked my head into Jack's office. "Jules done for the day?"

He didn't bother to turn from the computer. "I haven't seen her, so she's probably still working in the pro shop. Want me to go grab her?"

"Nah. I'll take care of it."

"Here." Jack stood and met my gaze as he pulled some cash from his wallet.

I took the folded bills from his outstretched hand. "Thanks. I'll pass it along."

He tipped his chin and went back to work, and I went in search of Jules. Down the short corridor, I spied her through a huge window. She stood behind the desk working at a computer, but her eyes looked red, almost as if she'd been crying.

She jerked her head upward to meet my gaze as I stepped inside, and her expression shuttered. My eyes narrowed as I examined her, but any trace of sadness was gone. "Ready to go?"

"Yep." Jules bent and grabbed her purse from a bottom drawer, then moved to turn off all the lights. She closed and locked the door behind us, then tucked the key into a zippered pocket of her purse. I watched each meticulous movement in fascination.

Side by side, we headed to my cruiser. Silence descended over us during the ride home, and by the time we arrived, I'd convinced myself that whatever I'd seen in her eyes earlier had been a trick of the light. We entered the house and went our separate ways, Jules heading to the bedroom while I hit the kitchen. It'd been a long ass day, and I needed a beer.

I cracked the top off a bottle and took a long swig. I wasn't sure why, but beer always tasted better from a bottle. I leaned against the counter nursing my beer, lost in thought as I stared out the window into the darkness.

A soft sound drew my attention, and I leaned around the corner. Jules stood in the middle of the hallway staring at the laundry chute. I tipped my head to one side, watching curiously as she opened the small door and peeked inside.

"What are you doing?"

She jumped at the sound of my voice, and the door slammed shut, the sharp crack of wood against wood filling the hallway.

"Oh! I…" She crossed her arms over her chest, and I could literally see her body quake where she stood. "I'm sorry. Curiosity got the best of me."

Eyes locked on hers, I approached slowly until I was right in front of her. I tipped my chin at the small door as I pulled it open. "Ever heard of a laundry chute?"

She shook her head, then peered into the small, dark space. "What does it do?"

I fought the smile pulling at my lips. "You drop your dirty clothes down there, and they end up in a hamper in the basement by the washer and dryer."

Her lips parted slightly, her eyes widening in amazement like a little kid's. "Can I try it?"

"Be my guest."

I stepped back and watched as she went into her room to gather clothes, then came back and dropped a large pile down the chute. "What now?"

This time, I did smile. "Follow me."

I opened the basement door off the kitchen, then flipped on the light and started down, Jules on my heels. At the base of the stairs, I turned right and headed toward the washer and dryer. A hamper sat on the floor next to them, now full of Jules's clothes. A huge smile lit her face, and my heart stuttered in my chest. It was the first time I'd seen her smile, really smile, since she'd arrived. For it to be over something so mundane blew my mind.

Her eyes darted toward the washer, then up to me. "I, um... would you mind if I use yours?"

"Not at all," I replied. I turned to go, letting her do her thing, but her small voice stopped me halfway back to the stairs. "Eric?"

I couldn't ever remember her calling me by my name before, and I closed my eyes briefly before turning back to face her.

"Could you, um, show me how this works?" Her voice was soft, her cheeks pink as if she was embarrassed to even have to ask. For the millionth time, I wondered who Jules really was and where she'd come from.

Masking my surprise, I approached and pointed to a knob. "You'll need to decide what temperature water you'll need, and how much."

Her brows drew together. "Do they all go in together?"

I pressed my lips together to keep from smiling and undermining her confidence. "The tags on your clothes will tell you how to wash them. Some materials are more sensitive than others."

I tried to relate it to her as best I could. "You know how some items can only be dry cleaned?" She nodded at my question, and I continued. "The rest of your clothes are like that, too. Some colors and materials do better in warmer water, some in colder. Let me take a look."

I picked up a shirt off the top of the pile and flipped it inside out, inspecting the tag along the seam. "This one says wash in cold. Let's start a pile for each."

We set out separating the clothes, placing each in their respective piles until I came to a pair of lacy pink panties. Almost as soon as my fingers grazed the material, I dropped them again, and Jules's face turned as pink as the fabric. She snatched them away, but not before I caught sight of the little black bows running in a straight line down the back, right where the crease of her ass would be. All I could envision was Jules in those tiny panties and nothing else.

She began to load the washer, and I turned once more to head upstairs, hoping the awkwardness would dissipate. I picked up a shirt that had missed its pile and carried it back to the washing machine. I reached around to drop it in just as she backed up. Her back hit my chest, bringing her body against mine, and we both froze.

For a long second, neither of us moved. I forced my fingers to release the fabric, dropping the shirt into the washer, then slowly withdrew my hand. Jules inhaled sharply as I brushed her arm in the process. Still, she didn't move. Holding my breath, I gently rested my fingertips in the crook of her elbow.

The curves of her tiny body fit perfectly against the planes of mine, the top of her head ending just beneath my chin. My fingers itched to settle on her hips and pull her further into my embrace. I wanted to feel every inch of flesh sliding over my own.

"Sorry." My breath stirred the wispy hair by her ear, and I felt the faint vibration deep in my bones as a delicate shudder racked her body.

"It's fine." Low and breathy, her voice was barely a whisper—but I heard it. Not fear. Not embarrassment. *Lust*. She wanted to be touched; she needed it.

I congratulated myself on her reaction but hated myself for the same reason. I shouldn't want to want her… but I did. Unable to break the connection just yet, I slid the pad of my thumb back and forth over her soft skin, reveling in the feel of her. Inhaling deeply, I gave her arm a gentle squeeze before reluctantly stepping away.

She was too young, too innocent and naïve. She was secretive and untrusting, and I didn't know if she would ever open up to anyone. I wanted to be her confidant, yet at the same time, it would be easier to pretend there was nothing between us. I was already feeling more than protectiveness, and I couldn't allow my attraction to her to dictate my actions. I'd learned firsthand what distrust could do to couples. Not that we were a couple—we weren't. Neither of us could afford that.

THIRTEEN

GIULIANA

I paused in the act of hanging a bright blue zip-up sweatshirt. "Will the resort have a spa?"

Confused Bahamian blue eyes met mine. "A what?"

I slipped the hanger on the wire rack, then turned my attention to Mia. "A spa. Massages, facials, manicures, that kind of thing. Mr. Prescott never mentioned anything. Are you guys planning to put one in?"

A bright smile lifted her lips. "It sounds so funny to hear you call him Mr. Prescott, like he's all professional."

Embarrassed heat flared across my cheeks. "It just feels strange to call him Jack."

It was too personal, too… friendly. I wasn't sure I ever wanted to be on such familiar terms with him.

Mia waved away my concern. "Everyone calls him Jack; he prefers it. Anyway, what were you saying?"

My gaze slid over her unpolished nails, and I bit my lip. "I don't know. It was just an idea."

She set down the shirt she held and propped one hand on her hip expectantly. "Tell me."

Those blue eyes pierced mine, and I caved. "I was just thinking… A lot of resorts like this have restaurants, shops, spas."

Mia nodded. "The restaurant is about another six months out. We're interviewing chefs right now. But a spa…" She tapped her chin in thought. "I hadn't even thought of it."

I shrugged. "Wouldn't it be nice for people to come down off the slopes after a long day and be able to get a massage? Or grab a new dress from one of the shops and have your nails done before dinner?"

Mia's smile grew. "See? This is the problem with men running stuff."

I gave a little laugh. "They rarely understand our needs."

"Exactly." She nodded. "Which is precisely why we need to tell them."

She grabbed my hand and pulled me toward the door.

"Wait!" I cried out, trying to dig in my heels. "Where are we going?"

"To tell Jack we need a spa!"

I let out a little laugh as she dragged me out of the shop and down the corridor. Jack lifted his head as we entered his office, and Mia pointed at me. "Tell him."

"Wh—" My eyes widened, and my gaze darted between Mia's face and Jack's. My heart raced, and my feet felt frozen to the floor under his dark stare. Every muscle went completely rigid as I clammed up, unable to speak.

Mia swooped in and saved me from the awkwardness of the moment. She slapped one hand on his desk. "We need a spa."

Those dark brown eyes turned to Mia, and his eyebrows lifted in a mixture of confusion and surprise. "What?"

"A spa. You know." She held up a hand in my direction and wiggled her fingers. "Massages. Manicures. That sort of thing."

Jack was shaking his head before she even finished. "More additions right now will throw us off schedule."

"But—"

"And that's without even discussing the licenses for a place like that." He pushed his chair back and stood. "I don't think we can swing it."

Mia crossed her arms over her chest. "Well, I want a spa."

One nearly black eyebrow arched as he stared at her. "We don't even know if it would be profitable. These are things that need to be taken into consideration before we just jump into something."

"They're always profitable. Aren't they?" Mia directed the question at me, and my mouth dropped open.

"Um…"

"Of course they are." She waved a hand as if it didn't matter. "Jules and I will check into all of the regulations and licenses we would need, and we can build a proposal from there."

Jack practically growled. "You can't just make decisions because you own half the company, you know."

"Please." Mia rolled her eyes. "It's a great idea and you know it."

"I didn't say it wasn't, but—"

She propped her hands on her hips and glared at her fiancé. "You're just being stubborn."

My stomach clenched as I watched his lips press into a firm line. *Please stop,* I mentally begged Mia. *Don't do it.*

"We'll run the numbers, but I'm not promising anything," he warned.

"Fine." Mia threw her arms up and flounced away. "But you know I'm right." She let out a small yelp as Mr. Prescott's hand whipped out and caught her on the bottom. My heart thudded to a stop in my chest, my breath suspending itself in my lungs as I took a step toward her. *Oh, God.* I wouldn't watch another woman suffer at the hands of a man. I moved instinctively, my only thought to save her from the same fate I'd suffered for the past few years.

I was reaching for her, ready to pull her out of harm's way as she whirled on Jack. Surprise jerked me to a stop when she let out a little laugh and threw herself at him. Mr. Prescott met my gaze as he wrapped one arm around his soon-to-be-wife's waist and pulled her close. I halted my hands midreach, then pressed them flat against my stomach in an effort to contain the mixture of unease and confusion swirling within.

My teeth sank into my lower lip as I tried to reconcile the soft slap in my mind. Mia trusted Jack never to hurt her, but my uncle hadn't always seemed abusive, either. I'd only experienced suffering instead of pleasure at my uncle's hands —but I was now seeing a different side of things. Touch wasn't always hard and punishing. Mia hadn't seemed to mind—just the opposite, in fact. I didn't know how I felt about that. My mind screamed one thing while my heart said another.

Jack's assessing eyes missed nothing as they bored into mine for another long moment before turning back to Mia. He cupped her face in one hand and stared down at her. Something indefinable passed between them, making me feel like an interloper. The connection between these two was like nothing I'd ever seen. Finally, he dropped a kiss on her upturned mouth. "On second thought, I think it's a great idea."

"Really?" Mia fairly squealed as she threw her arms around his neck.

He nodded. "I still want to run the numbers, but I think it'll make a great addition." His dark gaze slid toward me. "I think if anyone could make a go of it, it would be you two."

His compliment warmed me, and I could feel a blush stain my cheeks as I dropped my head and stared at my toes.

"Put together a proposal, and we'll have Carter take a look at it." He continued. "Briarleigh definitely needs a feminine touch. I'm sure I can count on you two to make that happen, right?"

I lifted my gaze to find him staring right at me. I knew what he was asking. Did I plan to stay long enough to help and see this through? I couldn't go anywhere else; not really. I had no family to turn to, and, though Mr. Prescott paid me each day, I owed Eric for letting me stay with him. It would be a long time before I was ready to move on.

Truth be told, I didn't want to leave. I liked it here. Though I didn't get out much, I liked the small town of Pine Ridge. It was quaint and quiet, and everyone knew everyone. That might not be so important to some people, but to me it meant the world. If a stranger showed up, everyone would know it by lunchtime at Rosie's. I was safe here. I liked my job, and I liked the Prescotts. And then there was Eric. I wanted to stay.

Mr. Prescott pinned me with his dark stare, and his brows lifted a tiny bit in silent question.

Swallowing hard, I nodded. "Yes, sir."

The lines of his face softened the slightest bit. "You can call me Jack." He offered a tiny smile, the first one I'd seen. "Mr. Prescott makes me feel old."

A grin pulled at my lips, and for the first time, I began to relax. This was where I belonged. Maybe one day I would move on, but I was safe here. Mia and Jack were, if not friends, exactly, close acquaintances. This was where I wanted to be.

Jack kissed Mia's forehead and gently pushed her away. "Now get out of here so I can get some work done. You're a damn distraction."

A huge smile split Mia's face as she pressed her hands together in a praying motion. "You'll love what we come up with, I promise."

"I'm sure." He threw a sly wink at his fiancée, one I'd

have missed if I wasn't paying close attention. There was so much emotion conveyed in that tiny gesture.

Mia bounced toward me. "I have to stop by my office real quick to grab my laptop. Meet you back in the shop?"

"Sure."

Bemused smile in place, I strode back down the hallway toward the pro shop. I still couldn't quite wrap my mind around what had just happened. Jack and Mia's relationship was strange to me. Even my parents hadn't been overly affectionate. My mother seemed to tolerate my father more than anything, and I knew he'd had several affairs during the course of their marriage. I knew what he'd done was wrong, but he was my daddy—I loved him regardless.

I think that was part of the reason my mother had so willingly stepped away when daddy died. She'd given me over to Uncle Massimo's care and could finally do what she wanted with her life. She no longer had to pretend to like a man she wasn't in love with.

Sometimes I wondered if she knew how awful Uncle Massimo really was. I'd like to think that she didn't, but who knew? Wouldn't she have fought to keep me instead of allowing him to sweep me right out of our house and under his wing?

The last time I'd seen her was when I'd selected my wedding gown. Though saying that I had any choice in the matter was an overstatement. Uncle Massimo had herded me away, never leaving the two of us alone.

"Hey."

I stumbled, caught off guard, and my head snapped toward Sam where he stood several feet away. My heart jackhammered in my chest, and I fought for control. "Oh, hey."

"You liking it around here so far?"

"Yeah, it's nice."

"Good." He awkwardly rubbed at the back of his neck. "So, um… did you get the flower I left for you?"

My eyes widened. "That was you?"

"Well… yeah."

He said it like he was surprised I even had to ask, and I quickly covered my blunder. "Thank you. I wasn't sure it was for me."

His stance relaxed, and his charming grin came out once more. "Of course. Actually…" His gaze darted away for a second before returning to me. "I was wondering if you might like to go out sometime."

I opened my mouth, then snapped it closed again, unsure exactly of what to say. Sam was nice enough, but I hated to hurt his feelings by turning him down. I bit my lip and shifted on my feet as the silence stretched between us. "I—I can't," I finally managed to stammer out.

His face fell in disappointment. "Oh."

"I'm sorry," I rushed to say. "I just… I'm sorry."

I couldn't explain why things would never work between us. Thankfully, he offered a tight smile. "No problem. I guess I'll see ya around?"

"Sure." I nodded, and guilt tugged at my heart as he turned away.

FOURTEEN

ERIC

Nodding to the few patrons still filling the booths, I strode into the diner and up to the waist-high bar in front of the kitchen. Cynthia exited the double swinging doors and offered me a pretty smile. "Food's almost ready. Let me drop this off and I'll grab it for you."

"Take your time." I propped one hip on a barstool and pulled my phone from my back pocket to check my emails.

"How's your houseguest?"

I bit back a groan and smiled across the bar at Rosie. "Just fine, ma'am."

I should have known she'd hear about Jules staying with me sooner or later. I'd stopped in over the past few days to pick up food, always ordering two meals—one for me and one for Jules. Trying to put off the inevitable, I made sure to talk with a different waitress each day. I was probably lucky it had taken her this long to nail my ass down. If there was gossip to be found, Rosie was sure to dig it up.

Her gaze jumped toward Cynthia as she passed us once

more, then it returned to me. "She's a good girl, that one. You helped her a lot."

I shrugged one shoulder. "I just did my job."

Rosie regarded me, one eyebrow lifting toward her hairline. "You help an awful lot of people, Sheriff. But only one's livin' with ya."

"Yes, ma'am." Saying anything else would be suicide. I refused to confirm or deny her suspicions, but I knew rumors would soon spread like wildfire. I wondered if any were making their way up to Jules at Briarleigh yet. What would she think of it? Would she be appalled… or flattered?

I touched the brim of my hat just as Cynthia brought me the bag of food and set it on the counter in front of me.

Rosie offered a sly smile. "See you tomorrow, Sheriff."

I rolled my eyes, hating that she was right. I'd seen Jules's meager supply of college-like food in the cabinets. It magically appeared one day, but I couldn't get it off my mind. I didn't know how she could bear to eat that stuff. It wasn't nutritional in the least, and she was still too fucking skinny. The day after I'd seen the cheap noodles and canned foods in my cupboard, I started ordering daily specials from Rosie's Diner.

Most days, I would order lunch and take it back to the station, so I wouldn't show up at home with two boxes of food. I typically told Jules that Rosie had sent too much, or that someone at the station didn't want it. The first night, she'd given me a strange look but didn't argue. Ever since, she had just kind of accepted it. She would take the food and head back to the bedroom, then eat in silence by herself.

I hated that she felt like she had to do it, but it was probably for the best. We danced around each other, trying to stay out of the other's space as much as possible.

I left Pine Ridge and headed up to Briarleigh to pick up Jules. She was waiting just inside the back door when I pulled up, and she was already halfway to the SUV before I put it in park. I picked up the bag of food on the passenger seat and held it while she buckled herself in, then passed it back to her.

"Hold this, would you?"

Silently, she accepted it and settled it on her lap. I found myself holding my breath, waiting to see if she would say anything. She didn't. I headed back down the mountain to my place, silence hanging heavily in the air. I didn't know any women who spoke as little as Jules. I hadn't talked to Jack recently, not wanting to look too suspicious, but I wondered if Mia was making any headway with her.

"Hey, I've got a surprise for you."

Her head swiveled toward me, a mixture of confusion and trepidation in her pretty green eyes. "You got me something?"

Shit. "Not exactly." I fumbled with my response as I hit the button to lift the garage door. "I just figured you were tired of relying on me, so…"

She turned toward the garage, and her eyes widened as her car was revealed inch by inch. "You brought my car back!"

"Yep." A tiny kernel of pride flared to life as a smile lifted her lips. The cop in me was loath to let her keep driving around without a valid license or registration, but if she came back to my place each night... Well, I was willing to make that concession.

She gestured over her shoulder. "I saw your truck outside, but I didn't think…" She paused. "You didn't have to do that. I'm fine parking outside."

"It's no problem." I put the car in park and cut the engine. "Besides, I'm in the cruiser 90 percent of the time anyway. Makes more sense for your car to be inside."

She hesitated, her fingers on the door handle. "If you're sure…"

"I am."

Her teeth sank into her lower lip. "What do I owe you?"

I refused to take any more money from her. "All Charlie did was look it over. You don't owe me anything."

Her voice was quiet but full of gratitude. "Thank you."

"You're welcome." I climbed from the car, somehow resisting the urge to reach across the seat and draw her into my arms. "Now, come on. I'm starving."

I held the door for Jules as we entered the house, and I set the bag of food on the scarred oak kitchen table. I gestured with my chin to the chair opposite me as I unpacked everything. "Sit with me?"

It was both a request and an order. I'd given her several days and plenty of time and space to herself, but I was itching for answers. Tentatively, she pulled out the chair and sat. It was the first time she had joined me at the table, and it sent a little curl of pleasure through me. I'd hardly seen her at all except each morning and afternoon when I took her to and picked her up from work. It was reassuring to know that if she didn't completely trust me, she was at least becoming more comfortable with me.

I settled in the chair across from her and began to eat. I wasn't quite sure how to begin, so I just jumped in. "How do you like Briarleigh?"

"It's nice," she said shyly. I waited for her to elaborate, but she remained silent.

"Are you settling in okay?" I prompted.

She nodded. "Everyone's been really helpful."

She was infuriatingly succinct, and it made me want to scream. Why did she feel like she had to keep everything all bottled up, even the mundane shit? It bothered me more than I wanted to admit. She'd been in my home for five days now, but I'd yet to learn anything about her. It was about fucking time that changed.

"They getting all ready for the grand opening?"

She swallowed her bite of food. "Yep. Everything's coming together."

"You getting the shop all organized?"

A nod.

"I heard you're helping Mia with wedding stuff."

Another nod. "I am."

I ground my back teeth together and fought the urge to snap at her. Jesus Christ, getting her to talk was like pulling teeth. "Sounds fun."

"It is." She opened her mouth as if to say more, then snapped it closed again.

My brows lifted. I knew she'd been about to say something else, so why'd she stop? "You must enjoy it," I offered, hoping she'd pick up the thread of conversation.

She used her fork to push her meatloaf around the Styrofoam carton before responding. Her voice was low and tentative. "I do. I miss it, actually."

It was the first admission I'd gotten from her, and it felt like I'd won the fucking lottery. Finally, after damn near a week, it was something. She didn't strike me as a party girl, though. I assumed she meant it more literally, but I didn't think she was old enough to have been married. The thought alone sent a strange pang through my heart. But once the thought took hold, I couldn't let it go. I found that I needed the answer, though I didn't want to examine the reasoning behind it too closely. "Were you married?"

Her eyes widened and she shook her head. "No. I… no."

She said it with such vehemence that it couldn't be anything other than the truth. Yet there was a flicker of something in her eyes when I'd mentioned marriage. Fear, maybe? Thankfully, I didn't have to pry, because she continued of her own will.

A tiny smile lifted the corners of her mouth. "My family celebrated everything. Weddings, birthdays, graduations, victories…" Here she trailed off for a moment, her gaze dropping guiltily to the table, the smile sliding off her face. "Anyway. Any excuse to have a good time, they did."

Past tense. She spoke of them with reverence, yet something had driven her away from them. If she wasn't married, I could only jump to the next logical conclusion and my original guess—a boyfriend who'd treated her like shit. I surreptitiously studied the bruise on her forehead that had finally begun to fade. It was a sickly yellow color now and considerably less swollen than it'd been when she'd first arrived.

I got angrier every time I saw it. I hadn't brought it up, and she hadn't either. Not that I expected her to. I had a feeling she'd be happy to bury the past wherever she'd come from and leave it at that. Didn't stop me from wanting to find out. One of these days, I swore I was going to learn the truth if it fucking killed me.

We chatted amiably for the next few minutes as we picked at our food. The mundane questions helped her to slowly open up and gradually, the single-word answers grew more elaborate. Finally, I pushed away from the table and carried my takeout container to the trash. Jules watched me, her eyebrows drawing together as I slipped into my coat and boots.

"Are you leaving?"

Surprised, I jerked my head toward her. She'd never asked before what I was doing or where I was going. True, most of the time I didn't leave the house much. This was a night for firsts, apparently.

I tipped my head toward the front porch. "We're supposed to get some more snow overnight. I'm going to bring in some more kindling in case we lose power."

"Okay." She nodded slowly. "Do you want some help?"

I almost refused, but the expression on her face had me rethinking my decision. She looked almost hopeful, and I couldn't bring myself to deny her. The task was an easy one, but if she wanted to help, then I wasn't going to stop her. "Sure."

She popped up from her chair and quickly grabbed her coat and boots from the mud room. I eyed her as she slipped into them. The jacket was leather, the cut perfect for her figure and obviously expensive, but it was too thin to really be of much protection, especially up here in the mountains. Same for the shoes. Her black leather boots were of good quality, but she needed something a little more substantial if she intended to be traipsing around in the snow.

"You should talk to Mia about getting a heavier coat and some snow boots," I observed.

She immediately shook her head as she zipped the coat up to her neck. "These suit me just fine. Besides, I don't really have the money to waste on clothes."

"Wouldn't hurt to ask."

"Maybe." From the tone of her voice, she may as well have told me to take a long walk off a short pier.

"I'm sure they'd be pretty reasonable with your employee discount." I didn't know if the workers got any type of discount or not, but if she needed appropriate clothes, I was damn sure going to make it happen.

"Oh. I didn't think of that."

"We can ask tomorrow." I pulled open the front door, and Jules sucked in a sharp breath at the bitter cold that rushed past our faces.

"It gets so cold up here."

"It can," I admitted. "I'd say it's not so bad once you get used to it, but I'd probably be lying."

Out of the corner of my eye, I swore I saw a flicker of a smile. "You're probably right. I'm not sure I could ever get used to this."

For some reason, I felt a little stab of disappointment at her statement. I'd known all along that she wouldn't stay. I wasn't even sure I wanted her to stay, and if I did, it was purely for her safety. At least, that's what I told myself.

"Here."

She held out her hands, and I placed several logs on top of her outstretched arms. I gathered an armload myself, and we carried them back into the house then stacked them by the fireplace. We made another trip outside, and I paused, staring up at the sky. Jules came to a stop next to me. For a moment, I almost expected her to speak, but she didn't.

I let out a soft chuckle. Of course she didn't. Jules was an observer. I'd never met a more intriguing, infuriatingly frustrating woman in my life. Instead of turning me off, though, it made me want to know more about her. I was dying to know where she'd come from, what had happened to her. What she was going to do next, where she would go.

I had no business asking these things. There were a thousand reasons I should let her go on her way and go about my life, not the least of which was that she was sexy as fuck. It was becoming harder and harder not to touch her. She was technically an adult, but she was still a good ten years younger than me. I felt old as hell next to her, though she'd never given any indication that it bothered her.

And why should it? She probably saw me as the sheriff, a figure of authority. Worse, she might even see me as a big brother or a father figure. Meanwhile I was panting away after her, jerking off to her image in the shower, imagining what she'd look like naked—or in those fucking pink panties. I should encourage her to move on—I needed to, for both our sakes. But the fact of the matter was, I liked having her around.

I wasn't stupid, though. Neither of us could afford anything more than the platonic relationship between us. I wasn't going to pine after a woman who wouldn't even tell me her real name. I could feel her eyes on me, so I cleared my throat and pushed away my wayward thoughts.

"It never ceases to amaze me how bright the stars are out here."

As if just now noticing, Jules let out a little gasp and

leaned further over the railing, like she could reach out to touch them if she got a little closer. "It's beautiful. I've never seen anything like this."

"I knew they were there, of course, but I grew up in the city where the lights drowned them out."

She nodded in agreement, but didn't say anything, still transfixed by the vista in front of her. I took that to mean she was from a city—a city large enough that she'd never really been out of it to see the stars at night. There was really only one city like that near where the car had been registered.

"The closest thing I ever came to seeing stars before I moved out here was the courtyard at the Tavern."

Jules cracked a tiny smile as she stared upward, her gaze sliding over the thousand little diamonds twinkling in the sky. "I know, right?"

As if suddenly realizing what she'd said, Jules went completely rigid next to me. That one little slip had told me so much. It'd been a gamble, but it'd paid off, and I barely managed to hold back a victorious grin. The Tavern was a high-end restaurant in Chicago—one she was apparently well acquainted with.

Playing it off, I kept my eyes focused on the sky. "They look beautiful, but it's kind of a bad sign."

"Why?"

I heard the hesitation in her voice, and I glanced at her across my shoulder. "Gonna be cold tonight."

Her shoulders relaxed, and she tipped her head slightly to one side in question. "How can you tell?"

I gestured with my chin to the few wispy white clouds hovering in space. "Clouds help form a barrier to hold in the warm air. Otherwise, the Earth's surface temperature radiates off more quickly."

I felt more than saw her turn back to me. "Is that true?"

"I think I know what I'm talking about. I've been around a

lot longer than you." I tossed her a wink. I needed to keep reminding myself of that fact.

Jules scrunched up her nose. "Sounds… fake."

"Fake?" I scoffed. "It's science."

"Hmm…" She hummed a little noise in the back of her throat. "I'm going to google it later."

I lifted a brow in her direction, and she quickly turned away—but not before I caught the tiny teasing smirk on her pretty mouth.

FIFTEEN

GIULIANA

"You are coming to the wedding, aren't you?" Mia asked.

I bit my lip, taking in the pleading look in her eyes. "Well, I um… I honestly wasn't sure I was invited."

"Of course you are!" she exclaimed. "Make sure Eric comes too. I'd like for him to be there."

I gave a little nod, completely unsure of whether I could make her request happen or not. I wasn't sure why she thought I held any sway over what he did. "I'll see what I can do."

She looked at me, then back at the room, half-full of merchandise. "Let's leave this for later. I have a better idea."

"Okay?" I drew out the word, my confusion evident in my tone, and Mia laughed.

"What we really need is a dress for you." My cheeks flamed, knowing she was probably right. She'd only ever seen me in yoga pants or jeans, the full extent of the wardrobe I'd brought with me.

"Are you sure you want me there?" I hedged.

She rolled her head slightly to one side and gave me a disbelieving look. "You're not getting out of it now."

I flattened my lips to hide a smile. "You're the best."

Mia cracked a little grin. "Don't let Jack hear that, but I'm glad someone understands."

I laughed as we gathered up our purses, then headed out the employee entrance to her car. Instead of the little rental she had last week, a black Range Rover SUV now sat in its place.

"It's beautiful," I said as I slid inside.

Mia rolled her eyes and started the car. "It was Jack's idea."

"Smart man," I quipped, and Mia grinned as she pulled out of the parking lot.

"He does have his moments."

Every time she mentioned Jack's name, she lit up with pure joy, and a tiny little spark of jealousy shot through me. Someday, I wanted that. I wanted a man who loved me and could put that kind of smile on my face every day. Though I didn't know their story, I was happy that they had prevailed.

Jack's intensity still made me a little uneasy, but it was hard not to love Mia. Part of me wanted to hold back, but the little girl who had grown up mostly in solitude wanted a friend, someone to confide in. I wasn't ready to spill my secrets, but I longed for camaraderie and companionship.

When Mia and I had last been in town, we'd stopped only at the diner and the general store. But buildings lined both sides of the main street, and I had recognized at least a church and a convenience store type drive-through, so I knew the little town held more than met the eye. I settled back into my seat, content to chatter amiably as we made our way down the mountain into the tiny town.

We parked in front of Rosie's Café, and I stepped out of the car, bracing myself against the bitter cold. The icy wind assaulted my exposed face, but the rest of me was warm thanks to my new coat and boots. I had—as Eric suggested—bought them at a hefty discount from Briarleigh's stock, and I was incredibly grateful for the thick material as I tucked my hands in the fleece-lined pockets. The sun was shining despite the few inches of snow that lingered on the sidewalks, and just the sight of it lifted my spirits.

Mia appeared next to me, and I turned my gaze on her. "So where are we headed?"

She smiled and shrugged. "Let's just walk and see what we find."

I wanted to laugh. "I can't believe you've never been here either. I was under the impression you'd been here for a few weeks now."

A funny expression crossed Mia's face. "I mostly stayed inside," she said haltingly.

Though I was curious, I decided not to pry. The cut on her forehead looked to be mostly healed, though she still sported evidence of some scrapes and bruises. I wondered once more if they were from Jack. She seemed crazy about him, though I'd learned that appearances could be deceiving. Was she staying with him out of some sort of obligation? I hoped not. It wasn't my place to ask, but I was here to listen if she needed a friend.

My head swiveled left and right, taking in the little signs hanging in the windows or over the doorways.

"Oh! Over here." Mia pointed across the street, and I allowed myself to be tugged along to the small boutique. We stepped inside, and I paused as my eyes scanned the small space. Both men's and women's clothing cluttered the overflowing shelves and racks placed around the room. Aside from men's on one side and women's on the other, there seemed to be no rhyme or reason to the placement of the items. Dresses and shirts were mixed in with pants, shoes and bags topping the racks.

A young woman somewhere between Mia's age and my

own bounced out from behind the counter. "Hi! Can I help you find anything?"

Mia and I shared a glance. "Actually, I'm looking for a dress for my friend's wedding."

She looked me over with an appraising eye. "Do you have something in mind?"

I gave a little shrug. "Not really. I was just going to... look around."

The girl must've seen my hesitation, because she laughed. "I'm sorry. Things are a little hectic in here right now. I'm Joey, by the way." Mia and I shook hands with her. "Nice to meet you. I've been helping my grandfather out, and I just ordered a bunch of stuff, but I haven't had much of a chance to get it organized."

"Well..." I said slowly. "What would you recommend?"

She looked me over again from head to toe, then held up a finger. "Hold on one second." She bustled around the racks, and I shared another surprised look with Mia before Joey exclaimed triumphantly, "Here it is!"

She trotted back over to us carrying a navy blue dress. "I'll grab a couple more if you want to get started."

"That would be great, thanks." I slipped the hanger from her fingers, then Mia and I headed to the fitting room in the back corner of the shop. I stepped inside and pulled the curtain across, then shrugged out of my coat. The navy blue material hung limply from the hanger, and I made a little face as I stared at it.

I didn't want to hurt the girl's feelings by not trying it on, so I quickly shed my clothes and slid the dress over my head. With an eye roll, I realized there were no mirrors inside the dressing room. I peeked my head out to find Mia there waiting expectantly. "Are there any mirrors?"

Joey appeared at that very second, her face twisted into an expression of remorse. "Just that one." She pointed down to a narrow mirror hanging over the back door.

I shoved the curtain aside and stepped out reluctantly. Mia's eyes lit up, and Joey let out a little squeal. My eyes widened as I regarded them. "Is that a good thing?"

"Oh, yes." Mia nodded emphatically. "Check it out."

I turned toward the mirror, surprised by the reflection. The dress hugged my curves in all the right places, the skirt hitting me just below the knee and swirling sensuously around my legs. The neckline dived down toward my breasts, giving a tantalizing peek of cleavage, while the ruffled sleeves fell gracefully down to my elbows. It was graceful and feminine, a complete contradiction to the way it had appeared on the hanger.

I turned and lifted a brow at Mia. "Do I even need to try the others on?"

"Nope." Her mouth tipped up in a smile. "I think that's the one."

I let out a little laugh, then turned my attention to Joey. "I don't think I can wear my boots with this. Do you have anything in a size six-and-a-half?"

She bolted off, then came back less than a minute later, holding a pair of beige heels. "Try these on."

I slipped my feet into them, reveling in the feel of the smooth leather. It felt like months since I'd worn a pair of high heels. Now that I'd gone so long without them, I kind of missed the way they made me feel. "I'll take them."

Back in the dressing room, I stripped everything off, then passed it through the curtain to Joey to ring up. Mia was wandering the shop when I came out, and she already had a handful of items draped over her arm.

Joey sifted through the racks for a minute before pulling out a sweater and holding it up for Mia's inspection. "This one is new, if you like it."

"Oh, yes." Mia practically snatched it from her fingers.

Joey let out a little laugh. "I thought you might. It seemed to fit with the rest of the clothes I picked out for you."

Mia turned a surprised look on Joey. "What do you mean?"

Joey's cheeks flamed bright red. "I was here when Carter came down for clothes a couple weeks ago."

"I had no idea," Mia replied. "Thank you. Everything was beautiful."

Joey waved her off. "It was no problem at all."

I watched the exchange with interest, wondering what I had missed.

"It's a long story," Mia said. "I'll fill you in later."

With a nod, I surveyed the large room, then turned back to Joey. "Um… Do you have any pantyhose?"

She bit her lip, and her cheeks turned pink again. "Promise you won't say anything?"

I flicked a glance at Mia, and we both nodded. Joey waved us to the back of the store, where she pulled out a large brown box.

Her voice was hushed when she spoke. "Some of the girls from the Fox Hole asked me to order things for them from time to time, and I keep the extras back here. My grandfather would kill me if he ever found out."

She untucked the flaps to reveal a heap of lacy, sexy lingerie, then passed me a package of pantyhose. A scrap of red caught my eye, and I held up the panties for inspection. "These are gorgeous."

They were surprisingly good quality too, the lace soft beneath my touch. Joey dug around for a moment, then pulled out a matching red bra.

"It's a set if you like it."

"She'll take it," Mia declared, and I shot her a look. "What?" she exclaimed. "Every girl needs sexy underwear."

No lie there, though I wasn't sure when I would ever have the chance to wear them. Still, I was reluctant to relinquish them. "Oh, what the hell," I said. The girls laughed, and Mia picked out her own set to entice Jack, although I was sure she didn't need any help in that area. We cashed out, then left with a wave to see Joey again soon.

SIXTEEN

ERIC

My heart beat furiously as I wound my way up the curves of the mountain, and my gut clenched as I recalled Jules's words from barely twenty minutes ago.

I need your help.

I hadn't thought twice. I'd swiped my paperwork off my desk and into my briefcase, strode out of the station, then hopped in the cruiser and headed toward Briarleigh like a bat out of hell. Relief assaulted me as the huge resort came into view. Gravel churned beneath my tires as I skidded to a stop in the employee parking lot just a few cars down from where Jules was parked.

I hopped out and hurriedly approached. Jules stood alone by the front bumper of the Cavalier, looking unsure as hell. Her arms were wrapped around her waist, and her cheeks were rosy from the cold, her brow furrowed with worry.

Swallowing down the urge to pull her into my arms and press her head to my chest, I addressed her. "What happened?"

With a shaky hand, she pointed toward the driver side tire. "This was flat when I came out."

I studied her for a moment. That was all? The way she'd sounded on the phone made me think she'd been hurt or, at the very least, scared. She still looked scared, but I couldn't figure out why. "Okay. We'll take care of it."

I moved toward the car, parked between two other vehicles that I assumed belonged to employees. Kneeling next to it, I checked the valve stem first. The fitting appeared to be tight, and I ran my hand over the side wall. "Could've picked up a nail or…"

I trailed off as my fingers slipped over a raised portion of rubber near the lettering on the tires. I'd missed the cut during my initial once-over. About an inch wide, it had been made by something sharp—most likely a knife. Whoever had done this definitely possessed some strength. It wasn't nearly as easy to puncture a tire as people thought.

I lifted my gaze to Jules, fighting the urge to snap at her. "Is something going on that you're not telling me?" She shook her head adamantly, and I took a deep breath before continuing. "Someone slashed your tire."

Her eyes widened. "But I… I didn't mean…" She blushed and broke off, her teeth digging into her lower lip.

I stared hard at her, willing her to come clean. "Jules." I waited for her to look at me. "Do you know who might've done this?"

She hesitated, then gave a little shrug. "I'm not sure."

Rising to my feet, I propped a hip against the fender and eyed her. "Tell me what you do know."

It was too damn cold to be having this discussion outside, but I couldn't bring myself to move toward the cruiser. I felt frozen in place, fear and anger and worry rendering me motionless. If I stepped any closer to her, I was afraid of what I'd do. Part of me wanted to grab her and shake her, demand she tell me the truth—the whole truth. A deeper, more dangerous part of me wanted to gather her into my arms and soothe her, hold her close and never let her go.

She blinked several times. "Well… There's this guy who works here—Sam—"

"Pickett?"

Her gaze jumped to mine, and she nodded. "I think so, yeah. Anyway, I met him last week when I first started here. Then one morning when I got into the shop, I noticed a red rose sitting on the counter."

Motherfucker. The picture began to crystalize in my mind as she continued.

"I ran into him yesterday, and he told me he was the one who'd left the rose. Then…" She trailed off and licked her lips, her eyes dropping to her toes.

"Then…?" I prompted, though I had a feeling I knew exactly what was coming.

"He asked me out," she whispered. Her pretty green gaze collided with mine, begging me to believe her. "I didn't want to hurt his feelings, but I didn't know what to do."

"It's fine," I managed to grit out, though it was anything but fine. I was going to wring that little shit's neck when I found him. "Is he working today?"

She shook her head. "I'm not sure. I don't think so."

She was probably right; after Jack told me he'd introduced Sam and Jules, I'd taken the liberty of checking into him. Though he worked full-time at the hardware store, he apparently picked up a few extra hours at Briarleigh now and then to help pay off his student loans.

"All right. I'll have Charlie tow your car down and replace the tire. Did you mention this to Mia or Jack?"

"No, I didn't even see it until I got ready to leave."

"Okay." For the first time, I noticed the shopping bags near the front of the car. "Were you in town today?"

She nodded. "Mia and I hit up a couple places for wedding stuff."

I scooped up the bags and strode toward the cruiser, then stowed them in the back seat. "Hop in. I'll give Charlie a call as soon as I drop you off."

Jules slid into the car and snapped her seat belt into place, then settled her hands in her lap. Her fingers fidgeted, and I could hear the faint click of her nails as she picked at them. I wanted to reach over the console and settle her, but I didn't. Instead, I put the car in drive and started back down the mountain, fuming over what had happened.

"Do you work tomorrow?"

Jules slid a look at me from the passenger seat. "No, thank goodness. It was my day off anyway, so maybe my car will be done by the time I have to go back."

I nodded, lost in thought, and silence fell once more as I drove toward my place. It was already almost dinnertime, and I debated calling Charlie out tonight. With a sigh, I decided to just get it over with. Dragging it out wouldn't make the situation any better.

I dug my phone from my back pocket and pulled up McBride's number. My fingers drummed the wheel impatiently as I waited for the call to connect, and I was rewarded a moment later when a gruff voice answered. "McBride's."

"Hey, Charlie, it's Donahue."

There was some shuffling in the background and the metallic sound of what I assumed was a tool landing heavily on the workbench. "Something wrong with the car?"

I heard the faint thread of defensiveness in his tone, and I rushed to reassure him. "Not with your work. Need a tire replaced if you have one in stock. 70R14." I rattled off the size and waited a long moment while Charlie checked his inventory.

"I got it. Need a tow?"

"Yes, please. It's up at Briarleigh in the employee lot."

Charlie grunted an acknowledgement and hung up before

I could say anything else. I dropped the phone into the cupholder and pulled into the driveway but didn't get out of the car. A quick glance at the clock told me the hardware store would be open for another half an hour or so. "Will you be okay by yourself for a few?"

Jules nodded haltingly. "Yeah. I'll be fine."

I didn't want to leave her alone any longer than necessary, but I wanted to get over to Pickett's Hardware to see if Sam was working.

Jules climbed from the car and made her way inside. I watched to make sure the door was closed before reversing out of the drive and heading back into town. Inwardly, I seethed as I approached Pickett's Hardware and slid to a stop in an angled parking spot. A bell over the doorway tinkled a happy little greeting, completely incongruous with the reason for my visit.

My gaze moved to the counter located along the left wall of the store, narrowing immediately on the person I was looking for. Sam started to smile, but it slipped from his face as soon as he saw my thunderous expression. His eyes widened, his shoulders stiffening as I stomped across the room, my footfalls heavy on the scarred hardwood floors.

He stood at the register counting cash, probably ready to close up shop for the evening, and he paused in the act of sorting the bills in his hands. He gave me an uncomfortable little nod. "Sheriff."

"Sam." I stopped a few feet from the counter and hooked my thumbs in my belt loops. "How's business?"

He eyed me warily, seemingly thrown by my nonchalant question. "A little slow, but you know how it is."

I lifted my chin at him. "Heard you've been working up at Briarleigh a little, too."

"Yep." He gave an abbreviated nod. "Figure it'll help pay off my student loans faster. My folks offered to help, but I want to do it myself."

I could understand that. It was a reasonable answer, even commendable, and I admired the kid for his sense of responsibility. So he liked to be in control; did that mean he was offended when something didn't go his way? "Can I ask you a couple questions, Sam?"

Social niceties over, he tensed. "Sure."

"Were you working here today?"

"Yes, sir."

"All day?" I clarified.

"Yep. Except lunch time," he amended. "I stopped over at Rosie's sometime after noon to grab a sandwich. Dad was feeling a little under the weather this morning, so I offered to open and close."

I contemplated what he was telling me. It'd be easy enough to verify his side of the story. With such a tight-knit community as Pine Ridge, someone was bound to know if he'd left the hardware store unattended and driven up to Briarleigh.

"You didn't happen to stop up at the lodge any time today, did you?"

"No, sir." He shook his head, his expression concerned. "Why? Did something happen?"

"Nothing you need to worry about." I rapped my knuckles on the counter. "Thanks for your time, Sam."

"Sure." He looked confused and more than a little wary, but I would find out soon enough if he was telling the truth.

I glanced at my watch as I pushed out the front door and stepped onto the sidewalk. Just after five o'clock. Most everything in Pine Ridge was closed or getting ready to shut down for the evening—except Murdoch's. I cut across the street at an angle, heading for the bar situated right next to Rosie's Café. As soon as the diner closed each day after lunchtime, the bar opened. I knew I'd find a good number of people inside, and I hoped someone would be able to answer my questions.

The door swung open, and a man stumbled out, bringing with him a smoky haze. The mandate on nonsmoking facilities was completely ignored by the residents of Pine Ridge, and I didn't bother to push it. Until someone pitched a fit, I was content to leave it as it'd been for the past hundred years. It didn't truly bother me, but I didn't spend much time at the bar myself. Though I hadn't smoked in years—not since my divorce—the smell triggered a faint urge to pick up the habit again.

I held the door wide as Herbert McElroy threw a surprised glance my way. "Thanks, Sheriff."

I nodded. "You good, Herb?"

"Yessir." He hiccupped, then straightened, and I sighed. This was the part about small towns that I both loved and hated. It was, for the most part, a quiet life. People worked hard during the day then headed to the bar to drink off the stress. In Herb's case, the older man had probably been filling his stool since the bar opened at two o'clock.

"Do you need a ride home?"

"No, sir." He shook his head emphatically, nearly losing his balance and tipping over again.

My hand shot out, catching his upper arm. "Come on. Let me take you home. It's too damn cold out to be walking in this."

It wasn't the first time I'd had to drive someone home. Herb only lived a few blocks away and odds were he'd be just fine, but I didn't want to risk it. I guided him to the cruiser, one hand on his shoulder, keeping my grip light and friendly but at the ready in case he stumbled again.

He practically melted into the passenger seat, and I rounded the SUV, frustrated. I'd hoped to get in and out, then get back to Jules. I knew she didn't want to admit it, but I'd seen the fear on her face. Whatever she'd been through in her past had done a number on her, and I recognized the fight or flight coping mechanism kicking into gear. She was ready to run again, no question.

I didn't know if there was any way to keep her from doing so the second she got her car back. I prayed that Charlie had a whole slew of customers to take care of before Jules. Maybe I could convince him to hold on to it for a bit; it would buy me another few days of knowing she'd be safe with me instead of on the run somewhere.

I shook the thought from my head. It shouldn't bother me nearly as much as it did. Jules was nothing to me—rather, she *should* mean nothing to me. The truth was, I cared way more for her than I wanted to admit, and that bothered me. I didn't like the responsibility of taking care of anyone but myself. I didn't even have a dog, for Christ's sake. I'd shunned any possibility of having a serious relationship after my train wreck of a marriage ended, yet here I was, desperate to keep Jules attached to me for however long I could have her.

What the hell was wrong with me? I was a fucking idiot, that was what.

"How's the store, Herb?"

"Eh." He waved a hand in the air. "Joey's takin' care of it."

I'd met his granddaughter, Joey, a handful of times. Herb had owned the local clothing store in Pine Ridge for the past several decades. After his wife passed away last fall, Herb had lost interest in the business. Joey had come up to help him out and had pretty much taken over. I'd hoped that having his granddaughter around would bring him out of his fog of grief, but losing his wife had taken a toll on the man.

"You like having her around?"

A grimace tugged at his lips. "She's always nagging me to take better care of myself."

I hid a smile. Maybe that explained why he was heading home so early. "She just wants you healthy."

Herb sighed. "I know. She's a good girl."

He poured himself from my SUV as I pulled up in front of

his house, then I turned around and headed back to Murdoch's. Inside, I spoke with the owner himself, who'd seen Sam at Rosie's during the lunch rush. Another two men had been in the hardware store today at different times, both verifying that Sam had taken care of them.

I propped an elbow on the door panel and rubbed my temple as I headed home, completely unsatisfied with the results my questions had yielded. Best I could do was pull the tire tomorrow and get a better idea on whatever had been used to puncture the thick rubber. It wouldn't help much; without the weapon itself, I wouldn't be able to tell who was responsible. Jack had recently installed cameras around the lodge, but the employee lot was more than likely out of view.

Jules was off tomorrow, but I'd stop in and speak with him, let him know what was happening. Maybe we'd get a lucky break, but I seriously doubted it.

SEVENTEEN

GIULIANA

The clock ticked loudly on the wall behind me, the only sound in the empty room. After a night of no sleep, I dragged myself out to the couch and curled up in the corner. Eric had folded the blanket and laid it over the back of the couch before he'd left for work, but his scent lingered, and I drew in a lungful of the musky, masculine smell.

Dressed in sweats and a thick sweatshirt I'd pilfered from Eric's closet, I felt like I couldn't get warm. Closing my eyes, I imagined I could feel the heat from his body seeping into mine, warming me from the inside.

What he'd told me last night chilled me to my bones. He'd apparently questioned Sam, who denied everything. Not only that—he had an alibi, and several witnesses saw him at the hardware store throughout the day. If it wasn't Sam, who could it be? Idle threats weren't my uncle's style; he would have shown up—probably with lots of firepower if necessary—and dragged me back to Chicago.

A loud knock came from the front door, making me jump.

On stealthy feet, I approached. Before I even neared the peephole, a familiar voice called out, "Jules? It's me, Mia."

I breathed out a sigh of relief as I slid the chain on the deadbolt and peeled open the door. Forcing a smile to my face, I stepped back to let her enter. "Hey."

She watched me warily as I closed up the door and relocked it behind her. "You doing okay?"

I exhaled, long and slow, knowing I wouldn't be able to keep it from her. Besides, she'd clearly already heard that something had happened; I might as well tell her everything.

"I'm fine. It was really no big deal."

She lifted a brow. "Really?"

I shrugged. I wasn't sure what she wanted me to say. Silently, I moved toward the couch and sank down in one corner. Mia followed suit and slid onto the cushion at the opposite end, just watching me, waiting for me to speak. "It was... scary, I guess."

I was still scared; I didn't know who to trust or what I was going to do. If I'd had my car, I probably would've been packed and on the road by now. Unconsciously, I picked at my nails, lost in thought.

Suddenly, Mia spoke. "Have you eaten yet?"

My eyes widened. "No, why?"

"Come on." She pushed to her feet. "Let's go grab lunch."

"I don't know..." My gaze skated over Eric's huge sweatshirt where it hung from my body.

"Can I offer some advice?"

My head tipped to one side as I contemplated her.

Mia drew a deep breath. "Never let them see your fear."

Not for the first time I wondered about her past and the fading bruises and cuts that marred her pretty face. It made sense. It was the mantra my father had lived by—though look how that'd ended for him. Shaking the thought away, I considered the subject at hand. Maybe it really was Sam or someone close to him who'd done the dirty work for him. I refused to let the person win. If they were just trying to scare me, they'd have to try a hell of a lot harder than that.

Slowly, I nodded. "Let me throw some jeans on."

Twenty minutes later, we pulled up in front of Rosie's diner and made our way inside. The lunch rush had passed, but half the tables were still full of lingering customers reluctant to go back to work. We slid into a booth towards the back of the restaurant along the wall.

A pretty waitress, her blonde hair cut into a cute bob that framed her face, smiled in our direction. "I'll be with you in just a second."

"No problem." Mia smiled and waved one hand at the woman, then she turned to me. "So, tell me the truth. How do you like it at Briarleigh so far?"

"Truthfully?" I grinned. "I love it."

The waitress appeared beside the table. "I'm Cynthia. What can I get for you?"

The menu was limited; Rosie offered only one special per day with few variations. Mia and I both ordered the pot roast with iced tea, and Cynthia bounced back to the kitchen to place our order. I turned back to Mia to speak but was cut off as another woman materialized next to our table.

"You must be Jules." The large-breasted woman propped a hand on her hip as she studied me.

I flicked a glance at the woman's name tag, which proclaimed her to be Rosie, the owner of this diner. "Yes, ma'am."

The woman caught the direction of my gaze and stuck out one hand. "Name's Rosie. Nice to finally meet you."

I slipped my palm into hers and shook. "You as well. I didn't realize my arrival was big news."

I wasn't truly surprised; in a town this small, I was sure a newcomer was a big deal.

"Hear you're staying with the sheriff."

I nodded. "For now."

"Just for now?" Rosie lifted a brow. "A pretty little thing like you livin' with the sheriff?"

A crash came from behind Rosie, and cold tea splattered my pants as the glasses Cynthia had been carrying hit the floor. I met her eyes as her face contorted into an expression of abject mortification. "You okay?"

My words shook Cynthia out of her shock, and she nodded furiously as she bent to wipe up the tea with a towel. "I'm so sorry."

I reached under the table to retrieve a hard plastic glass that had rolled underneath, and she accepted it with trembling fingers and a whispered "thanks" before turning tail and fleeing back toward the kitchen.

"Poor thing," Rosie clucked from beside me. "Afraid of her own shadow, that one."

Mia's brows drew together. "Is she okay?"

Rosie's expression turned hard. "Better off without that worthless husband of hers knockin' her around."

My mouth dropped open. "That's terrible!"

She nodded and turned her gaze my way. "Think she might have an eye on your sheriff."

"Oh, it's not like that." My cheeks heated as one thick brown brow arched toward her hairline. "We're just friends," I clarified.

Rosie took in my expression and let out a deep laugh. "Oh, darlin'. Don't tell me you believe that."

"I'm sure he doesn't—"

Rosie slapped one hand on the table, making me jump. "That man is in here every day buying lunch for you. Never done that before for nobody."

So it had been intentional. I hid a smile as I thought back on the excuses he'd given me each time he brought a meal home. They ranged from "Rosie gave me too much" to "I ordered it for Riley, but he doesn't like turkey." I'd known he was lying, though I couldn't help but be touched by the gesture. I'd almost refused the first night, but I couldn't bring myself to do it. He'd looked so insistent, almost pleading for me to take it. So I had. And he'd been bringing me dinner each night since.

She nodded at me, face serious. "He's a good man."

"He is."

Rosie persisted. "Man like that needs a good woman."

My smile immediately fell away. That wasn't me—it couldn't be me. I didn't deserve his generosity, and I would never be good enough for him. It stung more than I thought it would. "He does," I agreed softly. "He deserves the best."

Apparently sensing that I was uncomfortable with the turn our conversation had taken, Mia turned pleading eyes on Rosie. "Have you thought about making my cake?"

"I don't make cakes often, mind you"—Rosie lifted a brow in her direction—"but I'll make an exception for you."

Mia smiled beatifically. "And I can't begin to tell you how grateful I am for that."

"Won't be nothin' fancy," Rosie warned her, and Mia shook her head.

"We're keeping it low-key; I don't want anything over the top anyway."

I hid a smile while I watched Rosie examine Mia as if judging her authenticity. I was pretty sure Mia could convince anyone to do her bidding just by smiling and offering up a few kind words. The most amazing part was that she truly was as sweet as she seemed.

Rosie headed back to the kitchen, and I turned to Mia, unsure of what exactly I wanted to say. "So, this is kind of nosy… but I'm just curious."

She smiled. "Shoot."

"It seems like you could do anything you wanted for your wedding, but…"

"You're wondering why I'm not doing anything lavish?" Mia smiled knowingly. "I'm not interested in putting on a show for people. As long as I have Jack at the end of the day, that's all that matters."

The statement was so pure, so matter-of-fact that tears burned the backs of my eyes. I couldn't fathom loving someone that much, but I heard it in her voice, saw it in her expression. I couldn't help but wonder if I'd ever experience love like that.

On the heels of that revelation came another thought. Something had been bothering me for days; the closer the wedding came, the more I needed to know. I glanced uneasily at Mia. "Can I ask you a personal question?"

She tipped her head. "Anything."

"I just..." My eyes darted toward her forehead, and I lowered my voice. "That's not from Jack, is it?"

Her eyes flared wide with surprise. "Oh, my God, no! He's not..." She shook her head emphatically. "I had no idea you thought that."

"I'm sorry," I said, immediately contrite. "I—"

"No. I'm sorry." Mia's hand covered my own. "I should have said something sooner. Jack told me how uncomfortable you are with him. I didn't realize you thought he'd hurt me."

Her eyes took on a faraway quality. "Jack rescued me after a car accident a couple weeks ago. He's... amazing. Truly." Her gaze darted back to mine. "He would never hurt me. And he would never let anyone hurt you, either."

I dropped my gaze away from her assessing stare. How much could I reveal to her? "It's..." I took a deep breath. "I feel like I'm always looking over my shoulder, waiting for something bad to happen."

Her face softened, her eyes turning dark with empathy. "I can understand that."

I truly believed she did. "Do you ever feel like you're caught in the middle, kind of? Like you can't move forward, but you can't go back?"

"More than you'd know," Mia murmured. "Sometimes

you have to confront your past—if not physically, at least emotionally. What I do know is that, between Eric and Jack, you'll always be safe."

I nodded. "Thank you."

After Mia dropped me off more than an hour later, I contemplated what she'd said. The more I thought about it, the more I realized Mia was right. What had happened with my tires wasn't the work of my uncle. I wanted to stay, but I was worried that something else would happen. I still hadn't figured out who would have any reason to hate me or why, but I knew I was safe here—at least for now.

My melancholy thoughts turned to Eric. The more time I spent with him, the more I liked him. He stirred feelings in me that I didn't understand, and it was scary and exhilarating all at once. Unfortunately, he didn't seem to feel the same. I caught little glimpses from time to time, but he never made a move. I knew he cared about me to some extent, otherwise he wouldn't have taken me in. But was that all it was? Disappointment stabbed through my heart at the possibility. I wanted him to want me the same way I wanted him.

Something had changed between us the other night. We'd had dinner together for the first time and talked under the stars. I was terrified that I'd given away too much when I made a reference to Chicago. But Eric hadn't mentioned it since, and I decided I was overthinking things.

Eric returned home later in the afternoon, and we crossed paths only a couple of times before I headed to my room for the night. The weight of guilt pressed in on me as I curled up in the large bed. I briefly debated telling him of my past, but he'd done too much for me already; I couldn't drag him into my mess.

I buried my face in the pillow, breathing deep. It held a trace of Eric's unique masculine scent, and I wanted more of it. It was exciting somehow to know that his head had lain on this very pillow. I pressed my cheek to it, imagining what it would be like to wake up in this very bed and see his face on the pillow next to mine.

I immediately shook the thought from my head. He didn't want me—he'd made that perfectly clear by keeping his distance. Suddenly sad, I pushed off the bed and made my way to the chair. It was better this way—I was better off on my own where I couldn't drag anyone else down with my crap. I took a step toward the bed, then turned back. I eyed the pillow where it lay in the middle of the bed, a slight depression in the middle from my head. I couldn't relinquish it. It was the closest I would ever come to Eric, and I refused to give that up. Settling in the chair, I hugged the pillow close, wishing Eric were curled around me.

EIGHTEEN

ERIC

I punched the pillow then flopped over on my back and threw an arm over my face. I couldn't sleep, mostly because I hadn't been able to get Jules off my mind all night long. I should have known, should have seen it coming.

She was going to leave. And there wasn't a damn thing I could do about it.

Two nights ago when we'd talked, it had been damn near perfect. I felt like we were finally starting to make headway. Though she hadn't told me the whole truth of her past, she'd opened up at least a little bit. Today, though, there'd been a visible change in her behavior.

She'd avoided me as much as possible from the moment I walked in the door this afternoon. I knew what had happened yesterday had scared her, though I still wasn't sure exactly why. My only suspect had an alibi, and she couldn't seem to think of anyone else who might be responsible.

Over the past few days, I'd come to enjoy Jules's company, and I thought she finally felt safe. But the sight of her sitting cross-legged on the bedroom floor this morning, counting out bills as if her life depended on it, had killed whatever sliver of hope I harbored.

Goddamn it. I slammed my fist against the back of the couch, mentally cursing myself. I shouldn't have pushed her. I should have kept my fucking mouth shut instead of prying for details. But I couldn't help it. I wanted to know every damn thing about her. More than that, I wanted her to trust me. I wanted her to feel like she could come to me with anything. Instead, I'd scared her off. Fucking perfect.

The scanner sitting on the bookcase crackled to life, and Lucy's voice filtered into the otherwise silent room, ripping my thoughts from the woman in the bedroom just feet away.

"Code 20 in progress…"

I let out a groan as she rattled off the address for the domestic dispute—one I was intimately familiar with. These motherfuckers. I'd warned them last week that their shit was getting old, but the Johanssons were apparently up to no good again. I was tired of being nice. This time someone was going to jail. It probably wouldn't teach them a damn thing, but at least it would give us a few days' reprieve from having to deal with them.

I couldn't figure out why the hell, after a dozen years of marriage, they hadn't figured shit out yet. In my opinion, they either needed to work out the kinks in their marriage— however many of those there were—or get divorced already. Personally, I was rooting for the latter. I'd be happy if they went their separate ways—preferably to a different city altogether—and I never had to see either of them again.

I snorted. Wishful thinking, that. They'd both been born and raised here and planned to die here. Lucky us, we had the pleasure of putting up with their shit in the meantime.

Hawkins's deep voice followed immediately. "Central, this is 308. I'm en route to the location."

Pushing off the couch, I turned the dial on the scanner to shut it off. Fuck it. There wasn't a chance in hell I was going to sleep anyway. May as well join in. Besides, this would at least give me something to think about other than the fact that Jules planned to leave.

Rolling the tension from my shoulders, I traipsed to the spare room. Thank God I'd had the foresight to stash most of my clothes in here. At least I could get dressed without having to bother Jules while she slept. Quickly, I tugged on my uniform pants and pulled my vest on over my head, then I shrugged into my shirt and tucked it in. Getting dressed was so automatic, I didn't even have to think about it anymore. I picked up my duty belt and checked to make sure I had everything.

Jules had been tucked away in her room most of the evening, and I hadn't wanted to bother her by digging around in the safe. Instead, I'd dropped my stuff by the couch where it was within reach. I snapped my belt into place and did one more look-over. I never knew what the hell I'd run into, so I always erred on the side of caution.

Shit. I let my eyes close and my head drop back as I realized I'd put my extra magazines in the gun safe a couple nights ago. And the safe was in the bedroom. I brushed a hand down my face and debated my options. I didn't want to barge into the room while Jules was sleeping, but I hated to go out unprepared. Fuck.

Heaving a sigh, I made my way down the hall as quietly as possible. My heart sank as I neared the bedroom. She was sleeping with the light on again. I thought it was a fluke when I saw her light on last night. I hadn't even meant to notice, but I'd seen the rectangular outline around her door when I got up in the middle of night last night to use the bathroom.

Leaning my ear against the door, I listened for any sound within. I scratched softly, but it remained quiet. Taking a deep breath, I tested the handle. My eyebrows shot up in surprise when I realized it was unlocked. After everything, I hadn't expected that. In fact, I wouldn't have been shocked to find she'd barricaded the door with the dresser while she slept, as skittish as she'd been today.

I pushed the door open and peeked inside, my eyes sweeping the corners of the room. What greeted me damn near broke my heart. Instead of lying in bed, Jules was curled up in the chair in the far corner of the room. She was tucked into a tiny ball, like if she made herself as small as possible, she would go unnoticed.

She hadn't even bothered to pull the comforter off the bed or use a covering of any sort—the only thing she had was a pillow. Her entire body was wrapped around it, holding onto it like a lifeline, her head buried in the downy fabric.

A fierce protectiveness swept over me. I hated to see her like this, vulnerable and afraid. Part of me wanted to pull her into my arms and soothe her, promise that everything would be okay. I couldn't do a damn thing, though, because she wouldn't let me in. The helplessness rising within me was a foreign emotion. I'd been trained for most every situation, and yet this young woman eluded me. I had no way to help her because I had no idea what I was up against.

I hated it even more because I knew she'd never let me— or anyone else—see her like this. She would bottle everything up, lock it inside where no one would see it. She would fight her demons alone because she trusted no one to help. She was too strong, too goddamn proud, and it pissed me off.

Biting back a growl of frustration, I quietly strode to the closet where I stored the safe. The keypad beeped with each digit I tapped in, and I cringed, praying even that soft sound wouldn't wake her. The door of the safe unlocked with a metallic click, and I quickly grabbed two extra magazines from the top shelf. I closed up the door, making sure it relocked, and tossed one more look Jules's way.

She couldn't possibly be comfortable, her body crunched into that tiny space. Shadows played over the wall, making the circles beneath her eyes even more pronounced. She looked absolutely exhausted, and I briefly debated carrying her to bed. Just as quickly, I dismissed it. She obviously wasn't sleeping well, and I didn't want to risk waking her up.

With one last look at Jules, I quietly stepped out of the room and closed the door behind me.

NINETEEN

GIULIANA

The sound of organ pipes filled my ears, and stained glass windows glowed radiantly as the sun spilled through the colorful panes. The sound of Monsignor Francis's voice drew my eyes to the stooped little priest a few feet away on the altar.

My eyes dropped the length of my body, taking in the ornate lace gown. A chill swept down my spine as I recognized the dress Uncle Massimo had selected for me to wear when I wed Nikolai.

I felt a presence next to me, and I glanced across my right shoulder to the man at my side. His head was turned away from me, so I couldn't get a good look at his face. My gaze darted back to the priest as he droned on, and a collective cry of joy went up as he lifted his hands toward us.

No, no, no. This couldn't be happening. The man—Nikolai, I assumed—took my hand in his and tugged me to my feet. His grip tightened as I tried to pull away, his fingers digging into the back of my hand and putting pressure on the delicate bones. My cries were drowned out by the jubilant voices of friends and family joined together at the church.

I tried to dig in my heels, but people poured out of the pews and pressed in around us, sweeping me along, forcing me forward as Nikolai pulled me up the aisle. I swiveled my head left and right, searching for a sympathetic face. Surely someone would help me.

As we reached the tabernacle, the cathedral faded away and became the gathering room in my family's restaurant. It'd been elegantly decorated, white cloth-covered tables placed throughout the room. The pungent aroma from thousands of white roses rose in the air, and the sickeningly sweet scent filled my throat, causing me to gag.

I still couldn't make out the man's face, but everyone kept approaching us, shaking his hand and congratulating us. I tried to scream, but nothing came out. I was pulled around the room, through a sea of smiling happy faces.

All of a sudden, Daddy was there. He and Massimo stood in the corner arguing, and it sparked a memory I had long forgotten. Daddy and Uncle Massimo had argued bitterly about a week before Daddy died. Where was Eric? I glanced frantically around the room. Then, as if he'd heard me calling for him, Eric appeared.

I tried to break free and run to him, but the man grasping my hand held me back. Eric's face twisted in anger as the man refused to let me go. He reached for me, ready to pull me away, and I stretched out a hand for him. Our fingers brushed, but I was yanked backward, and he slipped from my grasp.

Over Eric's shoulder, I saw Uncle Massimo's face twisted into an evil glare. I tried to call out, tried to warn him before it was too late, but nothing came out. The knife glinted as it cut through the air, and I let out a scream. Massimo drew the blade across Eric's neck, and his eyes bulged as a bright red line appeared.

I ripped myself away from the man beside me and threw myself at Eric as he collapsed to his knees. He pitched forward, clutching at his neck with one hand and reaching for me with the other. Blood saturated my pristine white dress as I knelt next to him.

"No! Please!" I grasped his hands, begging him to stay with me.

Eric's lips parted, and blood trickled out. Hazel eyes met mine, and I leaned forward to capture the words leaving his mouth. "I'm sorry."

I let out a scream as arms grabbed me roughly from behind and drew me away. I fought against their hold, my eyes on Eric as a crowd formed around him, swallowing him up.

A familiar voice spoke next to my ear. "You're mine now."

I sucked in a breath as I jolted upright, sweat clinging to my skin, my body simultaneously running hot and cold. Harsh breaths heaved in and out of my lungs as I glanced frantically around the room. My heart pounded in my chest, and my mind raced with worry and fear.

Oh, God. Eric.

It took a long moment for the dream to dissipate, and I finally recognized my surroundings. I was in Eric's bedroom. I was safe. Another shiver racked my body as I mentally replayed the dream, and a tremor of worry sliced through me. My stomach twisted as I remembered Eric bleeding out in my arms and shook my head to dispel the image.

It had felt so real—I needed to see for myself that he was okay. Dropping the pillow to the floor, I bolted from the chair and raced from the bedroom.

Escaping into the dark hallway, I made my way toward the living room, padding quickly but quietly along the wood floor. It was cold beneath my bare feet, the sensation helping to ground me and bring me back to reality. The living room was dark, and I could feel the emptiness before I even stepped foot inside. He wasn't there.

Turning on a heel, I went to the spare room. Light spilled over the empty room as I flipped the switch, and my heart kicked into overdrive. Fear rose in my throat. Oh, God. Where was he? Was he okay?

I sprinted into the mud room and threw open the door to the garage. Even before I turned on the light, I knew I'd find it empty. Closing the garage door, I hastily made my way back to the kitchen. I flipped on the overhead light and scoured the counter for a note, anything that would indicate why he'd left in the middle of the night.

As my mind cleared, the pieces began to come together. His boots weren't in the tray by the door as they normally were. A quick glance around told me that his duty belt and heavy overcoat were gone as well.

My heart slowed to a more normal pace as it hit me. He'd been called out for something, probably an emergency at this hour. Dragging in a deep breath, I returned to my room. I couldn't do anything but wait and pray he was okay. I was overreacting. This was his job; he was called out at all hours of the day to help people, and he could certainly handle himself. I was sure Eric was safe wherever he was.

The heat of embarrassment washed over me as I headed back to the bedroom. I was glad Eric hadn't been here to see me overreact. I stripped off the sweats I'd been wearing, suddenly too hot. This time, I crawled under the covers and curled up in the middle of the bed. Here, surrounded by his scent, I felt safe. It made me feel connected to him in a way, and it helped to calm my rioting emotions.

I closed my eyes and imagined the snow falling softly outside. Almost immediately, I blinked them wide open again. What if it snowed so hard he got into an accident? Oh, God. I ducked beneath the covers, pulling them over my head as a thousand scenarios—none of them good—assaulted my brain in rapid succession.

Growing up, my father had done his best to shield me from the ugly side of his business, but that didn't keep me from knowing it existed. As I grew older, I heard whispers and rumors about my family. I knew I was different—that they were different. I'd never really experienced death firsthand until my father was killed.

I'd once thought him invincible, and it was the same thing I thought of Eric. He was so strong, so smart. He seemed to me like he could walk through fire unscathed, but death knew no bounds. It stole without remorse. I couldn't bear to lose Eric too. Somehow, he'd become incredibly important to me over a short period of time. I tried to tell myself it was just because he was a good man… but I knew better.

What I felt for him was more than friendly.

I couldn't get that scar out of my mind. It slashed across his throat, and there was no doubt it could have been lethal. I couldn't fathom the thought of something happening to him. Lying here was slowly driving me crazy. The last thought propelled me from bed. With no clear intention of where I was going or what I was doing, other than just not imagining the worst, I left my room.

I slipped around the corner into the dark kitchen and winced against the bright light of the fridge as I quickly retrieved a bottle of water. Cool air rushed over me, sending goose bumps over the flesh of my arms and legs.

My hand shook as I twisted the cap off and took a sip, but I knew it wasn't the cool blast of air that had me shivering. The bottle trembled in my hands, and I recapped it before I spilled any. Taking a deep breath, I leaned my forehead against the cool metal of the freezer door.

I turned around just as a lamp flickered to life in the living room. "Jules?"

My heart jumped into my throat at the sight of him, safe and unscathed. "Eric!"

Dropping the water bottle, I launched myself into his arms.

TWENTY

ERIC

I sighed as I sank onto the couch, glad to be free of the weight of my duty belt and vest. The plates inside my vest weighed damn near forty pounds alone, but I never went without them. I'd learned the hard way that they could mean the difference between life and death. Yeah, Pine Ridge was a sleepy little town for the most part, but you never knew when shit would go down in a big way.

I tipped my head toward the ceiling and had just closed my eyes when a soft sound caught my attention. From my position on the couch, I watched Jules skulk into the kitchen like a silent little kitten. Then… *Oh, God.* I saw her—*all* of her.

The light from the fridge glowed around her gorgeous, lithe body like a halo, over those sleek legs and pert, round bottom encased in a tiny pair of lacy black boy shorts. I couldn't tear my gaze away. Her cheeks swelled under the fabric, and I wanted to run my fingers over the creases, use my teeth to pull the panties from her body and put my mouth on her.

Oh, fuck. This was bad. So, so bad. It'd been stressful

enough over the past week, knowing she was under the same roof. But now… seeing her half-naked in my kitchen, clad only in a tiny, tight camisole and black underwear, I wasn't sure how much longer I could take it. My groin swelled in appreciation, pressing against the seam of my uniform pants as if trying to push through the fabric, begging to be inside her.

Shoving down the urge to pull her over my lap and sink deep into her warm, sexy body, I adjusted myself with one hand and stood. I took one more long moment to study her before flipping on the lamp to my right. "Jules?"

Her eyes met mine from across the room, flaring wide. "Eric!"

Before I could process what was happening, she was in my arms, her tiny body pressed to mine. I wrapped one arm around her waist and caught her against me. "Wh—"

I didn't even get a full word out before she was rambling, her hands moving over every inch of me she could reach, her voice frantic. "Oh, God, Eric! You're here, you're home! Thank God you're okay!" The warmth of her fingers burned my flesh through my shirt as she ran them across my chest and biceps, over my shoulders to cup my face. Those wide green eyes, full of relief, drew me in. "I woke up and you were gone, and I was so worried about you."

She'd been worried about me? Why? I tightened my hold on her. "Jules, what's wrong?"

Her arms tangled around my waist, and she buried her head against my chest, her perky breasts pressing against my stomach. I felt my arousal spring to life once more, the feel of her warm body against mine like heaven. She heaved a deep breath before speaking, those tight little nipples scraping my flesh through my shirt.

Oh, God, I'm so going to hell for this.

She pressed her cheek to my chest, right over my racing

heart. "I had this horrible dream, and I just… I'm so glad you're okay."

Tentatively, I ran one hand down her spine. "Everything's fine, Jules. I'm good."

She shivered—because of the cold or because of my touch, I couldn't tell—but the motion somehow brought her even closer to me. One bare thigh slid between my legs, and she tipped her head up, those gorgeous green eyes locking with mine. For a long moment, we stood frozen, staring at each other. Slowly, her hands moved. Palms splayed open, she caressed the expanse of my back before slipping them around my waist and up my chest. Every muscle in my body tensed as they coasted upward to rest on my shoulders.

"Jules…" Her name fell from my lips—a warning or a plea, I wasn't sure.

"Eric." One hand moved to cup my face, and my breath suspended in my chest as my good intentions dissipated into thin air.

Only inches away, I could've dipped my head and captured her mouth. She was asking for it—I'd seen that look a thousand times before. But never had any of the other women made me feel this way. She felt so fucking good and yet… she was too young, too pure. She deserved more than someone like me. I was broken in so many ways, and I wasn't sure I'd ever be whole again.

Besides, we both knew how this would end. I refused to start something when she was already planning to run. The thought pissed me off all over again, and I lashed out as the injustice of it all bubbled to the surface.

"You think this is what you want?" Quickly spinning her, I pressed her up against the wall and caged her in my arms. Her chest rose on a sharp inhale, the movement causing her breasts to brush against me. Just the slightest touch made my resolve waver, and I leaned into her the tiniest fraction, not ready to break the connection between us, no matter how tenuous.

I kept my palms planted firmly on the wall. I couldn't touch her—I wouldn't. Her skin would be my kryptonite, soft and silky beneath my fingertips. I was terrified I'd lose control and take her right here against the wall.

She smelled so fucking good, and I couldn't resist the temptation. Dropping my head next to hers, I drew in a lungful of her sweet scent—flowery soft and uniquely Jules. She tipped her head back as I traced the curve of her cheek with my nose. My lips barely brushed her soft skin, and the sensation sent fire licking down my stomach, my dick tightening at the feel of her. Of their own volition, my hips pressed forward, seeking the softness of her body.

This was all I could ever have of her, this moment right here. Closing my eyes, I inhaled once more, committing everything to memory—each contour of her pretty face, the sensual curve where her waist flared out to her rounded hips. I lifted my head and steeled my spine as I met those bright green eyes, the ones that haunted my dreams each night and would continue to haunt them long after she was gone.

"I'm not a good man, Jules. I don't make love, and I'm not gentle. I'm not what you need." She started to shake her head, and those beautiful lips parted, but I spoke over her. "And you're not what I need."

Confusion marred her brow, and guilt shot through me as a look of intense insecurity crossed her beautiful features. I hated the way I felt, knowing I was about to hurt her. With a heavy heart, I delivered the final blow. "Go back to bed, little girl."

Her head jerked as if I'd slapped her, and she flinched. I dropped my arms to my sides, and she pulled away from me. Head held high, shoulders straight, she walked stiffly back to her room and closed the door. The soft click was worse than if she'd slammed it, and I cringed.

Fucking hell. I wanted to put my fist through the wall. So goddamn beautiful, yet so untouchable. Why was life so unfair? She was everything I'd ever wanted and needed but couldn't have. Being with Jules was like standing outside the gates of heaven yearning for joy and comfort yet knowing I'd never be allowed inside. And that pissed me off. I'd never be good enough for her, and the knowledge was hard to stomach.

I stared at the closed door, wishing things could be different. I wished everything was different. I wanted to run down that hallway and pull her into my arms, beg her forgiveness for saying something so awful and untrue. I wanted to kiss her and hold her and make her want to stay with me.

I still knew nothing about her, but my body didn't care. I wanted her—only her. I'd been with women over the past couple years, but Jules… she was fucking special. And I had no idea what to do about it.

I wanted her more than I'd ever wanted anything, but there was so much between us. Age. The past. The truth. Could desire ever begin to overcome those things? After the things I just said to her, I doubted I'd ever find out.

It was for the best, I decided. Even if it hurt like hell.

TWENTY-ONE

GIULIANA

Arrogant, insufferable man.

Humiliation and anger coursed through me, still potent enough to make my skin burn hot.

"I'm not what you need. And you're not what I need."

I snorted. *Liar.*

I'd felt him. He may not *want* to want me, but he couldn't mask his desire. I'd seen it, deep and dark in those hazel eyes. I'd practically felt the lust emanating from him in great, rolling waves as he'd pressed against me, holding me securely between the wall and, well... a hard place. A *really* hard place.

I shivered just thinking about it. It felt so foreign, so scary and exciting at the same time. He wanted me... but would he ever give in to whatever this was between us?

Damn stupid man.

"In my opinion..."

I jumped as Mia appeared next to me. So completely wrapped up in my thoughts of Eric from last night, I hadn't even heard her approach.

"…if a woman is wearing an expression like that, a man probably put it there."

"Hmm?" I turned back to the mannequin in front of me, trying my best to play it off.

Out of the corner of my eye, I watched Mia cock her head and prop her hands on her hips. My shoulders slumped, and I dropped my chin to my chest as the air rushed out of my lungs on a hefty sigh. "Why are men so…?" I threw my hands up in the air as I turned to her, unable to come up with one specific word.

One eyebrow ratcheted toward her hairline. "Stubborn. Stupid. Ignorant." She gestured with one hand. "I can keep going."

Her sarcasm had me smiling. "Yes. To all of those. God, they're so frustrating."

"*They* in general or a specific *him*?" Mia inquired.

"Him. Just one."

"Eric?" she whispered conspiratorially, and I nodded. "What did he do?"

There was no hiding it from her. And, I found, I didn't want to. I needed to talk to someone—someone experienced —and get it off my chest.

"I'm just frustrated. I thought…" I waved a hand in the air. "It doesn't matter. He wants nothing to do with me."

"Oh, I don't believe that for a second." Mia tipped her head in contemplation. "He watches you like a hawk."

I dipped my chin and flicked a disbelieving glance her way. "He called me a little girl."

Her brow creased as she regarded me warily. "Like… in what context?"

I swallowed hard, the pain of his words spearing through me. "As in, 'go back to bed, little girl.'"

Outrage filled her eyes. "He did not!"

"Yeah, he kinda did." I adjusted one of the coats. "He thinks I'm too young, too inexperienced."

"Please." Mia waved a hand in front of her. "They all say that. Jack tried that crap with me, too."

I turned to face her, intrigued. "Really?"

She nodded. "I think I loved Jack the moment I saw him. But he was four years older, so he held off pursuing me for a long time."

Four years? That was all? Jack seemed so much older, so much more mature than Mia. Probably because Jack's demeanor was almost constantly cold and hard while Mia perpetually wore a smile.

I latched on to the last thing she'd said. "Four years isn't all that much. Not nearly the gap between Eric and me."

I wasn't brave enough to ask exactly how old he was, but I figured he was at least ten years older than me.

Mia lifted a shoulder. "It was a big deal when I was sixteen and he was twenty."

My jaw dropped. "You've been together that long?"

She followed my gaze to her engagement ring, and she smiled. "That's a story for another day. But"—she held up a finger—"the point is, men like those two always try to do the honorable thing. Or what they think is honorable."

I couldn't hold back a soft snort. "Idiots."

A grin cracked Mia's face. "Precisely."

I rubbed a hand over my forehead. "What do I do?"

She tipped her head in contemplation. "I've heard blackmail works wonders…"

We dissolved into a fit of laughter. Almost immediately, Mia clutched at her stomach, her opposite hand fluttering to the base of her throat.

I turned concerned eyes on her. "You okay?"

She swallowed hard and nodded. "I'm good."

"Are you sure? I—"

Mia bolted from the room before I could finish, and I followed her out of the pro shop and down the hallway as she shoved through the door of the bathroom. A metal stall door banged, and I quietly shut the door and locked it as she emptied the contents of her stomach into the toilet. I figured it was one of two things. Mia emerged a couple minutes later and threw me an apologetic glance. "I'm sorry you had to see that."

I waved one hand in the air. "Don't apologize. Are you feeling better?"

She nodded and moved toward the sink to rinse out her mouth. "As soon as I get it out of my system, I seem to be fine."

Well, that answered my question. "How long?"

She bit her lip. "About a week."

"Does Jack know?"

She shook her head emphatically, her eyes wide. "Please don't say anything."

"Of course not," I assured her. "How have you managed to hide it?"

She shrugged. "It seems to hit once in the morning, then I'm fine the rest of the day. Thankfully, I'm usually here when it happens."

I studied her. "Do you need anything?"

"Well…" She rolled her eyes skyward in thought. "I'm kind of hungry now."

My mouth dropped open in shocked amusement. "Mia!"

"What?" She laughed. "I'm pregnant. What do you want from me? Is it normal for cravings to kick in already?"

"I have no idea." I lifted one shoulder. "I don't know anything about babies."

I had a huge extended family, but I'd never taken care of children.

"Hmm…" She hummed a noncommittal sound. "What about you? Are you hungry?"

"Starving, actually," I admitted.

"All right." Mia grinned. "Let me brush my teeth, then we can head out."

Half an hour later, we were situated once again at Rosie's in a corner booth. Cynthia, the little blonde waitress, shot me an unreadable look as we entered, then murmured some excuse and ducked into the back. I wondered if what Rosie had said was true; did she resent me for living with Eric, even if nothing had happened between us?

"Sheriff takin' care of ya, darlin'?"

I smiled up at Rosie, though I felt a little pang in my chest when I thought of him. "Yes, ma'am."

We placed our orders and were talking more about the soft opening as well as plans for the spa when Mia's phone rang. Her brows drew together as she studied the screen then answered. "Hello? Oh, hey… Yeah." Her eyes darted across the table to me. "She's with me… Okay. Hold on."

My eyes widened as Mia silently extended the phone across the table to me. I slipped it from her fingers and held it to my ear. "Hello?"

"Jesus." Relief filled me as I recognized Eric's voice on the other end of the line. "I've been trying to reach you for half an hour. Had me damn near ready to drive up to Briarleigh to check on you."

"I'm sorry," I apologized, though I wasn't quite sure why.

"No, no, it's fine. I was just… checking in."

He was worried about me? A little glow of warmth flickered to life around my heart. "I'm fine. Mia and I took a lunch break."

"Okay." His end was silent for a long moment. "Your car is done."

"Oh? Do you want me to go get it? Mia can—"

He cut me off before I could offer to pick the car up. "No. I want to drive it first to make sure everything is okay."

"Are you sure? I don't want to put you out."

"It's no problem," he replied, his voice gruff. "I'll drop it off later this afternoon so it'll be there for you by the time you get done."

"Thank you."

"Sure."

The silence stretched between us for several seconds, and I traced a crack in the Formica tabletop. "So. Um…"

"Yeah. I guess I'll see you later?"

"See you later," I replied, then hung up. I met Mia's gaze as I passed the phone back to her. A smile curved her mouth, much like the cat that caught the canary, and I blushed. "What's that look for?"

"You know," she said impishly as she stowed her phone in her bag. "And you said he doesn't care about you."

"He doesn't—"

Mia pointed at me. "He tracked me down through Jack to find you because he was worried about you." She lifted a brow to drive home the point. "He cares about you."

A tiny smile curved my mouth as I dropped my gaze to the table. "Maybe."

"Don't give up on him," Mia said softly. "The right man is always worth fighting for."

I knew she was right. And maybe he did truly care about me. But what could I do as long as he continued to fight whatever was brewing between us? I wished he could see that what he needed was right in front of him; all he had to do was reach out and take it.

TWENTY-TWO

ERIC

I turned off the radio and focused on the sounds of the car. The tires hummed against the pavement beneath me as I drove toward Briarleigh, and it sent a faint vibration up through the seats.

I accelerated through a slight curve before the road started its steep incline. Trees flanked both sides of the road, a fresh layer of snow clinging to their boughs. The sun shone overhead, but most of it was blocked out by the tall pines.

Out of habit, I flicked a glance in the rearview mirror. The image of my cruiser filled the small oval, Riley at the wheel. It was a quiet morning, and so far, we hadn't passed another car.

The Cavalier appeared to be in good condition even though it was old. Egerton had apparently taken good care of it, but I would still feel better if Jules was in something newer and more reliable. The engine had over 200,000 miles on it, and I wasn't quite sure how much longer it would last even with proper maintenance.

From outside the vehicle, a flat crack cut through the

morning air. I'd heard that sound too many times not to know what it was. My initial assumption was that a hunter was in the woods—but the splintering of the windshield half a second later told me I was dead wrong.

Instinctively, my fingers tightened on the wheel as I ducked down in my seat. The tires slipped on a patch of ice, sending the car into a wild spin, and trees streaked past my window in a wild blur of green and white before the car slammed into the guardrail.

The airbag exploded in a puff of white, blasting against my chest and face, halting my forward motion as the seat belt snapped tightly across my chest. The car jolted to a stop, the rear end facing the opposite direction.

For a second, all was quiet. I braced myself for another shot, but it never came. Twisting my head, I peeked around the headrest to see if I could get a glimpse of anything. No movement came from the woods, and I took a moment to brush away the blood trickling from my nose.

I glanced around again. Considering the shot had come through the windshield, I figured whoever had shot at me was located somewhere up on the mountain. We would have to measure the trajectory to find out exactly where, and I planned to get the deputies up there as soon as possible to start looking around.

Rapid footfalls slapping against the pavement met my ears, and my door was wrenched open a few seconds later. Riley knelt low, using the Cavalier to conceal his body as he stared at me. His face was pale, his lips pressed into a firm line, and I could see the fear in his eyes. I held one hand up in reassurance. "I'm good." He gave a terse nod, and I continued. "Radio it in. We need all available units up here ASAP."

Riley spoke into the radio situated in his shoulder, and I mentally cataloged myself as well as Jules's car. Glancing briefly in the rearview mirror, I caught sight of my battered face, and I grimaced. I could feel that my nose was broken, and abrasions stood out starkly red across both cheeks and my forehead. Thank God for airbags—and guardrails. Otherwise Riley would've been pulling me up from the valley a thousand feet below, and I doubted I would be breathing.

Riley turned his attention back to me. "Squad is on the way."

The last thing I wanted to do was waste time by going to the hospital, but I knew there was no getting out of it. Regardless of whether I wanted it or not, it was basic protocol to check for a concussion. I wanted to be up on that mountain myself looking for leads, but my guys would have to take charge on this one. I eyed Riley as I extricated myself from the Cavalier. My body ached everywhere already, and I knew tomorrow was going to be a bitch.

For the past two minutes since the shot had been fired, all had been silent. I was both wary and grateful, but I didn't want to waste precious time. I motioned for Riley to move to the front of the car with me, downwind from where the shooter had been. "I want to check trajectory on that shot."

Riley gave a concise nod, his quick mind already working. Part of the windshield had caved in when the car connected with the guard rail, but the small round hole just to the left of center was still visible. Riley took off at a jog toward my cruiser and grabbed a kit from the trunk.

While he was gone, I craned my neck to peer inside the vehicle, looking for the bullet. I knew it hadn't struck my seat, but I thought I'd heard a dull thud as it hit the back seat. Sure enough, I found it about four inches below and to the left of the headrest.

Riley approached again with a long dowel rod. Positioning himself at the right front fender of the car, he carefully slid it inside the small circular hole the bullet had left in the windshield. I guided it the rest of the way through until the base of the rod touched the slug lodged in the back seat.

I shared a quick glance with him. From the angle, it appeared the shooter would have been located north of me and off to the right side of the road. Using a pair of forceps from the case, I dug the bullet out of the seat. It was a .22 caliber, a common enough size for a rifle. Everyone in Pine Ridge had at least one in their household.

"We need to get up there and assess the scene, see if we can find anything." From the base of the mountain, I heard the faint wail of a siren as the ambulance wound its way up to us. I knew my deputies wouldn't be far behind, and I was grateful for the quick response. My head ached, and I blinked to clear away the black spots dancing before my eyes. Flashing red lights preceded the ambulance's arrival and I turned to Riley. "Can you do me a favor?"

He dipped his chin. "Sure thing, boss."

My breath rushed out of my lungs on a sigh. "Can you send someone to pick Jules up, take her back to the house?"

I knew they'd require me to be treated down at Kalispell General, and there was no way I'd be released in time to get her.

"No problem." He paused. "You think…?"

"Yeah." I didn't have to be a genius to know what he was thinking. I'd driven the Cavalier only once before today, and that had been more than a week ago when she'd first arrived in town. "Just make sure she's safe 'til I get there."

Someone would answer for this. But first, I needed to talk to Jules—and find out what she was hiding.

TWENTY-THREE

GIULIANA

The cruiser pulled up, and I pushed out the door, heading toward it. My steps slowed, and my feet turned to lead when I saw an unfamiliar face in the driver seat. The man rolled down the window separating us. "Hey. Jules, right?" I nodded. "I'm Riley. Eric sent me to get you."

Warning bells went off in my head. "Why? Where is he?"

His face contorted into an expression I couldn't read. "He was in an accident."

Those five little words stole my breath, and my knees buckled. I grasped the sill of the door to keep myself upright. "What happened? Is he okay?"

Riley studied me. "He'll be fine. They took him down to the hospital in Kalispell—standard procedure. He asked me to take you to his place until he gets home."

I quickly debated my options then climbed into the car. I pulled the seat belt across my chest, and Riley hit the button to roll up the window before putting the car in gear. The trip to Eric's was silent, and I breathed a sigh of relief as we pulled into the driveway. I turned surprised eyes on him when he cut the engine and made to climb out. He answered my unspoken question before I voiced it.

"I promised I'd stay here until he got home."

I nodded, but the whole situation seemed strange. For the next several hours, Riley sat at the kitchen table, intermittently taking phone calls and answering emails while I paced the small house. I still didn't fully trust him or what he told me, and I probably wouldn't until I saw Eric for myself. Riley still hadn't told me exactly what had happened, and that bothered me.

The crunch of gravel came from outside, and I glimpsed a flash of red through the kitchen window as the vehicle pulled into the driveway. Barely a minute later, Eric entered the house.

"Hey, boss." Riley moved toward the door. "You good?"

Eric nodded. "See you tomorrow."

Riley tipped his chin in acknowledgement, not offended by Eric's curt tone in the least, and he made his way outside. I heard Eric's harsh exhale as he closed and locked the door behind Riley, his broad shoulders tense.

I sucked in a breath as he turned to fully face me for the first time. A bandage stretched over his nose, and there were dark bruises beneath both eyes. I had the sudden irrational urge to run to him, throw my arms around him, but his posture stopped me cold. For nearly a minute, we stood there in silence just staring at each other.

Finally, I swallowed hard and forced the words out of my constricted throat. "Are you okay?"

It was a silly question, and the answer was fairly obvious —of course he wasn't okay. He nodded anyway. When he still didn't say anything, I continued. "What happened?"

He studied me for several seconds then tipped his head toward the kitchen table. "Let's sit."

He didn't take his eyes off me as I moved around the table and sat gingerly in one of the hard oak chairs. "Had some trouble with your car today."

"Is that what caused the accident?" He nodded, his hesitation so brief that I almost didn't catch it—he was lying to me.

I dropped my gaze away before summoning my courage and meeting his stare again. "What really happened?" My voice was barely more than a whisper, and he exhaled through his nose before speaking.

"Someone shot at me."

"What?!" I was out of my seat, hands planted on the table as I leaned toward him before I realized I'd moved. My gaze raked over him before jumping back to his. "Someone shot at you?" Eric's face remained impassive as he returned my stare, and I sank back down into my seat. "You're serious?"

He nodded. "While I was driving to Briarleigh."

It all made sense. The broken nose, the abrasions. They were from an airbag. Oh, God. He could've been killed. I pressed one hand to my chest as bile rose in the back of my throat.

A soft sound drew my attention back to him. "We're still trying to figure out who's responsible."

I knew with surety that it hadn't been my uncle. If he was the one who'd shot at Eric, I wouldn't be having this conversation right now; I would be on my way back to Chicago while the town prepared for his funeral. The only other person I'd had any kind of contact with recently was Sam—and he'd been cleared of slashing my tires. Besides, why would he shoot at Eric? It wasn't worth going to jail just for retribution.

I shook my head again. "Who would do something like that?"

Eric's gaze darkened as he stared at me. "I don't know, but you can be damn sure I'm going to find out."

His words sent a chill down my spine. The look in his eyes told me he wouldn't stop until he'd gotten whatever answers he was looking for.

TWENTY-FOUR

ERIC

I leaned back in my chair and stared at the water-stained ceiling. The cells were empty—kind of a surprise there, since it was Christmas. Seemed that holidays and full moons brought out the worst in people, often landing them in jail for the night.

So far, I hadn't encountered shit. The one time I actually needed something to happen, it was quiet. Why the hell couldn't someone do something stupid so I could haul their ass to jail? Then I wouldn't have to think about Jules every second of the day.

Every time I closed my eyes, I saw her soft curves, smelled her sweet scent—saw that stricken look when I'd cut her down like the asshole I was. Goddamn it. And that was precisely why I could never have her. She was too fucking pure for me. Even when I'd turned her down, she'd taken my rejection with grace and dignity. She hadn't thrown things, hadn't yelled, hadn't even said a word. The following morning she'd acted like it never happened.

Things had gotten progressively worse after the shooting incident. I knew Jules was holding back; she knew something. Whether it pertained to her past or to whoever was responsible, I didn't know. Over the past three days, we'd barely spoken at all and avoided each other whenever possible. It was exactly what I'd wanted. And I fucking hated every second of it.

Things on that front were at a standstill, too. The fact that someone had shot at me—at Jules, rather—still had the power to send fire roaring through my veins. I replayed the events of that day, thinking through each step. When I'd spoken with Mia, she and Jules were eating at Rosie's.

It was possible the shooter had seen Jules in town and assumed Mia had taken her down to pick up the car during her lunch break. Charlie parked the vehicles outside when they were ready to be picked up, so the shooter may have made the connection and headed through the woods to lie in wait.

For at least the dozenth time, I flipped through the report that Riley had compiled from the deputies' findings from the scene. Over the past few days, the guys had been busting their asses to find the person who'd fired at me, and they had cataloged every finding along the mile-long trail stretching between the general store and the spot on the mountain.

Partial treads from a man's work boot. A shell casing that we'd sent in to be analyzed. Fibers from an article of clothing, probably some type of outdoor or hunting wear, judging from the coarse material. A plastic wrapper from a Mountain Dew bottle that had seen better days. Various other pieces of trash picked up along the way.

The clothing emporium in Pine Ridge only carried a dozen or so styles of boots, so Riley stopped there first and got one of each pair to verify against the tread we pulled from the scene. It was easy enough to compare. The size ten-and-a-half men's Red Wing work boot was one of the most popular sold at the Clothing Emporium.

When I spoke to Joey, she told me that she would pull sales for the boots as far back as she could. With the holiday and her grandfather's lackluster attempt at keeping book over the past year, she apologetically told me that it might take several days.

Truth be told, I wasn't totally optimistic anyway. If someone took care of them, boots like those could last several years. We would have to sift through every purchase, question each suspect, in order to find out who'd been up there. Judging from the tracks to and from the scene, it appeared the person had approached on foot.

It was just over a mile from the tree line on the main road to the back of the general store, and I imagined the shooter had parked somewhere behind the plaza. The trek would've been easy enough to make for someone adept at spending time in the woods—which narrowed it down to about 70 percent of Pine Ridge's population.

A soft scuffling sound outside drew my attention toward the outer office, and I leaned back in my chair to check it out. I bit back a groan as a familiar form appeared in the plate glass window beside the front door. With a muttered curse, I pushed out of my chair and strode to the front door.

I twisted the lock on the doorknob to unlock it, then slid the chain on the deadbolt over to release it. I knew most people in Pine Ridge didn't bother to lock their doors at any time of day, but as a city boy born and raised in Chicago, it wasn't a habit I was able or willing to break. I insisted on the safety of myself and my men at all times and kept the doors locked whenever possible.

I opened the door and stepped back, allowing Cynthia to enter. She stepped inside with a smile, bringing with her the sugary scent of freshly baked cookies. I closed the door but made no move to invite her back to my office. I refused to lead her on, to give her any hope of anything ever happening between us.

After a long moment of uncomfortable silence, she held up the tray in her hands. "Merry Christmas, Sheriff."

I offered her a tight smile. "Merry Christmas."

I slipped it from her hands, careful not to touch her as I did so, then set it on Warren's desk. My deputies would enjoy them tomorrow when they got in. I personally had no intention of indulging in them. I casually leaned one hip against the desk and crossed my arms over my chest as I regarded her. "What brings you by today?"

She clenched her hands together at her waist, her mouth twisted into an expression of discomfort. "I knew you were here all by yourself, and…" She gave a little shrug. "The cookies are fresh. I baked them myself."

"Thanks. The guys will enjoy them."

Her face fell, and part of me felt like an asshole for hurting her. Still, I refused to encourage her. Her gaze darted around the room before finally landing on me again. "So, I, um… I thought maybe we could do something sometime?"

She framed it up almost like a question, as if she were afraid to ask, and my heart went out to her for having the courage to speak up. "Cynthia, I really appreciate the offer, but…" I shook my head. "I can't. I'm sorry."

Her eyes narrowed on me, flashing with fire. "So it's true then?" I refused to dignify her impertinence with a response. Unfortunately, she pressed on. "You should know better than to fall for some girl just because she has a pretty face," she remarked bitterly.

I seethed inwardly but refused to let her see that she'd affected me. "And you should know that my business doesn't pertain to you."

My soft words hit their mark with surprising force, and

her face twisted into a stricken expression of hurt and remorse. "I… I'm sorry. I should go."

"I think that's for the best," I agreed as I moved toward the door. Cynthia paused in the doorway as if she wanted to say something else, then decided against it. With a slight nod, she hurried out onto the sidewalk to her car, and I locked up behind her with a sigh.

I hated to hurt her feelings, but she needed to know that there was nothing between us. Not now, not ever. There was only one woman who might ever be able to tempt me out of my bachelor status, but I wasn't sure I had the courage to pursue Jules, no matter how much I cared for her.

With all honesty, I could say that I was jaded from my first marriage, which had been a disaster of epic proportions. It hadn't started out so badly, but then, they never did. In the beginning, Steph had been sweet and sexy, and she seemed to care for me. But the reality was so much darker than the truth.

Steph and I were so young when we got married—too young. We first met junior year when she transferred into my school, and I fell hard for her pretty face. She was kind of a mean girl back then, but I'd written it off as Steph adjusting to life in her new high school. She'd been terribly possessive, jealous of my friends and any girl who tried to talk to me. I continued to make excuses for her bad behavior, because, well… I was in love. Or as my football coach used to say— young, dumb, and full of cum.

I'd seen the pale scars on her wrists soon after we started dating and, with me doting on her, things seemed to get better. But the more possessive she got, the more we fought, and she picked the habit up again. She was so worried about losing me after graduation, she said, that she couldn't stand the pain. She'd promised to stop if I married her. And it worked—for a while.

When it was good, it was good. But when it was bad, it was volatile. We fought like cat and dog, but she drew me back in after each fight with tears and apologies, claiming that she couldn't live without me. She'd even gone so far at one point to tell me after a particularly bad breakup that she considered killing herself. No more idle threats with shallow cuts; she was at her breaking point. She said I was too harsh and demanding, and I felt guilty for pushing her that far.

I should've seen the red flags, should've known that those manipulations were just the beginning of a tumultuous downhill slide. I had no doubt that she liked me and was attracted to me, but she certainly didn't love me. She loved that I dressed up in uniform each day after going through the academy and joining the force in Chicago, but that's where it ended.

She didn't seem to care that the job could be dangerous or that I could be hurt. Some nights men didn't make it home. Instead of being concerned for my welfare, she seemed to thrive on the drama of it. She'd become jealous and antagonistic when I explained once that there were details of my job I couldn't divulge. She resented that and saw it as a betrayal.

I remembered her words from that day, still ringing clearly in my ears. "It's a choice. And if you can't talk to me about your job, then what else are you hiding?"

I'd laughed at her. "Are you accusing me of cheating on you?"

She threw a temper tantrum, and I told her I was going to leave and give her some time to herself to figure things out. The words she'd thrown at me still had the ability to chill me to my bones. "If you leave, I'll tell everyone that you're abusive and you rape me."

I'd never lifted a hand to her, but the conversation had been an eye-opener. I'd never been more ashamed in my life to have to go to my chief and explain the situation. The very next day, while she was at work, I moved in with my partner,

Ric. I'd had to leave half my shit at our house, but breaking ties had been worth it.

When she realized I was gone, she called me up, raging and screaming. Finally, she broke down and begged me to come back, even going so far as to entice me with sex. I felt bad and was tempted to fall back into the rhythm we'd established, but her betrayal and threats eclipsed all the good memories we'd made. There was no fucking way I would risk having sex with her and knocking her up. It was literally the worst thing I could imagine.

Since then, I had resisted a serious relationship, certain that it would feel just like my marriage had ten years ago. As sheriff, I had a certain reputation to uphold. If I needed the satisfaction of a woman to warm my bed, I made sure to seek them out at least one town over. I didn't want to stir up the drama by dating someone in my own backyard. That way, if things didn't work out, no one was the wiser. We could go our separate ways and not have to worry about running into each other every day. No one over the past few years had struck my fancy—until Jules.

I didn't know what it was that drew me to her like a moth to flame; it didn't make sense. I felt lust and passion for her, even protectiveness. But that's all it was, all it could ever be. I fucking hated secrets, and I hated more the fact that she refused to open up. I couldn't be with someone who held her cards so close to her chest the way Jules did. I needed to know where I stood with someone.

With her, I never knew what to think. Sometimes she was so aloof, so inaccessible. Other times, her eyes burned with longing, but for what I didn't know. Freedom? Me? I'd be stupid to hope it was the latter. I didn't want someone I couldn't trust. And that was the crux of the matter. I didn't know if I could trust Jules or not because she was so damned closed off.

Even as the thought crossed my mind, I knew it wasn't

completely true. Jules was a vault of secrets, but she was nothing like my ex-wife. She had nothing to hold over me, rarely even spoke to me if she didn't have to.

Which was precisely why her actions the other night had shocked the hell out of me. There was no way she could feel anything for me, not the way I did for her. She'd been fueled by fear and worry, still half asleep. Though I had to admit, she seemed fully aware of what she was doing at the time. Turning her away had made me physically ill. Since then she'd been coolly polite but distant, and it had damn near killed me.

Part of me wanted to breach the gap, to put everything on the line and tell her how I felt. The trepidation that sat like a stone in my gut kept me from taking that leap. For so long I'd lived my life just going through the motions. After the incident back in Chicago, I'd shut myself off completely. Tired of the political bullshit and not able to go back to my job, I'd come here to heal, both mentally and physically. I hadn't allowed myself to think about the future; rather, I spent my time living only in the present when my head wasn't stuck in the past.

I never intended to be sheriff, but the people had coerced me into it, and I found that, for the most part, I enjoyed it. Things around Pine Ridge were typically pretty slow, and sometimes it grated on my nerves. It was almost a culture shock coming from the bustling busyness of Chicago, where something was always going down. The worst thing to happen around here was usually a drunk and disorderly conduct or domestic dispute. The recent incident with Jack and Mia at Briarleigh was the most action I'd seen since moving here nearly three years ago.

That horrible day stood out in my mind like it happened yesterday. There was no saving him, though God knew I tried. The loss still hurt sometimes, and memories flooded my brain. The members of our SWAT team had all been close, but

Ric was like my brother. I still wasn't sure exactly where it had all gone wrong, but I remembered the gut feeling I had walking in there that something wasn't right. The events of that day left two FBI agents dead, as well as my partner, Ric.

We'd infiltrated a warehouse to aid in the interception of contraband smuggled in by one of Chicago's most notorious crime syndicates, and shit hit the fan almost immediately. The firefight hadn't lasted more than two minutes, but I remembered every second as if it had just happened yesterday. About thirty seconds in, Ric went down—a bullet had slipped between the ballistic plates of his vest and lodged itself in his lungs.

When I thought we had them neutralized, I did chest compressions to keep him breathing until a medic arrived. So focused on him, I hadn't heard the soft footsteps behind me. Before I even knew what was happening, my head was jerked back and a knife slipped between the bottom of my helmet and the top of my vest.

With his dying breath, Ric lifted his pistol and shot the man, killing him. Thankfully—though I wasn't sure how—the blade had just barely missed my artery. The laceration had severed my vocal cords, and the corrective surgery they'd performed at the hospital had returned it almost to normal. Though we'd eliminated one monster that day, it was kind of like cutting the head off of a snake—another would just pop up in his place, probably a family member who'd been groomed for the job since birth.

Losing my teammate and suffering from near-fatal injuries had me rethinking my life. Before, I'd never hesitated before to put my life on the line. I lived for the rush. But life changed, and so did people. Now I was… comfortable, if not entirely happy.

I sighed as I glanced around the quiet office, wondering not for the first time what Jules was doing today. Though Jack and Mia had invited us over for Christmas dinner, we'd both declined. This wasn't my first holiday alone, nor would it be my last. The thought of Jules not being around this time next year stung more than it should have, and I pushed down the disappointment.

Maybe after she left, I would make more of an effort to date. I just had no idea how I'd ever find someone who made me feel a fraction of what she did.

TWENTY-FIVE

I opened the door of the oven once more to check on dinner, then closed it up and nervously wiped my hands on the towel as I glanced at the clock. The digital green numbers told me that it was already after six o'clock, a good hour past the time when Eric normally got home.

I wondered if he was still avoiding me. For the past few days, we had pretty much danced around each other in uncomfortable silence. He pretended to ignore me, and I did my best to not let on how much it bothered me.

My ears perked up as I heard the door of the mud room open, then close again. There was shuffling as I imagined him hanging up his coat and toeing out of his boots as he did every time he entered the house. Several moments later, Eric stepped into the kitchen. His face was drawn, exhausted, as if he hadn't slept in several days. He looked exactly the way I felt. His head tipped back as he sniffed the air appreciatively.

"Something smells good."

Growing up, we'd had a chef who made all of our meals.

This was my first time really making a meal, and I'd scoured the internet for the perfect recipe. I'd followed it to the letter, and it smelled divine. I was immensely proud of the way it'd turned out.

I willed my pulse to slow as a nervous smile lifted my lips. "I figured you didn't have a chance to eat today, so…" I lifted my hands in a little shrugging motion.

Eric eyed me from where he stood just outside the kitchen. "You cooked dinner for me?"

"Well…" I rolled the hem of my shirt between my fingers. "I wanted to thank you for everything you've done, and I couldn't really afford to get you a gift so… this was the best I could come up with on short notice."

His head tipped slightly to one side. "You didn't have to do this."

He made no move to come closer, and the hope that had begun to bloom in my chest quickly died away, turning to embarrassment. Was he going to refuse my gift? I stared at him. "I know. I wanted to."

For a long moment we just stared at each other, then finally, he shook his head. "I can't accept this."

Disappointment and humiliation mingled in my gut, and I swallowed hard. "Right." I threw the dish towel on the counter. "You can bring me dinner every night under the pretense that Rosie sends extra home with you, but I can't make you dinner to show my appreciation for taking me in when you didn't have to?"

Face carefully blank, his lips parted to speak. "I don't…"

I gave a short laugh when he trailed off. He could refuse to eat a simple thank-you dinner, but apparently he couldn't bring himself to lie to my face. "You don't know what I'm talking about? How about the fact that Rosie told me you order two meals each day? I know damn well you only eat one of them, so who is the other one for?" Thoroughly frustrated at his complete and utter lack of communication, I started to push past him out of the kitchen.

"*Capotosta*," I muttered under my breath.

A strong hand wrapped around my arm and whirled me back to him. I let out a little gasp as the motion brought my face only inches from his. "What did you say?"

Anger welled up, spilling over, and I planted my hands on his chest, shoving as hard as I could. His huge body didn't even move, and the feel of his hard chest beneath my fingers only served to infuriate me more, reminding me of my attraction to him—and the magnetic pull between us that he continued to fight. "It means you're bullheaded, you arrogant son of a bitch."

His eyes flashed and his nostrils flared, his fingers tightening around my bicep. He gave a little jerk, and my body swayed the slightest bit toward him. He drew in a deep breath, then exhaled, the feel of his breath warm against my face. His thumb softly stroked the skin of my upper arm as he stared down at me. I waited for him to say something— anything—but he remained obstinately silent.

I gave him one last chance. "Will you have dinner with me?"

Something flickered in his eyes, but he remained quiet for a long moment. Finally, he gave an almost imperceptible shake of his head.

My heart dropped to my toes and I pulled out of his hold. The bridge of my nose burned as tears rose, and I quickly turned away to keep him from seeing the moisture gathering in my eyes. Spine straight, I headed down the hallway, determined to keep my composure. I could practically feel his gaze on my back as I moved away. Part of me hoped he'd come after me, but I knew he wouldn't.

Just a few more steps... Inside the bedroom, I closed and locked the door then let the angry tears fall. The man was absolutely maddening. He wanted me—I knew he did—so why was he fighting it? He tried so hard to control his emotions, his reactions to me, and I wanted to smack that look of indifference right off his face. I wanted him to look at me with unrestrained desire—not the quick glimpses that flashed in his eyes before he tamped them down. Why couldn't he see that I wanted it, too?

Men thought they owned and controlled everything, and I was sick of it. I was tired of having no authority over my own life. Never had I been able to make my own decisions. My entire life had been planned out from the day I entered this world. I'd always known that I would grow up, marry a made man, and live a life of luxury surrounded by secrets and funded by dirty money.

I'd hated the idea then, and I hated it even more now. Maybe it was because I'd had a taste of what life outside the *famiglia* could be like. A tiny piece of me missed my home, the men and women I'd grown up with. But all of it had been fabricated—everything arranged to strengthen the bonds between families and different factions. Just like my marriage to Nikolai was intended to settle a feud between the *famiglia* and the Bratva.

I swiped angrily at my tears. My virginity was just a commodity to be auctioned off to the highest bidder. I deserved more than that. I wanted to be the one who got to decide what to do with it. It was my right, damn it. For the past twenty years, I hadn't had a say in anything—not my clothes or hair, and certainly not my behavior. Every day had been strategically planned out, a revolving door of tutors and tailors. I didn't have the chance to just be me.

I was seen as merely an object, not a person. But Eric—he saw me. I knew he did. I saw the desire deep in those eyes, the temptation thick in that growly voice. I was no longer the broken girl he'd picked up almost two weeks ago. He'd shown me what it was like to feel safety and comfort, and I wanted to show him my appreciation. More than that, I wanted control over my own life, over my body. I was so tired of watching over my shoulder, always waiting for the other shoe to drop.

I wasn't stupid enough to think that my uncle would give up looking for me. He would hunt me down on principle alone for running away. Moreover, I'd foiled whatever plans he'd had to soothe affairs with the Russians. If he didn't need me so badly, I knew he'd kill me for that.

I hadn't been around men other than family members for most of my life. Bodyguards followed me like oversized shadows, but I'd never had a boyfriend. I'd been deprived of the most normal teenage relationships. I read articles online, and I felt the pull of desire deep in my core when I looked at Eric.

I'd never felt about a man the way I did with him. I was attracted to him, and I knew he was attracted to me too. Maybe Eric didn't want any more complications. I'd already turned his life upside down and was basically living with him. Was that why he was hesitant to deepen our relationship? He'd seen me at rock bottom, sleeping in my car, still bruised from the altercation with my uncle.

Eric was honorable, kind, and caring. Over the past couple of weeks, he'd taken it upon himself to fulfill the role of protector. But that wasn't what I wanted from him. I'd be lying if I said he didn't make me feel safe—I'd never felt more secure with another man. I just wanted… more. I wanted to be desired, loved.

He was nothing if not noble. As sheriff, I expected nothing less. But was that it, or was it… more? Was he afraid to give into temptation? Maybe Mia was right. Did the gap in our age bother him that much? I just had to show him that I was ready for more. I'd done pretty much everything I could think of to make him see me as a woman. But he wouldn't act on his desires. He would never make the first move if he thought it would be taking advantage of me. I would have to completely bare my soul, put myself out there for him.

Part of me understood why he was hesitant to act on his desires—because I was absolutely positive that's what I saw in those striking hazel eyes. I didn't know if he was capable of deeper affection or not, but I needed to find out.

The thought of rejection made my knees tremble, and I sank down on the bed. I really had two choices. I could keep going the way things were, my heart hurting every time I saw him, or I could make one last attempt to make him see me as more than just a friend and roommate. My heart was already cracked. What was the worst that would happen? If he told me no, I would pick myself up, pull myself together, and move on.

I was determined to make one last overture to win him over. If this attempt failed, I would leave him alone for good. Of course, if this didn't work out, it would probably make things so awkward between us that I would have to leave.

Was I ready for that? I wasn't sure I had a choice. Being here with Eric, slowly falling for him but knowing that he may never return my feelings was breaking my heart. I couldn't continue to put myself out there only to be shot down every time. Deep down, I knew he was worth the fight, and I was willing to give it one last try.

I took my time brushing out my hair so it hung down my back in loose, tousled waves. I used the makeup I'd borrowed from Mia to bring some color to my face and dressed carefully in the red lingerie I'd purchased from Joey's shop. Taking one last long look in the mirror, I took a deep breath and gathered every last ounce of courage before striding out to the living room.

He sat on the couch, and I saw surprise—and lust—flare in his eyes before his expression shuttered once more. His knees were spread wide, and I moved between them, so close

I could reach out and touch him. I forced myself to meet his gaze. "You said you don't make love."

Every inch of me trembled, and I steeled my spine against those eyes, hooded now as they studied me. He blinked, the only indication that he'd heard me, and with a sharp inhale, I rushed on. "I want you to fuck me."

TWENTY-SIX

ERIC

Shock pinned me to the couch, the sound of that dirty word falling from those perfect, sweet lips damn near inconceivable. I wanted to bend her over my knee and paddle her ass red for thinking it, let alone saying it aloud. I wanted…

Goddamn it, I wanted to do exactly what she asked and fuck her so hard she forgot how to speak altogether.

The woman in front of me wasn't the reserved girl I'd met twelve days ago. She was a goddess—a walking, breathing temptation. Though she was still too thin, her lithe, nubile body was perfectly rounded in all the right places. My hands ached to take her breasts, feel the tight little nipples outlined beneath the lace of her bra. I curled my fingers into my thighs, desperately trying to rein in my desire.

She had no idea what she was asking. I leveled a hard stare at her, hoping it would break her. But Jules stood stubbornly, statue-still, the only sign of her distress the faint twitch of her fingers at her side. Anger consumed me. She wanted to push me? I'd play her game and give it right back, twice as hard.

I grasped the backs of her legs and yanked her toward me. I caught her as she stumbled, lifting her so she was spread over my lap. Her hands moved to my shoulders, gliding upward to the back of my neck. The sensation of her nails scraping the sensitive skin sent a bolt of pleasure straight to my groin.

My arousal leaped between us, pressing eagerly against my zipper. The heat from her core was so close, I could feel it through the fabric of my pants. I wondered with sick curiosity if I'd have a wet spot from where she rested on my thighs.

I cupped her roughly. "You want me to fuck you?"

My fingers slipped past the barrier of her panties and glided along her lips. I barely managed to hold back a groan as I dipped a finger into her channel. Holy fuck, was she wet. I pressed a second finger deep inside her, delighting in her sexy little gasp as she dropped her head forward, burying her face in the crook of my neck.

"So fucking tight, baby." Her head tipped to one side, allowing me better access, and I bit her neck. "Do you want me inside you?"

The jerky motion of her head must've been a nod, but I needed her words. "Yes or no?"

I sank my teeth into her skin again, and she hissed in a breath. "Because I want to feel you. I've been dreaming of being buried deep inside you, watching you come."

Jules let out a whimper and wiggled on my lap, bringing her closer to me. Her nails dug into my shoulders, spurring me on. Fingers still buried deep inside her, I fisted my free hand in her hair, wound it around my wrist, and yanked hard.

Her back bowed, thrusting those perky, perfect tits toward me, and my cock jumped at the sight. I wanted to see what was beneath the sexy red bra, imagining what she'd look like bare. Would her nipples be large or small? Dusky pink or brown?

"I want to fuck you long and hard and rough." I pressed my thumb against her clit, moving in small circles. "Is that what you want?"

"Yes," she breathed. "Oh, God…"

She broke off, panting heavily as the walls of her core tightened around my fingers. I'd be damned if I was going to let her come on my hand. Hell, no. She was only going to come with me inside her—multiple times if I had any say in the matter.

She let out a cry of distress as I pulled my hand free of her pretty red panties. "No! Don't… Don't stop, please!"

Her pleas fueled me, breaking the tenuous grip on my resistance. Unable to hold back, I fused my mouth with hers, drinking in the taste of her sweetness on her plump lips. The sensation was erotic as hell. I pulled on her hair, breaking the kiss, and her nails cut into my shoulders as she let out a needy moan.

"Eric!"

Two syllables. That's all it took for me to lose my mind and my control. Slamming my mouth over hers, I stood with her still in my arms and stalked toward the bedroom. Maneuvering from memory, I made my way to the bed until my thighs bumped the mattress.

Ripping my mouth from hers, I tossed her on the bed. Her breasts jiggled as she landed with a bounce, and she let out a sexy little gasp as I caged her in my arms. I'd give her one last out. "Last chance, sweetheart."

Her teeth burrowed into her lower lip, and she shook her head. I lifted an eyebrow. "Is that a yes or no?"

She grabbed the fabric of my shirt and pulled me toward her. "Don't stop."

Ah, fuck. I groaned into her mouth as her tongue tangled with mine. Reaching between us, I popped the button on my fly and worked the material of my pants down my legs. Breaking the kiss, I unzipped my shirt and tossed it to the floor, then shucked my boxers.

Yanking open the drawer of the nightstand, I grabbed a condom. I stroked my cock with one hand as I ripped the foil packet open with my teeth, then rolled the thin material over my straining erection.

Jules stared at me from where she lay on the bed, propped up on her elbows, and her tongue darted out to wet her lips. I could see the faint glistening in the bright moonlight, and my cock jumped. I needed to be inside her. I was on fire, ready to burst, and I couldn't wait another second to feel her.

I hadn't lied to her earlier—I'd fantasized about this moment hundreds, if not thousands, of times this past week. She was gorgeous, so young and naïve, but so damn tempting at the same time. The sexy little vixen shifted her legs, shielding herself from view. A feral smile broke over my face. I was going to get very well acquainted with that part of her very soon.

I climbed onto the bed and prowled over her, prying her knees apart. My favorite assets were still covered in red lace, and that just wouldn't do. Reaching behind her back, I flicked the clasp on her bra and drew it up her arms, then tossed it over my shoulder.

Jules's hands moved to cover her breasts and I shook my head. "Huh-uh, gorgeous. You're going to let me see you. *All* of you," I emphasized as I took her wrists and lifted them over her head. The motion pushed her breasts higher, and my attention zeroed in on them. I rubbed a palm over one tiny pink tip, and it pebbled under my touch.

Jules arched her back at the sensation, and I dropped a kiss on her navel, then moved south. She lifted her hips as I slipped my fingers beneath the waistband of her panties. The backs of my fingers grazed the soft skin as I pulled them down her legs. She slipped her feet free of the material, then automatically tried to clench her legs together again. I lifted a brow. "What did I just say?"

She blinked up at me, and I halted my movements as I stared down at her. "I asked you a question."

She licked her lips nervously. "You… you want to see me."

Her legs reluctantly fell open as I tugged on one knee. "That's right, baby. I want to see every…" I trailed my lips up her inner thigh, punctuating each word with a kiss. "… single… inch."

Her hands moved next to her hips, fisting in the comforter. Deciding we'd both endured enough teasing for the evening, I levered myself over her. Her eyes were closed, teeth cutting into her lower lip. I cupped the side of her face. "Look at me."

Her eyes popped open.

"That's better." I brushed my lips over hers. "I want those beautiful eyes on me."

The crown of my arousal bumped her core, sliding along her folds, and I fought to hold back a groan. She was soaking wet, primed and ready for me. Dipping my head, I devoured her mouth as I lined myself up with her.

I rolled my hips, thrusting into her fast and hard. Almost immediately Jules's nails cut into my skin, and the tightness of her sheath sent up a red flag in the back of my mind.

Jules's back arched, her legs stiffening where they clenched my hips, and a keening cry ripped from her throat— not the good kind. Her face was contorted in agony, her teeth cutting into her lower lip as if to keep her cries from escaping. I froze, and the world around me stilled as all the pieces of the puzzle slowly fell into place.

She was a virgin? Deep in the recesses of my mind, I didn't want to believe it, but I knew what I'd just felt, and a sickening dread filled my stomach.

Her nails dug into my biceps where she gripped me, trying to hold me close and push me away at the same time. "Eric!"

Why the hell hadn't she said anything? Fuck. *Fuck!*

The tortured plea in her voice damn near broke me, and I had no idea how to make it better. It would hurt worse if I tried to pull out right now. Her body was strung tighter than a bow, her muscles clamped down on me like a vise. I pushed my anger aside and tried to soothe her. "Shh, baby, just relax."

Her chest heaved as she struggled to draw in air, and I worried she might hyperventilate. Her eyes were wide and wild as she fought me. "I can't… It's…"

I cupped her face with one hand and forced her attention to me. "I've got you, sweetheart. Look at me."

Her expression bespoke of a mixture of fear and pain, and her arms flailed frantically as she tried to extricate herself from my hold. Using my body weight, I pinned her to the bed, then grabbed her wrists and pressed them over her head. "Jules. Look at me."

With an anguished cry, she blinked those beautiful, heartbreakingly sad eyes up at me. "Take a deep breath, honey. I'm right here."

Her chest rose on a shaky inhale, and I released her wrists to run one hand over her hair. "That's it, baby girl." I wiped up a stray tear with the pad of my thumb. "Just relax."

Burying her face in the crook of my neck, she nodded. I started to retreat, but her arms automatically wound around my shoulders. "Wait."

Her head moved against my throat as she shook her head. "Not… not yet."

I remained still, suspended over her, before I gently pulled back to look at her. "Tell me what you want me to do."

"It doesn't—" She broke off and swallowed, then continued. "It's better now."

What the hell did that mean? It'd been years since I was with a virgin, and reading between the lines was fucking impossible. "I need you to tell me what you want, Jules. Do you want me to stop?"

Her teeth dug into her lower lip as she averted her gaze, then hesitantly shook her head. "No. I want..."

Grasping her chin, I redirected her gaze to mine. I needed to hear the words—I needed to see those beautiful eyes when she told me. I wasn't going to let her second-guess it, and I sure as hell wasn't going to keep going if I thought she was conflicted. I was *not* going to be a regret tomorrow morning. "Look at me when you speak."

Her eyes widened a fraction, but she gave a timid little nod.

"Tell me exactly what you want." She'd come to me earlier for reasons I couldn't begin to understand—especially now— begging me to fuck her. If she still wanted it, she was going to have to ask. "I want to hear you say it."

She swallowed hard. "I want you."

"You want me to... what?" I wasn't going to give her an inch.

Irritation flared in those pretty orbs, and she smacked my chest. "You know what."

I captured her tiny hand in mine and trapped it between us. "Maybe, maybe not."

Looking unsure as hell and more than a little pissed, she hissed out what I'd been waiting to hear. "Fuck me."

"Good girl." I unfurled her hand and placed a kiss on her palm before replacing it on the pillow over her head. Framing her face with my hands, I dipped my head and kissed her long and slow. Sweeping my tongue into her mouth, I tasted her, devoured her. I'd started to soften while I waited for her to make up her mind; now my erection came back full force. Beneath me, her body began to relax, and Jules threw herself into the kiss, matching me stroke for stroke.

Her inner walls strangled my cock, and I rolled my hips, testing her readiness. She sucked in a breath but didn't shy away. Instead, her pelvis lifted as if she needed to get closer. I knew exactly what she was feeling in that moment. Even though I was buried inside her, it wasn't enough. I wanted to claim every inch of her, mark her—make her mine. I wanted to burn my presence into every cell of her body so my touch was the only one she would ever remember.

I dropped to my elbows and slid my hands through her hair, cupping her head and lifting her face to meet mine. The weight of my body pressed her into the mattress, and her tight little nipples scraped my chest with every breath that filled her lungs. Ready to explode, I wanted to take her hard and fast, but I clamped down on the urge.

Taking my time was fucking torture, but if I was ever going to do one thing right by this woman—it would be this.

TWENTY-SEVEN

GIULIANA

Every complication in life slipped away as Eric's mouth came down on mine again. He teased me, his lips grazing mine whisper soft, our tongues sliding sensually over one another's.

Unsure exactly of what to do with my hands, I moved them from his shoulders, then slid them up to the back of his neck. My nails scraped over his short hair, slightly damp with perspiration.

A growl rumbled up from his throat, and disappointment gripped my heart as he tore his mouth away from mine. It lasted but a second as he kissed my forehead, my cheeks, over the curve of my jaw.

I shifted restlessly beneath him, needing more. He was still seated deep inside me, my flesh throbbing and contracting around his shaft. He felt huge, stretching me to the limits. I knew it was supposed to hurt the first time, but I'd never imagined that.

The memory of the pain when he'd thrust inside me was

still sharp and startlingly clear. Yet my core throbbed with need, the pain replaced with the desire to find a fulfillment I so desperately needed.

"You sure about this?"

I lifted my hips a fraction, testing the pain. It still felt like too much—uncomfortable but not painful. "Yeah."

Pushing himself up so I was caged between his arms, he rocked his hips against mine, pulling out the tiniest bit before sliding back in. I met his thrust and curled my legs around his, urging him deeper. I bit my lip and shifted my hips, trying to find release. Above me, Eric's face was pulled into a concentrated mask, and his muscles rippled beneath my touch as he slowly pumped in and out.

My insides felt like they were on fire, the feeling of the condom unnatural and uncomfortable as it scraped along my flesh. I didn't even care about an orgasm anymore. I winced against the pain, praying he would finish quickly. Suddenly, he stopped moving. Was he done already? My eyes popped open and collided with his hazel ones.

"You're trying too hard."

I turned my head to the side, blinking against the tears that filled my eyes. "I'm sorry."

My voice cracked, and I bit my tongue to keep anything else from escaping. I clamped my eyes closed so I wouldn't have to see the disappointment in his. I knew I wasn't what he wanted or expected. He'd probably been with dozens of experienced women who screamed his name in ecstasy when they fell into bed with him. And here I was, a fraud who'd tricked him into taking my virginity.

One huge hand took my chin and guided it toward him. "Jules. Look at me." I blinked up at him through burning, watery eyes, and he searched my gaze. "What's wrong?"

I shook my head. "Nothing."

I just wanted him to finish. I wanted this to be over already.

His brows drew together. "Am I hurting you?" When I bit my lip and started to shake my head, he pressed up on the underside of my chin with his thumb. "The truth."

I licked my dry lips and whispered the word. "Yes."

Though he tried to hide it, his face contorted into a slight grimace as he slowly pulled away from me. I saw disappointment etched into every line of his face, and it sent a hot bolt of shame lancing through me. "I'm sorry."

"You have nothing to be sorry for." He softly kissed my lips, then pushed off the bed.

Embarrassed, I pulled a corner of the comforter over my body and curled into a little ball. My legs still shook, otherwise I'd have run to lock the door behind him so I could wallow in pity alone. Not that a flimsy lock meant anything. Unfortunately, Eric wasn't gone but for a few seconds. He lifted the comforter and slid in behind me, holding me close.

We lay in silence for several minutes before I gathered the courage to turn toward him. "I'm sorry."

His hand stroked down my spine. "Sweetheart, you don't need to apologize."

"I do. I…" I trailed off, my cheeks flaming. "I wanted to be good for you."

Gentle fingers swept up and down my back, comforting in their light and reassuring touch. "Had I known, I would have gone slower, taken my time."

I bit my lip, glad he couldn't see me. "Is it always like that?"

He hesitated for a moment. "I've heard the first time can be… overwhelming. Once your muscles get used to it, the pain goes away."

"I'm not sure about that," I said dubiously. "It felt like I was on fire."

He leaned slightly away to look at me, and I blushed. "I'm sorry, that was awkward. I shouldn't have—"

"I want you to tell me." He cupped the back of my neck in his palm. "Whatever it is, I want to know."

"It's just… It hurt every time you moved," I admitted, embarrassment burning my cheeks. I couldn't believe I was telling him this.

He looked pensive. "Do you have any allergies?"

I shrugged. "I don't think so. Why?"

"I've heard of some people having reactions to condoms. Maybe that's why you were so uncomfortable."

Despair settled over me. "So, what does that mean? We can't have sex?"

He hesitated so long, I wasn't sure he'd answer. "We could," he said slowly, "but there's still a risk… You know, even if I don't come inside you."

More than anything, I wanted to feel the way I had when he'd first swept me into his arms, riding high on passion.

"What do you want to do?" I whispered, afraid of his answer.

Hazel eyes bore into mine. "I'm clean, and I assume you are…"

He trailed off, leaving the statement open-ended as if waiting for me to decide. Emboldened by his words, I nodded as I slipped a hand between us and brushed my fingers over his shaft. It jumped as soon as I touched it, already starting to harden again, and Eric let out a soft hiss. "Need a yes or no, sweetheart. What's it gonna be?"

I kissed his throat, the short hairs abrading my lips as I nipped at him. "Yes."

Pushing my shoulder, he rolled me to my back and settled between my thighs. "I want you to tell me if it hurts."

Snaking a hand between our bodies, he tested my readiness. I sucked in a breath as his fingers sank deep inside me, the moisture from my core easing their way.

"I love that you're so wet for me." I felt my face flame at

his dirty words, but my embarrassment was forgotten a moment later as his mouth landed on mine, insistent and needy.

He pulled his fingers free and fisted his shaft, then pressed the rounded head to my entrance. I held my breath, waiting for the inevitable pain as he slipped an inch inside. His tongue distracted me as he continued to press inward until he slid all the way home. Hot and hard, skin on skin, I let out a whimper.

Eric lifted his head. "Good?"

I nodded, and he rolled his hips, pulling out and thrusting in again. The slight burning sensation remained, but it was eclipsed by the silky heat of him filling me, better than anything I'd ever felt in my life. Each stroke came a little harder, went a little deeper, and I pressed my heels into the backs of his legs, urging him to go faster.

Perspiration beaded on his brow, and I felt the slickness of his skin as I ran my palms over his shoulders and upper back. I kissed the base of his neck, my tongue darting out to taste the salty manliness of him.

He slowed his pace, dipping his head and fusing our mouths together. As his tongue stroked languidly over mine, his arousal teased my entrance in slow, shallow thrusts. I lifted my hips to take more of him, but he resisted, pushing backward instead.

Unwrapping my legs from where they were wound around his waist like a pretzel, he lifted them over his forearms. The angle pushed him deeper inside me, and we both let out a little sigh of satisfaction. Each pass fanned the fire inside my core to life. I let out a little groan as my muscles contracted around him, holding him tightly.

Eric's heated gaze swept over me and I curled my fingers into the comforter, needing something to hold on to. My legs trembled, nervous anticipation humming through my veins. I felt vulnerable, exposed. Never before had I shown this part of me to anyone—I'd never even been naked in front of another person before.

"Can you feel that, Jules?"

"Yes," I breathed, unable to formulate a more articulate response. It was all at once too much and not enough, heaven and hell mixed into one. A myriad of sensations built up, my emotions ping-ponging back and forth. Heat raced through my body, the fire that had been building in my core suddenly flaring into an inferno.

My muscles contracted, and I let out a silent scream as pleasure like I'd never known crashed over me. I couldn't think, couldn't breathe; I couldn't do anything but hold on as he swept me away to a place higher than the stars.

He plunged in and out, ragged breath leaving his mouth, sweat glistening on his chest. Two more hard thrusts and he pulled out, his hot seed splashing over my lower belly. He collapsed over me, his head burrowed against my neck. His chest rose and fell rapidly, the curly, springy hairs teasing my nipples.

Energy depleted, I was barely able to form a catlike smile. Turning his head, he dropped a kiss on my collarbone. Before I was ready to let him go, he lifted his body from mine.

"Don't move." He punctuated the order with a kiss, then slid off the bed. Thirty seconds later, he was back with a warm cloth. He ran it over my center, cleaning me, wiping up the evidence of our lovemaking.

Completely sated, I snuggled into the covers and allowed my body to relax. I was almost asleep when Eric climbed back into bed. He slipped one arm beneath my head, so I was pillowed on his bicep. The other arm came around my waist and pulled me close.

I let out a little sigh of pleasure. "I want to do that again."

What sounded like a rough chuckle left his lips. "Me, too."

Fingers splayed proprietarily over my stomach, he tucked

my bottom against his hips. He nuzzled my hair aside and kissed the spot just below my ear. "Sleep, beautiful."

I snuggled further into him as exhaustion pulled at me, and I handed myself over to its mercy, happy to be wrapped in Eric's arms, right where I belonged.

TWENTY-EIGHT

ERIC

I felt her relax as she dropped off to sleep, her head resting heavily against my shoulder as the tension drained from her muscles. My body was exhausted, but my mind refused to settle. Why hadn't she said anything?

I stared down at the woman in my arms, curled into me like a contented little kitten—far from the she-cat who'd hissed and spat at me in the kitchen earlier. Now it all made sense.

I couldn't fight this thing between us anymore; Jules was mine, and I wasn't going to let her go until she asked to be set free.

I closed my eyes and managed to doze for a bit until she shifted next to me. Unused to sleeping with someone, my eyes popped open. In the dim moonlight, I saw that Jules had rolled to her back.

The motion had caused the sheet to fall, exposing her torso to my view. Her pretty, pert breasts were revealed in stark relief in the moonlight, the tips pebbled as the cool night air washed over them. Almost immediately, I began to harden, needing to feel her wrapped around me once more.

My palm rested on her stomach, and I skimmed it upward, over her flat tummy to the soft swell of her breasts. I stroked the underside of one with my thumb, and Jules rolled toward me again, her lashes fluttering as she woke from her deep sleep. Burying my nose in her hair, I inhaled deeply. She was the sweetest thing I'd ever seen.

I palmed a firm, round breast, delighting in the way the tiny tip peaked immediately for me. She let out a sexy little gasp as I tweaked and pinched, her hips writhing against mine.

I kissed the slope of each breast before making my way up her neck and dropping a kiss at the corner of her mouth. Grabbing my head, she guided my lips to hers. Our teeth clashed as the kiss grew frantic.

"Eric!"

I shook my head. "I don't want to hurt you."

"Please, I want… I need…"

I knew exactly what she needed—I needed it too. I wanted to feel the connection between us, to feel her silky heat wrapped around me.

Maneuvering so I was settled between her thighs, I stroked my fingertips over her cheeks. "Look at me." Her eyes flickered open, startlingly green even in the dim light. "You sure?"

She nodded and licked her lips but didn't say anything else. I loved her shyness, loved that she trusted me. It scared the shit out of me at the same time, but I couldn't stop the flare of pride that filled my chest.

Slipping one hand between us, I gently prodded her folds. "Tell me if I hurt you."

She nodded, teeth cutting into her lower lip, eyes closing in bliss as I slipped inside her. Hot and wet, she was tight as hell, still swollen from our lovemaking only a few hours before. I took her gently, slowly, drawing out her orgasm until she came on gasping cries, calling out my name, raking her fingernails down my back.

I thrust deep one last time, then fisted my shaft as I moved over her, releasing my seed on her stomach. I couldn't help the slight swell of disappointment each time I had to pull out. I wanted to come inside her, with her hot, tight body wrapped around mine.

Exhausted, wrung out, Jules lay there, hair fanned out over my pillow. I swore I'd never seen anything so beautiful. I grabbed the box of tissues off the nightstand and hastily cleaned her, then slid in beside her. As if she was the positive charge to my negative, she immediately moved into my arms, melding her body to mine. I never felt more whole than I did with her by my side.

"Are you okay?" I whispered the words against her hair, and she nodded.

"Yes."

"Sore?"

She shifted her legs. "A tiny bit."

I kicked myself for not taking things more slowly with her. "Why didn't you tell me you were a virgin?"

Her lashes fluttered, and her teeth sank into her lower lip before she answered. "I wanted you to be my first. I was afraid you wouldn't do it if I told you the truth."

I barely held back a snort. No shit. Her first time should've been special. Damn, I wish I'd known; I would've done a thousand things differently. But I'd never dreamed a woman as beautiful as Jules would be a virgin. I swallowed hard. The thought of another man touching her made me see red. I didn't want another man looking at her, let alone touching her.

Worse, I couldn't help the warm flow of satisfaction that flooded my heart, making my chest feel tight. I was her first—she'd chosen me. It was an honor I didn't deserve but wouldn't take back even if my life depended on it. The possessiveness I felt for her was unnatural. I wanted her all to myself for as long as she would allow, whether it was until next week or a year from now.

I slipped one hand into her hair and pulled her against my chest. For now she was mine—only mine. I kissed the top of her head, cuddling her close. Her head was pillowed on the space between my shoulder and chest, and I hitched her thigh over mine. Every inch of us was sealed together all the way down to her cute as fuck little toes where they skimmed my calf.

This—this was where we belonged. I'd fought it for so goddamned long, and I was tired of it. I didn't know what it was about her, but I needed her by my side. She made me feel whole in a way I hadn't for the past three years. Yes, she had her secrets, but I had mine too.

Maybe one day we'd be brave enough, comfortable enough, to open up to the other. I prayed she stayed long enough for that to happen. If I had any say in it, she wasn't going anywhere—not for a long damn time.

TWENTY-NINE

GIULIANA

I woke draped over Eric, legs tangled together, my cheek pressed to his chest, the soothing beat of his heart pulsing next to my ear. My body was deliciously sore from last night, and it was still strange to think of it having been invaded so fully.

It should have been awkward, but being with Eric was as natural as the sun rising in the eastern sky, spilling its golden glow throughout the room. The softness of his skin stretched over hard planes of muscle, the heat of his flesh seeping into mine… This was my safe space—exactly where I belonged.

I swept one hand over the chiseled muscles of his chest. The springy dark hair tickled my nose as I turned my face into him and breathed deeply, drawing the very essence of him into my lungs. I needed his touch like I needed air; I wasn't sure how I'd ever existed without him.

One hand rested at the small of my back, and his fingers curled ever so gently into my flesh, letting me know that he was awake. I turned my head and placed a kiss on one sculpted pec.

His hand coasted up my spine, then back down to cup one rounded globe of my bottom. "Morning, beautiful."

His voice was thick with sleep, rougher than normal, and it brought a smile to my face. "Coffee?"

"Oh!" My eyes popped open at the reminder, and I bolted upright. "I completely forgot. The kitchen is a mess—"

"C'mere." Eric's strong arm stopped my movement, and I allowed him to pull me back to him. "I need to apologize."

"For what?" I leaned back to see him better. His gorgeous hazel eyes were filled with remorse, and I couldn't help but reach out to him, placing my palm on his cheek. He turned into my touch, closing his eyes briefly before speaking.

"I'm sorry I was an asshole about dinner. You have no idea how it made me feel to see you'd done that for me."

He paused, looking unsure and abashed. "I thought staying away was best for both of us. I resisted you for so long, and that nearly put me over the edge. I'm sorry, baby. You've been nothing short of perfect, and I've been a complete dick."

"Not completely," I whispered.

A tiny smile touched his face. He brushed a strand of hair off my cheek and tucked it behind my ear. "I was, and I'm sorry. Can we have a do-over? I'm off all day, and I want to spend it with you."

"Okay."

He lifted one thick eyebrow. "Just okay?"

I cracked a self-conscious smile. "I'd like that."

"Good." His lips brushed my forehead. "I don't know about you, but I need some caffeine."

He gently shifted me to the side, and I grasped the sheet, yanking it up to cover my chest as he swung his legs over the side of the bed. In the heat of the moment with a blanket of darkness enveloping the room, it hadn't bothered me. Now I felt on display. It was still new despite the fact that he'd explored every inch of me at length last night, and I was embarrassed to show myself to him.

Eric had no such compunction. He stood, showing off every chiseled, well-endowed inch, and I watched shamelessly. His back muscles rippled as he stretched his neck from side to side, and my gaze traveled downward to his ass. Tight enough to bounce a quarter off, toned flesh covering the sinewy muscle. His legs were thick and hard, the bluish tint of his veins standing out in relief. He was absolutely fascinating.

I blushed when he turned toward me, catching me ogling him. "Like what you see?"

I bit my lip and averted my gaze, completely embarrassed at having been caught red-handed.

He leaned forward and pressed his hands to the bed on either side of me. I clutched the fabric of the sheet between us like a shield, and his gaze dropped to it for a moment before meeting my eyes again. "I like what I see, too."

With a swift, hard kiss, he pushed away from the bed and strode to the closet. My heart raced at the sight of him, at the multitude of new emotions welling up inside me.

Eric passed me a shirt with a sinful smile, then took his time stepping into a pair of dark sweats. He gestured with his chin to the shirt in my hand. "I'll be waiting for you."

I watched him exit the bedroom, thinking bemusedly that there was a wealth of meaning behind those words.

THIRTY

ERIC

Jules sat up and stretched, long dark waves falling nearly to her waist. I swore I'd never get tired of looking at her, feeling her skin next to mine.

We'd spent the entire day together, and it constantly amazed me how much I enjoyed my time with her. I wasn't nearly ready to leave her and go back to work tomorrow; I wanted to lock the doors and block out the world so it was just the two of us.

After lunch, we'd fallen back into bed for another round of lovemaking, then dozed off. Now the sun had begun its descent, the last few rays of light illuminating her perfect form.

Arms stretched high over her head, she arched her back sensually, showing off sleek muscle and smooth skin that I couldn't wait another second to touch. Looping my arm around her middle, I pulled her down to me. "Come here, gorgeous."

She allowed herself to be pulled down, twisting to face me as she did so. I stared down into those gorgeous green eyes that swallowed me every time. Not just green—a hundred shades mixed expertly together to create a masterpiece unique only to Jules.

"What?" Her brow furrowed, and I smoothed the tiny wrinkle with the pad of my thumb.

"I could stare into your eyes forever."

Oh, Jesus. Did I really just say that out loud? I mentally cringed, waiting for her reproach. It never came.

"Yeah?" One eyebrow hitched up, along with the corner of her mouth. Her expression, bemusement mingling with disbelief, made me want to vanquish all of her doubts, soothe her fears.

I managed a nod. "They're beautiful. Like nothing I've ever seen."

My gaze swept upward from her eyes, over a sleek, dark eyebrow that was currently ratcheted toward her hairline. She relaxed her expression as I ran my thumb over that very same eyebrow, circling one gorgeous green eye to outline the plump roundness of her high-set cheeks, her olive complexion glowing a soft gold in the afternoon sunlight.

"Everything about you is absolutely..." Was there even a word for how beautiful she was? "Exquisite."

Her eyes widened with surprise and pleasure. "Better watch saying things like that, Sheriff."

I brushed my thumb over her full lower lip, and it quivered under my touch. "I mean everything I say, Jules."

Quit while you're ahead, dumb shit.

"I know." Her words came out on a shaky whisper.

Had I ever felt like this before? I didn't think so. There was some indefinable quality here, and Jules and I just... fit. She was made for my body. She was sweet and strong and independent. I wanted to know the story of her past, of what made her *her*. And I wanted to help write her future.

I ran my hand down the column of her neck, over the curve of her shoulder, along the dip of her waist, and around her hip. She trembled beneath my touch, but her gaze never wavered from mine.

Her legs shifted restlessly, and I slipped one knee between hers, hitching her thigh over my hip. My fingers splayed over her bottom as I sealed us together from hip to chest, wanting to feel every inch of her. "Stay with me, Jules."

Her lips tipped up in a tremulous little grin. "I am staying with you."

Beneath the nonchalant words, I heard the faint strain of nervousness and anticipation. I skimmed my fingers over the sensitive skin of her bottom, and she shivered in my arms. She knew what I was asking—she had to. Still, I had to know. I had to get it off my chest.

I wanted her here with me just like this every day. I wanted to crawl into bed every night and pull her close, then wake next to her and kiss her perfect, sweet lips each morning.

"Not because you have to. Because you want to."

She studied me for a moment, as if gauging my sincerity. Then she threw me completely for a loop. "Sometimes you scare me."

I jerked back, the words dousing me like cold water. "What?"

She shook her head and ran a hand over my chest, her touch light and soothing. "Not like that. But because, like this"—with barely a breath of space between her skin and mine as she snuggled back into my arms—"it would be so easy to fall for you."

I stared down at her, turning her words over in my mind, praying what she'd said was true. Was she serious? Those guileless green eyes only inches from my own told me yes.

Don't do it, don't do it, the voice inside chanted. I ignored the warning. "I wish you would."

"Why?" She breathed the word, making my pulse race.

I'd never felt this way before, not even with my ex-wife.

Jules made me feel like it was my first time, like the past slipped away, leaving only her and me. I wasn't ready to let her go yet—maybe not ever. Ignoring the voice in my head screaming at me not to, I jumped. "Because I'm already falling for you."

"Eric…"

My name on her tongue held a reverence I'd never heard and wasn't sure how to deal with. She didn't trust me—didn't trust my words. I'd have to show her with my body just how much I wanted her.

Rolling to my back, I took her with me, settling her over my hips so her hot core pressed against my hard arousal. Moving both hands to her hips, I lifted her slightly until she was suspended over me. Pressing down on her lower back, I rolled my hips up to her, thrusting as deep as possible.

This connection between us… it was fucking incredible. Like this, we were one entity; I had no idea where I ended and Jules began. Her chest still pressed to mine, I swore I could feel the beat of her heart beating in tandem with mine, both of us perfectly in sync.

I dropped my gaze to where her lips hovered just inches above my mouth. Her tongue darted out, wetting the flesh of her plump lower lip, and I closed the distance between us to steal a searing kiss. Her mouth parted, and I swept inside, my tongue tangling with hers.

I couldn't explain the profound feeling of possessiveness that swept over me. She'd never done this before, had never trusted another man enough. Only me. It made me feel… invincible. I was the only man who'd ever been inside her, and I swore on my life I'd be the last.

In that moment, I didn't care what had happened to either of us in the past. Together, we would overcome it; we'd beat the odds. She made me stronger, better. And I… I was already falling in love with her. It should have sounded absolutely insane—but it didn't.

Crazier things had happened. Falling for a woman I'd known for barely two weeks—who did that? But I couldn't deny the feeling between us. For the first time in years, I let my heart lead me, and it felt fucking amazing.

We'd begun first as strangers, then roommates. And, now, lovers. This was by far the best dynamic of our evolving relationship. I wanted to learn everything about her, prove to her I was good enough—I wanted to give her a reason to stay with me.

Seemingly of their own volition, my hands roamed her body. Over the curve of her ass, down her legs where her thigh muscles contracted with each rolling thrust, back up to her perfectly rounded hips.

I wanted to brand her, burn my touch into her flesh so she'd only ever feel me upon every inch of her body. She was mine. I was going to claim her so fully, she'd never want anyone else.

THIRTY-ONE

I'd never known this feeling existed, this connection between people. He kept his touch firm, almost possessive, as his hands skimmed over my body. I wanted them all over me—his large rough hands, his mouth. Once, I'd been held captive by fear; now his touch set me free.

Then something changed. The hand on my back slipped up my spine, pressing my body to his, sealing us together. The rocking of his hips slowed, turning sensual and passionate. Suddenly, it hit me, and my heart flipped over in my chest. This… this was making love.

Framing his face with my hands, I stared into those intense hazel eyes. The ones that said I was beautiful, special… worthy. Only Eric had ever made me feel that way—and I loved it. I'd never been comfortable in my own skin, but here, with him, I felt like I was exactly the way I was supposed to be.

Giving myself over to the sensation, the tingling in my core built and exploded outward. At the same moment, his cock hardened, and his muscles stiffened as he pulled out, spilling his seed on his stomach, my name a ragged groan on his lips. Exhausted, I sank down on him, our bodies sealed together with a sheen of sweat and desire.

I lay with my head on his chest, sated and content, a comfortable silence over us. His fingertips trailed over my arm, from my shoulder to elbow, then back again. His chest rose on an inhale.

"Do you want kids?"

I felt my eyes widen as I whipped my head up to look at him.

"Not right now." Eric chuckled and brushed his lips across my forehead. "Though we might be tempting fate if we keep going like this."

He pulled back a tiny bit and stared down at me. God, those eyes. They cut through me, so deep and intense, as if he could see straight into my soul and read me like a book. He seemed to know every desire, every need before I even expressed it. He was so much more than I could have ever anticipated.

Him asking me to stay had taken my breath away. For a fraction of a second, I'd seen the vulnerability, the insecurity deep in those hazel depths. He was such a strong man—the strongest I'd ever known. While my family had hidden behind firearms and larger-than-life personalities and lots of big talk, Eric did none of that. He didn't need to. He exuded power and confidence like it flowed through his veins instead of blood.

I bit my lip and contemplated his question. *Do I?*

Though I was surprised he'd broached the subject, the idea of having children didn't terrify me. Especially with a man like him. The thought of having a family—a real family —made my heart race with unbridled joy.

What bothered me was the thought of never seeing my relatives, my hometown, ever again. Chicago was home to me. Could I walk away from my family, from Mama and

Matteo? Could I go the rest of my life without seeing either of them again? I missed Mama, but not like I missed Daddy.

Once again, I wondered what Uncle had done when he found out I had left. Was he still hunting me? In his eyes, I would've lost the thing of greatest value—my virtue. He could still bring me back and marry me off out of spite, if not to Nikolai then to someone equally as awful.

Part of me wanted to go back home just on principle. I hated the thought of leaving all that money behind. Not that I needed it—my life here with Eric was infinitely better. Still, I resented the fact that Massimo had won in that regard. Daddy would be disappointed in me for not fighting for what was rightfully mine.

I couldn't even approach legal counsel or the FBI. Most of the money was dirty, not on any books anywhere, so a lawyer would do me no good. I knew Massimo was on the FBI's watchlist, but I knew nothing of his dealings. He made sure I was always sequestered away, never to see or hear anything.

In retrospect, I should've tried harder to gather enough information to blackmail him. Though guards had been stationed all over the house, maybe I would've been able to find at least something. Now I would never know.

I wondered if Matteo might help. He was the only person close to me, and he disliked Massimo as much as I did. But when it came right down to it, I knew that Matteo was loyal to a fault. He would never betray his father—not even for me.

I debated telling Eric everything, but I couldn't risk it. I knew what my family represented to a man like him; I couldn't bear to see the look in his eyes when he found out what I truly was. The last few days had been the best of my life, and though I felt guilty about not telling him the truth, I wasn't ready to give it up just yet.

I would have to make a decision and make it soon. I couldn't continue to live like this, existing just on the periphery of happiness. Though my fear had begun to recede,

I was always aware of the fact that Uncle still could still come for me. I kept an eye out anytime I was out in public. The only time I truly felt safe was with Eric.

And speaking of Eric... What I was doing wasn't fair to him in the least. What if things between us progressed; what would I do then? What if someday he wanted to marry me? My heart threatened to beat out of my chest, both with excitement and fear. He was bound to learn who I was eventually; I needed to tell him. But not yet.

"Jules? You okay?"

Swallowing hard, I turned to face him. His brow was drawn into an expression of concern, and I felt my lips curve into a smile of their own volition. God, he was so handsome.

Laying a hand on his chest, I nodded. "Sorry, I was just thinking. I think I do want kids eventually. With the right man," I added.

When I thought about a family, about having kids, he was the man I pictured next to me. Solid and dependable, he was everything I'd ever dreamed of. I didn't dare tell him that, though. "What about you?"

"Someday." His mouth curled into a soft smile as he brushed a strand of hair away from my face. "With the right woman."

My heart beat a rapid tattoo, pleasure and hope threatening to burst right out of my chest. I was terrified to read too much into his words. His hand came up to frame my face, tilting my chin up to meet his gaze full-on. "You'd be a good mom, Jules."

Strong fingers delved into my hair. I knew I needed to tell him everything; but this wasn't the time. I would give him one thing, though. I cleared my throat. "Giuliana."

His eyes flared, and his hand paused running through the long strands of my hair to cup the back of my head. "Is that what Jules is short for?"

I licked my lips and nodded.

A gorgeous smile broke over his face. "I love that. It suits you—exotic and beautiful."

The hand on the back of my head pulled me down, pressing my cheek to his chest, right over his heart. I snuggled against him, completely content for the moment. I didn't know how long this would last, but I wanted to soak up every second.

THIRTY-TWO

ERIC

For at least the dozenth time, I flipped through the report that Riley had compiled from the deputies' findings up on the mountain a week ago. Except for the holiday, Joey and Riley had spent every day digging through all the old sales receipts since Herb had resisted any kind of computerized inventory system for years.

So far, they'd managed to find fifty-two purchase receipts. I'd sifted out the ones belonging to residents who'd either passed away or who I assumed would be unable to make the trek through the woods.

Riley had called for backup immediately following the incident, and they'd converged on the scene eight minutes after the shot was fired. Warren and another deputy had followed the trail in an attempt to chase the shooter down, but he was long gone. I assumed it was a he; men were more prone to crimes involving firearms. Still, I couldn't rule out any of the women in town. Plenty had grown up hunting and shooting with the local boys.

The person had less than half an hour to make it from the

scene all the way back to the general store. Considering the snow and semi-rough terrain, that wasn't much time. That meant he would have to be hustling pretty quickly, hence me ruling out the elderly suspects.

That left us just about thirty leads to track down and investigate, which was still a fucking nightmare. Although this was a small town where cordiality abounded, I knew it wouldn't be easy. Some people would resist cooperation sheerly on principle of having their privacy invaded.

I'd run background on each of them, checking for priors, but not much had turned up in that department. Only four residents had prior arrest records. Two had been charged for being drunk and disorderly, another for a DWI. The fourth was Josh Drummond, Cynthia's ex-husband and my former deputy. I dismissed him, since he was still in lockup down in Kalispell. Two of my deputies were out questioning the other three suspects, but I wasn't terribly hopeful.

I flipped the page and my attention zeroed in on the item that had the potential to make or break this case—a shell casing that had been recovered several feet from the tree. My mouth curved in a grim smile of satisfaction as I stared at the photo. It had been tagged and sent out several days ago for the ballistics experts to study.

Each gun left its own identifying mark on a bullet when it left the chamber, and I prayed the striations matched something previously in the system. Moreover, I hoped for something even more substantial—fingerprints.

I would bet my life that the shooter had tried to locate the casing, which explained the disturbed snow all around the shooter's location. Knowing that he had only a few moments before we would converge on the scene, he probably left it in haste when he couldn't find it, then started his trek back across the ridge.

We almost missed it, too. Considering the shooter had been aiming south, the casing would have ejected to his right

—exactly where the fresh layer of snow had been tossed. Instead, it had been found more than three feet in the opposite direction, a tiny indentation in the snow that had gone almost completely unnoticed. The only thing I could imagine was that the shell casing had ejected with so much force that it ricocheted off a tree, sending it several feet to the person's left.

Thank God for metal detectors and diligent deputies. It was the only big lead that we had, and I hoped to hell the person had been careless enough to leave a print, even if just a partial. It would be more than we had at the moment, which was jack shit.

It was a typical quiet morning, and Riley and I were the only two here. Visible through the open doorway of my office, he sat relaxed, feet propped on his desk, a similar report on his lap. "Still no word on the shell casing yet?"

Riley shook his head but didn't bother to tear his gaze away from the papers in front of him. "Not yet, but I kind of expected a delay with the holiday."

I snorted. I had, too, but it would be nice if they would expedite the process a little bit, considering I was the one being shot at.

Correction: Jules was the one being shot at. Suspecting—knowing—that she was the intended victim still had the power to infuriate me, and a haze of red burst across my vision. The shooter had been aiming for the driver of the Cavalier, which was typically Jules. No one would've been able to watch me pick the car up from McBride's then trek nearly a mile across the mountain to get into place. There simply wasn't enough time.

Whether the shooter had missed me intentionally or by sheer luck was anyone's guess. It was possible he'd misjudged the mark—or the shot may have been a warning. The glare of the afternoon sun more than likely would've obscured the shooter's view through the windshield, and he may not have been able to discern the driver until I was close enough. If he noticed that I was inside instead of Jules, it would explain why no second shot had followed the first.

Though I hadn't come right out and told Jules my speculations, I had a feeling she knew. That brought me to my next question: what else did she know? She was carrying a hell of a lot of baggage that she still refused to admit despite our recent intimacy.

And, just like that, my brain switched gears, drawn by Jules's undeniable lure. The woman was absolutely incredible, and there was nothing I wouldn't do to keep her safe. I wanted her by my side for… well, a long damn time. Even though she'd been with me for only a couple of weeks, I couldn't imagine life without her. Going back to my old life, quiet and boring, seemed inconceivable. Jules made me want things I hadn't realized I was missing.

I liked coming home to her each night. I loved falling into bed with her, making love, then waking up to her beautiful face each morning. She'd somehow managed to unlock the deepest, darkest part of my heart that I'd buried away years ago.

Hope for the future filled my heart completely, leaving no room for the pain and distrust of the past. I still hoped that one day she would let me in as I had done for her. We were better together; I wanted to help shoulder the weight of her fear so she could finally move on.

First, though, I needed to figure out who the hell was behind this and put it to rest once and for all. Ironically, Sam Pickett's name had shown on the list of names Riley had compiled, and that was one lead I wanted to track all on my own.

THIRTY-THREE

GIULIANA

The morning of Jack and Mia's wedding dawned clear and bright. Though I knew it was freezing outside, the first bright rays of light spilled in through the window, bathing the room in its soft golden glow, giving it a warming effect.

The heat of Eric's huge body at my back warmed me from the inside, and I snuggled closer. His heavy arm draped over my midsection lent me a feeling of safety, security.

Completely attuned to me, Eric's arm tightened around my waist, pulling me infinitesimally closer. His lips found the back of my neck and nuzzled the soft skin, and one thumb brushed the underside of my breast just as I felt his morning erection pressing against my bottom.

"Mmm…" The faint vibration stirred the hairs on the back of my neck and reverberated through my body. "Morning, beautiful."

I turned my head to steal a sweet kiss. "Morning."

He brushed a strand of my hair back and tucked it behind my ear. "Sorry I woke you up last night when I came in."

He'd been called out late last night and had returned in the wee hours of the morning. I'd felt the slight change in air pressure as soon as he'd cracked open the bedroom door. He slid silently in next to me, his cold skin pressing against mine, heated by sleep. One huge hand had slipped up the outside of my thigh then around to my most intimate parts. He'd made love to me, slow and sweet, and we'd fallen asleep amidst the tangle of sheets more than an hour later.

I turned on my side to face him, and a smile broke over my face. "Feel free to wake me up that way any time."

"Good to know." He closed his eyes and rolled to his back, taking me with him so I was sprawled over his chest. I dropped my head into the crook of his neck, and his chest rose and fell on a contented sigh as his arms curled around me, holding me tight. "You feel so good."

His thick erection prodded the folds between my legs, and I lifted my head to peer down at him curiously. "Again?"

Eyes still closed, a smile curved his mouth. "With you, babe, I'm always ready."

His hands smoothed down my back and over my ass as I wiggled my hips against his. "Is it normal to have this much sex?"

He barked out a laugh, and those sexy hazel eyes blinked open to meet mine. "God, no, woman. You're going to be the death of me." He nipped my lower lip when I pouted, then soothed it with a soft kiss. "But at least I'll die happy."

I shot a quick look at the clock on the nightstand. "We might have to postpone it for a few hours."

I was supposed to be at Briarleigh in an hour and a half, and I still needed to shower and get ready.

"Probably a good idea," he agreed. "Pretty sure the tank's empty. I don't think I could get off right now if I wanted to."

I bit my lip to contain a smile. "You seem to recover pretty quickly."

"Only because you turn me on so damn much."

I dropped a kiss on his lips. "Why don't you go back to sleep for a bit, since you only got a few hours last night?"

A wicked grin lifted his mouth. "I'd rather have you in here with me."

I kissed him once more. "You'll need your energy for later."

With a soft sigh of regret, he let me go. "You're right."

I paused in the act of rolling from the bed. "I'm sorry, I don't think I heard you. What was that again?"

He blinked up at me for a second before my teasing tone registered. I let out a little squeal and squirmed away as he swatted my ass. "Just you wait."

I tossed him a smile as I slipped on his uniform shirt then made my way into the bathroom. I couldn't tamp down my happiness. Being with Eric was… easy. Fun. Freeing. Once he'd opened up, he was nothing like the man I'd met just weeks ago on the side of the road.

An hour later, I was washed and made up, and I was just slipping the navy dress over my head when Eric came into the bedroom. The scent of body wash emanated from his still-damp skin, and droplets of moisture clung to the hair on his chest and at the vee of his abs. The sight made my mouth water; I wanted to run my tongue over every inch and lick them up one by one.

He faltered midstride and stared at me, one hand moving to the knotted towel draped low on his hips. "What's wrong?"

"Nothing's wrong. Just…" I shook my head, struggling to come up with the right words as I moved toward him. "You."

One eyebrow lifted toward his hairline. "I'm wrong?"

"Definitely not." I slid my hands over his pecs, and he grasped my hips, pulling me close. "You're everything right."

One palm lifted to cup my face, and hazel eyes stared into

mine for several long, heart-stopping moments. Then his gaze dropped to my mouth. The feel of his lips against mine was so much more than a kiss; it was a claiming of my body, the stealing of my soul. Whether he intended it or not, Eric owned every inch of me.

He broke the kiss and rested his forehead against mine. We were so close that our chests brushed with each inhale, and I took a tiny step closer so my body was flush with his. I'd never known a connection like this was possible. There was no place I'd rather be.

I turned my head and pressed my cheek to the space over his heart. "The wedding is going to start soon."

"I know."

"We should get going."

"Okay."

Still he didn't release me, nor did I move from his embrace. A tiny smile tugged at the corners of my mouth. I pulled back and tipped my chin up to look at him. "Are you coming?"

A sexy grin tilted his lips. "Not yet."

A laugh broke from my throat, and I slapped his chest. "Is that all you can think about?"

"Always." One hand slipped up to the back of my neck, and he lowered his mouth to mine. I broke away from the kiss several long moments later, both of us breathing heavily.

"Okay. For real this time," I insisted, pulling away from him with a little laugh. "We've got to go."

We managed to finish dressing and get to the car without any more distractions, and a giddy smile lit my face as we wound our way up the mountain to the resort. Eric glanced at me from the driver seat, and I met his gaze, my heart full. His arm rested on the console between us, and he flipped his hand over, palm up. I slid my hand into his, intertwining our fingers, and he gave my hand a little squeeze.

I'd questioned it several times over the past few days,

what this feeling was between us. Now I knew for sure. It didn't matter that we'd only known each other for a little over two weeks; the things he made me feel—the desire, the attraction, the need…

I loved him.

THIRTY-FOUR

ERIC

I extended one hand to Jack. "Congratulations."

"Thank you. I owe you one."

He owed me nothing; I was just glad that both of them were okay and everything had worked out the way it was supposed to. We stood silently for a moment, each of us reflecting on the past few weeks and the changes they'd wrought. I had a woman I cared about—deeply. I glanced toward her, watching her move around behind the buffet table like she'd done it a thousand times.

"Jules seems to be fitting in okay." I hadn't checked in with him for a while, but she seemed to be in her element here. She was more open, more… free.

"She's a hard worker. Mostly keeps to herself."

That didn't surprise me in the least. She was still skittish with most people. I nodded. "She's a good girl."

Mia glided toward us, a huge smile on her face. She greeted me with a friendly hug, and I returned the embrace, if a bit awkwardly, and smiled down at her. I jerked my head toward Jack. "You're going to have your hands full with this one."

"Oh, I know it." She grinned up at him, and he wrapped one arm around her waist, pulling her close.

I glanced between the two of them before my attention was drawn once more across the room to Jules. A man approached the table where Jules stood, and I could see them talking. A polite smile crossed Jules's face before she turned her attention to the next person. But the guy didn't leave.

Instead, he stepped off to the side, closer to Jules. I saw her shift uncomfortably, and my blood began to boil in my veins. I murmured a "congratulations" to Jack and Mia and stomped across the room, intent on reaching her.

I studied the man as I approached. He didn't look familiar, so I figured he was part of Jack's crew. The man glanced at me, then promptly returned his attention to Jules. It felt like a slight, and I had to check myself before I lost my temper. Instead of my typical uniform, I'd dressed in slacks and a button-up shirt.

I reached them just in time to hear the tail end of the conversation. The man leaned in just a little too close to Jules, an expression on his face that I didn't like. "I'm in town for the next few days. Can I take you to dinner?"

Jules looked up at me as I slipped around the table and moved next to her. It was on the tip of my tongue to tell the guy to piss off, that Jules was mine, but I bit my tongue. She was an intensely private person, and I doubted she would like me claiming her in front of everyone.

Jules stumbled over her words as she turned her attention back to the man in front of her. "I... I'm flattered, but I'm kind of seeing someone."

He straightened, his face falling. "I understand."

"I'm sorry," she apologized as the man moved away.

I rolled my eyes. She was really too innocent for her own good sometimes.

"How is everything going?" I deliberately brushed the back of my hand against hers, and she lifted her face to mine, a shy smile playing over her lips.

"Everything's going really well."

I nodded. "Looks nice."

I didn't remember much of my own wedding; it'd been more than ten years ago, and I'd all but blocked it from memory. What Jules and Mia had created was simple but classy. I liked it. "You guys did a good job."

"Thanks." Jules practically glowed with pride.

Over the next hour and a half, I chatted with people and watched the newlyweds interact. I was kind of surprised that Jack and Mia weren't taking a honeymoon yet, even an abbreviated one, until after the lodge opened. The afternoon wore on, and Mia finally convinced Jules to go home.

"Rosie will take care of the food, and we can clean the rest up tomorrow," Mia assured Jules.

"If you're sure."

"I am." Mia gave her a hug. "Thanks for all your help."

I did the same, then shook hands once more with Jack. "Congratulations."

I helped Jules into her coat and, with a firm hand on the small of her back, guided her outside. After hours of watching her flit around the room clad in only that sexy dress, I was ready to strip it off of her. I held the door for her as she slid into the passenger seat, then I made my way around the car.

Dusk had just begun to settle over the land, turning the sky a deep violet. I started the car and put it in drive, then I reached over the console and laid a hand on Jules's thigh. She glanced across her shoulder at me and spread her legs ever so slightly in invitation.

Lust shot through me, and I dipped my fingers lower to stroke her hot center through the satiny material of her pantyhose. A heavy sexual tension filled the air, and I couldn't fucking wait to get her home. I was already hard for her, unsure of whether we would make it into the house before I buried myself deep inside her. My dirty thoughts were cut short as the radio in the cruiser crackled to life.

"Son of a bitch," I muttered, mostly to myself. I could let the deputies handle it, but I hated to shirk my responsibility. Besides, many of them were probably still at Jack and Mia's wedding, and I didn't want to ruin their fun for something as ridiculous as the Johanssons raising hell again.

I shot Jules an apologetic glance as I pulled to a stop in the driveway. "I'm sorry, baby, I promise I won't be long."

She squeezed my hand and leaned across to give me a heartfelt kiss. She pulled back and held my stare for a moment. "I'll be waiting for you when you get done."

I couldn't help the grin that cracked my face. Though I wasn't sure what all her promise entailed, it sounded damn good. Sliding my fingers into her hair, I cupped the back of her head and pulled her closer for another kiss. I didn't think I would ever get enough of her.

Jules slipped from the car, and I watched the gentle sway of her hips as she crossed the garage and paused just inside the doorway to the house. She turned and blew me a kiss, which I returned with a little wave. My chest tightened as I reversed out of the driveway and headed back toward town.

I wasn't sure what it was about her, but I wanted more of it. Nothing about us made sense. With at least a dozen years separating us, I knew she was from a completely different world. I would never be able to give her the things she was accustomed to, yet she never complained.

She was such an enigma, somehow both incredibly worldly and terribly naïve. Strong, smart, and independent, she needed a partner who would value her. I wanted to be that man. The more time I spent with her, the more reluctant I was to let her go. I'd felt from the beginning that she was special; now I knew I would fight heaven and hell to keep her safe and win her love.

Thoughts of her filled my brain as I approached the Johansson's residence, and I started in surprise when I saw another cruiser already in the driveway. One of my deputies, O'Neill, lifted his hand in greeting as the front door of the trailer closed and he headed down the stairs.

I slowed to a stop but didn't cut the engine as I rolled down the window. "What's going on?"

O'Neill lifted one shoulder. "False alarm."

My brows lifted toward my hairline. "Fight's over already?"

O'Neill shook his head. "No fight at all, it sounds like."

That sounded… off. "Everything seem okay?"

"As good as they'll ever be."

I tipped my chin at him. "All right then. See you tomorrow."

I rolled up my window and put the car in reverse, then backed out of the drive. My mind spun as I contemplated what had just happened. Had someone called in a fake tip? I knew the Johanssons were a nuisance, but what reason would someone have to call us to their location if nothing was going on?

The call had come in just after Jules and I left the wedding, I verified as I glanced at the clock. Knowing that most of the force was still at Briarleigh, had someone used this as a distraction to lure me away from Pine Ridge? The recent trouble with Jules hovered at the forefront of my mind, and worry shot through me.

My phone rang, jarring me from my dark thoughts. Surprise snapped my eyebrows together when I saw it was the sheriff down in Kalispell. "Rooney. What can I do for you?"

"Sorry I didn't let you know sooner; I just found out about it myself."

"What's that?" Dread congealed in my gut, and somehow I knew before the words even left his mouth.

"Josh Drummond was released last week."

Fuck.

"Thanks, Sheriff." I hung up without waiting for a response and pressed down on the accelerator. I was two miles from home when the emergency tone on the SUV's radio went off, and I could hear the faint trace of panic in Lucy's voice as she spoke.

"All listening units report to 7438 Woodlawn."

What the fuck? I was struck speechless at the sound of my own address. I palmed the button to tell her she'd made a mistake when a scream cut over the channel, turning my blood to ice.

THIRTY-FIVE

GIULIANA

I paused at the entrance to the house, one hand on the doorknob. Heart swelling in my chest, I blew Eric a kiss as he backed out onto the main road and drove away. The bright red glow of the taillights bled into the distance, and I touched the button to lower the garage door as I headed into the house.

As soon as I stepped inside, I slipped off my heels, then stooped down to pick them up. Hooking my fingers inside the toes of the stilettos, I let them dangle from my hand as I meandered further into the house.

Without Eric here, I felt no rush to get ready for bed. Instead, I made my way into the kitchen and pulled a glass down from the cupboard. I filled it with water from the tap and sipped at it as I stared out the window, lost in thought. I could see the tire tracks from Eric's truck in the light dusting of snow, and I wondered how quickly he'd come back to me.

Setting the empty glass aside, I pushed away from the sink and floated down the hallway toward the bedroom, marveling at how much things had changed in just a few weeks. I paused to look at the pictures decorating the walls and the top of the dresser. Though I'd seen them before, I took several moments now to really study them.

I remembered the first time I'd seen this photo of Eric with the members of his SWAT team. It'd been barely a month ago, and I'd been fresh on the run, still terrified of my own shadow. Eric had seemed so hard, so cold. Never smiling, none of these photos truly represented the man I'd come to know. Eric was protective, yet he was also sensual and caring, always focused on my needs over his own.

A soft creak of floorboards met my ears, immediately followed by the quiet click of a door. I turned toward the doorway. "Eric? Is that you?"

I took a step closer and paused at the threshold where the bedroom met the hallway. A figure stood backlit by the kitchen light, but I knew immediately that it wasn't Eric.

"I thought you were smarter than that."

The strange voice made my blood congeal in my veins. Dropping my shoes, I grabbed for the bedroom door just as the man rushed forward, a wicked knife gleaming in the light. The door slammed with a bang and I threw my weight against it, my fingers fumbling with the lock. It clicked into place just as the door jumped in its frame, shaking under the force of the man's blow.

"You bitch!"

I backed away, legs trembling as I glanced frantically around the room, searching for a weapon. The door shuddered once more as a booted foot collided with the wood.

"I'm going to kill you!" he screamed from the other side.

My eyes landed on the gun safe, tucked away in the closet, and my heart skipped a beat when I saw the radio sitting in its cradle on top. The door rattled again as the man on the other side tried to break it down, and I lunged for Eric's radio.

I clumsily hit several buttons, trying to find any

connection to call for help. A loud splintering met my ears, and I screamed as the wood around the doorknob cracked under the strain when he kicked at the door again.

Dropping the radio, I darted toward the nightstand and grabbed the first thing I could reach. Snatching up the lamp, I ripped the cord from the wall and held it poised, ready to throw. The door flew open, and I jumped as it slammed against the wall. The man stood outlined in the rectangle, eyes wild, chest heaving.

I didn't hesitate. The lamp was awkward and unwieldy, but I put as much force behind my throw as possible. The man ducked as it struck the doorjamb and shattered, sending slivers of porcelain through the air.

"You fucking cunt!" he screeched, swiping at a trickle of blood on his cheek.

He sprinted forward, and I scrambled over the bed to put as much distance between us as possible. The knife glinted as it slashed downward, barely missing me and slicing through the comforter instead. Praying that Eric would forgive me, I snatched up one of the photos on the dresser and flung it across the room. It clipped the man on the shoulder, and I used the distraction to dart toward the doorway.

I screamed as his hand fisted in my hair, and the sharp bite of pain brought me to my knees. Completely defenseless, I twisted and writhed under him, trying to roll to my back. I cried out in pain as the blade sliced across my forearm. I flailed my arms, and tears blurred my vision as I struggled against him. I tried to wedge my knees between us to push him away, but he was too big—too strong.

The man situated himself over my hips and pressed the heel of his hand under my chin, the blade levered against the soft flesh of my throat. I clawed at the hand constricting my airway, and I fought to draw in breath. Blood trickled down my arm, but I paid no attention as I pushed against his hold on my neck.

My head whipped to the side as his hand connected with my cheek. "Look at me!"

I forced myself to meet his gaze as his fingers dug into my cheeks and turned my face to his. The man studied me. "Do you know who I am?"

Stricken with fear, unable to speak, I tried to shake my head.

"I know who you are." I jerked my head away as he trailed a finger over my jaw. He stared down at me, a cold smirk twisting his lips. "You really should wait until the door closes before you go inside."

My eyes widened. I wondered how he'd gotten inside. "What… what do you want?"

He growled low in his throat. "He took everything from me."

I tried to shake my head again. "I don't—"

"Everything! I lost my wife, my house, my job." I flinched as spittle flew from his mouth and spattered my face. "All because of him!"

"W-who?" I managed to choke out.

"Donahue!" His fingers tightened on my face and he slammed my head back against the ground. "He's the reason Cynthia left me. It's all his fault!"

My eyes widened. *Oh, God.* I remembered the story Rosie had told us that day at the diner; Eric had helped Cynthia press charges against her abusive ex-husband—the man in front of me.

"Please, I—"

"He took everything from me," he murmured. "Now I'm going to show him how it feels."

My heart skipped a beat as I stared into his eyes, feverish with hate. I refused to go down without a fight. Shoving against his hold, I twisted my body and kicked my legs as hard as I could in an attempt to throw him off. I screamed, venting my rage, and adrenaline kicked in.

I punched upward and vindication shot through me as my fist connected with his cheek. The cut reopened, and a trickle of blood oozed down his face. The man let out a grunt of pain and slashed downward with the knife. I threw my head to the side just in time, and the blade slammed into the carpeted floor with a muted thunk.

I flailed one arm wildly, fingers groping. My hand connected with a solid object and my stiletto appeared in my peripheral vision. Hooking my fingers in the toe of the shoe, I swung it upward. The man jerked back just as the sharp heel connected with his face, and it sunk into his eye socket with a sickening squish. He screamed, his face morphing into an expression of pain and anger as one hand flew to his face.

Several emotions swelled up inside me, each battling for prominence. Satisfaction. Horror. Surprise. My stomach roiled and disgust won out as fluid seeped from the wound. Digging my heels into the ground, I shoved my body backward in an effort to scramble away from him.

Loud curses met my ears as a claw-like hand fisted in the fabric of my dress, halting my movement. The man lifted the knife high and I raised my arms to shield myself from the blow. The loud boom of gunfire filled the air, and the man jerked back, his good eye registering surprise as a red spot bloomed high on his chest. His hand loosened and I rolled away, clambering to my hands and knees.

A strong arm came around my waist, and I screamed, fighting against the iron grip.

"Jules! It's me, baby. I've got you, I'm right here."

The familiar roughness of Eric's voice finally permeated my fog of fear. A second set of footsteps approached, and another man wearing a deputy's uniform appeared in my peripheral vision. Tearing myself from Eric's grasp, I sprinted for the bathroom and made it to the toilet just as my stomach convulsed.

I was dimly aware of him speaking with the other man,

then he dropped to his knees beside me. He rubbed my back with a gentle hand all the while murmuring soothingly. When I was done, he scooped me into his arms and carried me from the bathroom.

Peeking over his shoulder, I saw that they'd closed the bedroom door. Thank God for that. My stomach rolled once more at the memory of that grisly scene, and a shudder shook my body. Eric's arms tightened around me as I burrowed my head into the crook of his neck. Using one hand, he grabbed several dish towels from the drawer next to the sink, then he sank into a chair.

"Let me see." His voice was thick and gruff.

Silently, I held my arms out for his inspection. The cuts didn't appear to be especially deep, but now that my adrenaline had worn off, I was aware of the pain. I flinched as Eric wrapped a towel around the worst one to stem the flow of blood trickling from the wound. He repeated the process with the others, then tucked my head to his chest and pressed his lips to the top of my head.

He didn't say anything else. Strong arms wrapped tightly around me, he cuddled me close until the sound of sirens approached. The strobe of red and blue lights filled the window as the ambulance pulled into the driveway and seconds later, two paramedics entered the house, their faces grim.

The tallest of the two men looked at Eric. "Sir?"

I felt Eric tip his head toward the hallway. "O'Neill is in the bedroom with Josh. Thanks, Wally."

Wally nodded and strode that direction. The door flew open once more, and two more deputies strode in. I recognized Riley from the day he'd picked me up at Briarleigh. The tension drained from his shoulders, and relief relaxed his expression as his gaze landed on Eric and me.

"Bedroom."

Riley and the second deputy started down the hallway at

Eric's terse directive, and I snuggled closer to him. The remaining paramedic offered me a small smile, and Eric gently nudged me where I sat on his lap. "Come on, sweetheart. We need to get you to the hospital for evaluation."

"No." Turning to face him, I clutched at his shirt. "I don't want to go."

"I need to make sure you're okay."

Josh may have been responsible this time, but I still had no idea where my uncle was—if he was still looking for me. My name being on record somewhere was infinitely worse than the few defensive wounds on my hands and arms.

"I'm fine, I promise." I gestured to the medic standing by the door. "He can do just as good a job. Please don't make me go."

Eric gingerly touched the towel covering one of the shallow lacerations. "Sweetheart—"

"Please," I begged, an almost irrational fear taking over. After what had happened tonight, I couldn't bear to be away from him. "Don't let them take me away."

He hugged me fiercely, his voice pitched low for my ears only. "No one will ever take you away from me. I'll never let that happen." He pulled back just enough to meet my gaze. "Never. You get me?"

I stared into his hazel eyes for a moment, tears clogging my throat. Finally, I nodded.

He studied me for another long moment then pressed a kiss to my forehead. "Everything's gonna be fine."

Eric nodded to the remaining medic. "Emmett, can you check her over, get her cleaned up?"

"Sure thing, Sheriff." The medic ventured a bit closer and set a bag on the table.

Eric shifted me off of his lap and settled me on the chair, still warm from his body. He framed my face with his hands. "I'll be back in a bit."

With one last gentle kiss he strode away. I watched him go, my love for him filling my heart and pushing down the remnants of fear.

"How are you feeling?"

I turned my gaze to the medic in front of me and sent him a look rife with incredulity.

"Right," he said with a tiny quirk of his lips. "Stupid question."

I remained silent as Emmett worked. With large but gentle hands, he cleaned and dressed the wounds on my arms. "Don't need stitches," he remarked as he applied antibiotic ointment to the worst one and wrapped gauze snugly around my forearm. "That's a good thing. Try not to get this wet for the next twenty-four hours. After that, just need to change them a couple times a day until they heal."

I nodded as he lifted a small penlight to my eyes. "Look right here."

I jumped in my seat as a brief knock came from the front door. A moment later it swung open, revealing Jack and Mia. She entered the house first, and my mouth gaped open in shock at the sight of her as she rushed toward me, dressed now in sweats, her hair still twisted up in an updo from the wedding. "What are you doing here?"

Mia flapped her hands in the air as if to dispel my question and answered it with one of her own. "Are you okay?"

"I'm fine." I turned a challenging look on Emmett, daring him to say differently.

Emmett patted my shoulder. "You're all good. No concussion, nothing major. Don't hesitate to yell if you need me."

I tried to smile but knew I hadn't quite managed. "Thanks."

Jack moved over to the living room to give us some space. Mia stood silently beside me as Emmett packed up his bag, then joined Eric and Wally in the bedroom where Josh was. *His body*, I mentally corrected myself with a shudder.

Mia laid a soft hand on my shoulder. "Are you hanging in there?"

I swallowed hard. "Just… scared more than anything, I guess."

"Understandable. What happened?"

"Cynthia's ex-husband showed up."

Mia's pretty blue eyes widened as she slid into the chair next to me. "The one who…?"

Her words trailed off, and I nodded. "He blamed Eric for taking Cynthia away. Said he was going to show Eric how it felt to lose everything."

We were silent for several long moments before Mia finally voiced the question I'd been dreading. "What are you going to do? You can't stay here."

I shrugged helplessly. Not only was the house now a crime scene, but I didn't think I could bring myself to go back into that bedroom ever again.

She pursed her lips in thought. "My dad's cabin is just a few miles from ours."

Mia hesitated, and I sensed there was more to the story. "But…?"

She eyed me shrewdly. "There's something I have to tell you."

"Did someone die there?" I quipped, trying to be funny.

My humor fell flat when her gaze didn't waver. "Not exactly."

Several minutes later, I sat back in my chair, stunned by her story. "Anyway," she continued, "I moved into Jack's place, so Dad's cabin is available if you don't mind staying there."

"Are you sure you're okay with it?" I asked. "I mean, it belongs to you."

Mia waved away my concern. "I'd be happy if you would stay there. Plus, we'll be close by in case you need anything."

I was truly touched by her offer. "You have no idea how much I appreciate this."

She smiled. "Just repaying a favor. Eric helped us; now it's our turn to help you guys."

Tears stung my eyes as I pulled Mia into a hug. Surrounded by friends like Jack and Mia, with a man who cared for me as much as Eric—I felt safe in a place that finally seemed like home.

THIRTY-SIX

ERIC

I threw another quick look at Jules—probably the tenth during the past minute. It was as if I needed constant affirmation that she was here; she was safe. Barely ten minutes ago, the medics had gone home, and I'd helped the funeral director, Dick Chancellor, load the body into the back of the hearse.

Riley was gathering Jules's clothes and toiletries at her direction. I hadn't decided where to go just yet; there were no hotels in Pine Ridge, and I hated to drive an hour down to Kalispell.

"How about Dad's cabin?" Mia asked, throwing a look at Jack. "It's clean now, and no one uses it."

I flicked a glance at Jack, remembering what had happened the last time we were at her dad's place. I knew he was thinking the same thing, because he looped an arm around her shoulders and pulled her closer.

Mia leaned into Jack, her voice soft as she continued. "I told her the story."

I nodded, unsure of what to say. I hated charity, despised

accepting handouts from people. But this wasn't for me—this was for Jules. Somehow I managed to swallow my pride and stick out my hand. "Thank you."

Mia grinned, the smile lighting her whole face. "You know this means we'll be neighbors."

I chuckled. Only here in the country could you call people four miles away your neighbors. "I'm not sure how I feel about that."

Jack tipped his head at Mia. "She seems to think Jules will make a good babysitter."

I blinked at him as his words sank in. "Wow, man. Congrats," I murmured, holding out a hand. "That's awesome."

Jack shook my hand, and I pulled Mia into an awkward one-armed hug.

Mia tipped her chin up to me. "If you want, we can go get things ready for you."

"I would appreciate that. We should only be a few more minutes, then we'll be up."

"Sounds good."

They left, and I meandered over to Jules where she sat at the kitchen table. Dropping into the chair next to her, I studied her. "You doing okay?"

Her pretty green eyes met mine, a sad wariness evident in their depths. "Fine."

There was a quiet reservation to her demeanor, as if she had begun to shut down and erect the protective walls around her heart once more. Would this send her running for good? I hadn't had much of a chance to speak with her since I'd walked in on the scene straight from hell, though I wouldn't have known what to say regardless.

"Jack and Mia have offered to let us stay at her dad's place."

"I know."

I hesitated for a moment. "I don't want you to feel like

you have to go if you don't want to. If you'd rather be in a hotel or by yourself…" I trailed off, not wanting to finish the thought, and she stared at me.

"What about you? Where will you be?"

"Wherever you are." The response rolled automatically off my tongue. "As long as you want me."

Her eyes glistened with unshed tears. "I will *always* want you."

Cupping the back of her head, I pulled her to me for a hard kiss. Part of me worried that, after everything that had happened this evening, I was going too fast. My mouth hesitated on hers for a second, waiting for her to pull away. Instead, her arms wound around my neck as if she couldn't get enough.

A discreet clearing of a throat from behind had me pulling away. Jules and I shared a little smile before I turned to Riley. "Got everything?"

"Yes, sir."

"Appreciate it."

Jules stood. "Thank you for everything."

"My pleasure, ma'am. Glad you're okay." Riley touched the brim of his hat and turned his attention to me. "Boss."

I accepted the bag he held out and nodded. "Thanks again."

With that, Riley headed out, and I locked up behind him then bustled Jules out to the car. I'd come back for anything we'd forgotten; the only thing I needed right now was Jules in my arms.

She stared out the window as we drove up the mountain past Briarleigh. "They live all the way up here?"

"Yep. Jack and Mia's place is right off that road there." I pointed off to the left. "We're going another mile or so north."

Jules made a soft sound of appreciation as we pulled up in front of the late Mr. Hamilton's cabin minutes later. "It's beautiful."

I parked next to Jack's Tahoe and grabbed the bags from the back of the truck before following Jules up the wide porch. Lights blazed brightly as we stepped inside, and Mia met us by the front door.

"New sheets are on the bed. Jack's getting a fire started right now."

As she spoke, Jack unfolded from his position next to the fireplace. "Good to go."

"Thank you so much." Jules hugged her, then Jack and Mia slipped out the front door, leaving us alone. Seemingly lost in thought, Jules wandered toward the fire. I locked the front door and turned down the lights before approaching her.

I settled my hands on her hips and she leaned into me as I wrapped my arms around her waist. For several seconds, I stared into the fire before speaking. "I didn't know what to think when I got that call."

Her head twisted around to look up at me. "You heard?"

"You must've hit the emergency button on my radio by accident." And thank God she had. Our radios were equipped with GPS, and the emergency button relayed a message to dispatch with the fallen officer's location—or, in this case, Jules's location. Another minute may have been too late.

She turned back toward the fire and nodded. "I tried to call for help, but I couldn't figure it out."

I pressed a kiss to the top of her head. "You did fine."

She snuggled further into my embrace, and my dick, already at attention, nestled between the rounded curves of her ass. "I really loved this dress. Now I never want to see it again."

Unable to keep my eyes off her, I glanced down. The dress hugged her curves, and the deep vee gave me a tantalizing peek at her cleavage. "Want me to get rid of it for you?"

"Please."

Dipping my head low, I nipped her earlobe, causing her to suck in a breath. As she tipped her head for better access, I trailed kisses down the column of her neck. My hand slipped over the dip in her waist, then moved around to the front to where the fabric of the dress parted. I ran one fingertip along the edge of the fabric, then delved inside to cup her breast.

From my vantage point behind her, I could see the lace of her bra, and I peeled the fabric down. My thumb flicked over her nipple, bringing it to an erect point. Her head dropped back against my shoulder, and her little shudder of pleasure reverberated through me.

My fingers found the tie on the side of her dress, and I tugged gently on the string, the motion erotic as she slowly spun to face me. The fabric of the dress loosened, and I pushed it over her shoulders, gliding my fingertips along her collarbone and curve of her neck, then down her arms until it fell to the floor in a whisper of fabric.

I studied her for a minute. "You sure you want it gone?"

Tipping her chin upward, she stared at me. "I don't want any reminders of tonight."

With a concise nod, I scooped the fabric off the floor and, with one smooth motion, tossed it in the fireplace. Jules and I watched as the flames licked over the material, consuming it until the dress was no more than a pile of ash.

"Thank you," she whispered.

"I need to feel you," I whispered back, my voice rough. I needed to touch every inch of her, reassure myself that she was whole and hale. Mortality pressed in on me, knowing I'd come so close to losing her. "Tell me you want this too."

She turned in my arms. "I want you, Eric. Only you."

I skimmed my hands up the expanse of her back to flick open the clasp of her bra. It slid down her arms and landed silently at our feet. She stood before me wearing nothing more than a blush and a tiny scrap of panties—the same pink panties I'd been fantasizing about since I saw them that day in the basement.

I dropped to my knees, kissing my way between the valley of her breasts and down her stomach. "Did you wear these for me?"

The pink of her cheeks seemed to intensify, but she offered a nonchalant little shrug. "I thought you liked them."

"Very much." I slipped my index finger beneath the material, and her hands sank into my hair as I placed an open-mouthed kiss to her hip bone. "I've been dreaming of seeing you in these since the first time I saw them."

"Do you like me better in them or out of them?"

My eyes widened in surprise as I met her gaze. "Out. Definitely out."

THIRTY-SEVEN

GIULIANA

Hooking his fingers inside the waistband, he drew the panties down my legs, a lascivious grin curving his mouth.

"Come here, baby."

Folding me in his arms, Eric drew me down beside him on the rug. Behind me, the fire crackled and popped, throwing its dancing light over the room. It illuminated Eric's face, and I traced the hard planes with my fingertips. They trailed lower to the silvery scar low on his throat, and I gently caressed it, thankful that he was here with me. One of these days I would be brave enough to ask what had happened. But not today.

He was so beautiful it made my heart hurt. I didn't tell Eric that his face was one of the last things I'd seen when Josh had wielded that knife over me. I was grateful for this moment and that fate had given us a second chance.

I swallowed hard. "Thank you for saving me. I…"

"You saved yourself." Eric studied me for a long moment and tucked one hand in my hair. "You're so brave, baby. So incredible."

His lips crashed down on mine, and I allowed myself to be lost in the kiss, swept away from all the bad memories. The fabric of his shirt scraped against my nipples, sending a ripple of pleasure through me and reminding me that he was still fully dressed.

Wedging one hand between our bodies, I fumbled with the buttons on his dress shirt. Distracted by his tongue sweeping over mine, I couldn't free them from their tiny holes, and I let out a little growl of frustration.

"Patience, pretty girl." He chuckled. "I got you."

He rose up above me and quickly stripped out of his shirt, then pushed his pants and boxers down his legs. I watched in breathless anticipation as he pressed the swollen head of his cock to my entrance and pushed. I let out a soft sigh of satisfaction as he filled me; with our bodies fused, hearts beating as one, I finally felt complete.

Twining my arms around his neck, I clutched desperately at him, never wanting to let go. Eric rocked against me, thrusting in a slow, tortuous rhythm. Suddenly he gave one powerful thrust—then he paused, seated deep inside me. I shifted my hips, urging him to move, but he remained frozen.

"I was so fucking scared," he murmured against my lips. "I thought I'd lost you."

I opened my mouth to speak, but he cut me off with another hard, fierce kiss. He framed my face with one hand, directing my gaze to his. His eyes were dark, full of emotion. "You're mine, Jules. *Mine.* I love you so goddamn much."

Afraid my heart might burst from my chest if I tried to put my feelings into words, I dug my nails into his shoulders and dragged him back to me. He claimed my mouth once more, tongue sweeping over mine, sucking and licking every inch of my mouth. His muscles contracted as he pulled out, then slammed back in, taking my breath away.

Surrounded by the heat of the fire, Eric's body wrapped around mine, I began to spiral out of control. A low buzz filled my ears as electricity zipped along my nerve endings. My legs tightened around Eric's waist as he thrust hard and deep, sending me over the edge with a ragged cry. His pace increased, and he pumped in and out several more times before pulling out and letting out a soft groan as he came.

He lay heavily on top of me, and I turned my head to speak against his ear. "I love you."

They were the easiest three words I'd ever said.

Soft, warm lips brushed the back of my neck, and I shifted in Eric's arms. "Again?" I grumbled without heat.

His deep, rusty chuckle vibrated through me. "Can't blame a guy for trying."

I grinned and rolled toward him, love filling every inch of me as I stared into his hazel eyes. "You're going to be the death of me, you know that?"

"As long as you're by my side, I don't care when or how I go," he replied.

This man never ceased to surprise me. I pressed my palm to his cheek. "I love you."

His arm tightened around my waist and pulled me closer, as if he could meld our bodies into one entity. "Love you, baby. So much."

Sometime in the middle of the night, Eric had scooped me into his arms and carried me to the bed in the loft upstairs. Our lovemaking that time had been slower, more tender and loving. I couldn't decide which was my favorite. He wrought so many emotions in me, and I knew I wanted to spend a lifetime sorting through them.

We still hadn't talked much about the events of last night, but I knew I'd have to get it over with sooner or later. When Eric drew a deep breath, I knew my time to address it was right now.

"I hate to do this, but I guess now's as good a time as any. I need to head down to the station in a few to file an official report, and I'll need your statement."

I tipped my chin up to him. "Any chance we can come back here after we're done?"

A sexy grin curved his mouth. "I suppose I could find a couple reasons to take the day off."

One hand wandered to my breast, his thumb circling my nipple and drawing it out to a tight peak; the other went to my bottom as he rolled to his back, pulling me astride him.

I rotated my hips against him, his erection already straining and hard, eager to be inside me. "When did you say we have to leave?"

"That's the advantage of being sheriff," he remarked as he lifted my hips and guided his cock to my slick entrance. "No one will notice if I'm ten minutes late."

I sank down on top of him with a hiss. "Can we make it thirty?"

THIRTY-EIGHT

ERIC

Jules lay draped over me, still firmly in my embrace. I wasn't sure I'd ever let her go. Maybe if she asked nicely... but I seriously doubted it. After we'd filed Jules's official statement this morning, I'd taken the rest of the day off. The guys all understood, and after everything that had happened, I needed the reassurance of her body next to mine.

The results had come back this morning on the shell casing we'd found from the shooter's spot on the mountain. It was, in fact, a positive match to Josh. If only we'd gotten that report yesterday. It could have saved so much heartache.

From what I'd been able to piece together, Josh had been waiting for Jules when we got home yesterday evening. He'd called in the domestic dispute as a diversion, then sneaked into the house behind her. The garage door had a sensor on it that would prevent it from closing if something was in the way. I imagined that Jules had hit the button to close the garage, then entered the house, never realizing that the door hadn't closed the whole way.

I fought a shudder and hugged her more tightly to me.

Our chests rose and fell in tandem, my heart beating in rhythm with hers. This thing between us was so much more than sex. It was more than mutual attraction. A lifetime ago, I thought I loved my ex-wife. That was nothing compared to the way I felt with Jules. This love was pure and unadulterated, and she meant more to mean than anything in this world.

But with love came the inevitable fear and anxiety. Would she ever give me a glimpse of her past? My heart stuttered in my chest, and I swallowed hard, my throat suddenly dry. The last thing I wanted was to drive her away; but I had to know.

"Jules?"

"Mmm?" She sounded sleepy and sated, and it sent my pulse racing. I loved her so damn much it hurt.

"You know you can talk to me about anything, right?"

Her muscles tensed under my touch, and she took so long to respond that I was afraid she wouldn't. "I know."

"You ever going to tell me?" She knew what I was asking; there was no mistaking it.

Another long pause, then— "Someday."

Her voice was soft, reserved, but I heard the truth beneath the surface. Someday, when she trusted me, when she was ready, she would open up and tell me everything.

I nodded, my chin brushing the top of her head. "I'll be right here until that day comes."

She was silent for a long moment. "I promise I will. Soon."

I hoped that was true, but I wouldn't push her. I pulled her close once more and pressed my lips to her hair as she nestled her head against my shoulder. "Love you."

I decided it didn't matter, because in this moment, everything was perfect. Jules was here in my arms, and that was enough for now. All I wanted was to hold her tight and never let her go. And that's exactly what I did.

There's never a dull moment in Pine Ridge! When Jules is kidnapped in broad daylight, Eric will do anything to bring her home safely—even if it means going back to the one place he swore never to step foot in again. Keep reading for a sneak peek of <u>Beautiful Deception</u>!

BEAUTIFUL DECEPTION

GIULIANA

I stood at the counter and peered out the kitchen window into the bright morning light reflecting off the heavy layer of snow that had fallen last night, turning the backyard into a winter wonderland. Without warning, a pair of strong arms slipped around my waist.

"Morning, beautiful."

I leaned into Eric's warm body and tipped my head to the side, allowing him to drop a kiss on the slope of my neck. "I missed you last night."

"I know." I could hear the regret in his voice. "The Johanssons were at it again."

As sheriff of the small town of Pine Ridge, Eric took his job seriously. He was often called out in the middle of the night and though he had several deputies beneath him, he'd told me once that he felt an obligation to personally see to the citizens' safety. There was no doubt in my mind that he knew every single resident of Pine Ridge by name, and his protective and caring nature was evident in the way he handled his duties.

"I'm sorry." I snuggled further into his embrace. "I'd say I hope they'd learned their lesson, but..."

He chuckled, and his warm breath wafted across my cheek. "If they haven't figured it out yet, I doubt they ever will."

I wiggled my hips against his and felt the hard ridge of his arousal pressing into my bottom. His hands left my waist and slid down to the curve of my hips, his fingers curling into my flesh and pulling me close. I glanced at the clock and bit my lip. "Don't start something you can't finish."

He growled low in my ear, then nipped the soft flesh, making me jump. "I always finish, and so do you."

"But I can't take time to appreciate it properly," I complained without heat. I shivered as his mouth moved downward, his teeth skimming the cords of my throat.

"Only because I want to make sure you're properly taken care of."

It was true; he was notorious for spending an inordinate amount of time ensuring I derived as much pleasure from our lovemaking as possible, as many times as possible—and I loved every second of it.

"I would," I said regretfully, "but I have a meeting with Tony and Mia this morning to go over plans."

I loved my job at Briarleigh Lodge and Resort, a beautiful retreat for vacationers situated at the top of Mount Washington in northern Montana. Jack and Mia Prescott, the owners, were amazing to work for. Barely ten years older than myself, they were more like friends than employers. When I'd suggested the addition of a spa a couple of months ago, they'd immediately hopped onboard. Since then, Mia and I had been working nonstop to get everything ready for its grand opening. It had taken a lot of research and the application of multiple licenses, but everything was finally starting to fall into place.

"What time will you be done?"

I shrugged. "Probably normal time, as long as nothing crazy happens between now and then."

"Tonight then." Eric spun me in his arms and stared down at me for a moment. "But I'm not letting you go without this."

He took my mouth in a hard kiss, his tongue sliding over mine, and my knees went weak like they did every time he touched me. I'd never felt so cherished, so loved, as I did with him. I would forever be grateful that he found me on the side of the road that day nearly three months ago.

Born into the Capaldi crime family, I was a mafia princess and only daughter of the capo of the Chicago outfit. When my father was killed three years ago, my uncle took over, and things changed drastically. In an attempt to align the Italian and Russian families, Uncle Massimo arranged my marriage to the Bratva captain, Nikolai. My uncle was abusive and cruel, often locking me away in the dark, stifling closet for hours at a time, but I'd heard the swirling rumors that Nikolai was worse; his first two wives had disappeared without a trace, and I refused to be another statistic. With little more than the clothes on my back, I ran and never looked back. As I stood in the circle of Eric's arms, I had never been more thankful for anything in my life.

He broke the kiss, and I stared up at him, studying his features. He was a hard man, stronger than anyone I knew, but he would never hurt me. He'd saved me more times than I could count, not only from external threats, but from myself as well. In those early days, I'd been tempted to flee at the first sign of trouble. Eric had slowly coaxed me out of my shell, urging me to believe in him. And I did—I trusted him with my life.

"You okay?"

His brows drew slightly together as he stared down at me, and a smile slowly spread over my face. "Perfect."

He stared at me dubiously, and I tightened my hold on his

shirt where it was still clenched in my fists. "I was just thinking about how lucky I am."

His expression softened, and he pulled me infinitesimally closer. "You've got that wrong, babe." He dipped his head and brushed his lips over mine, soft and sweet. "I'm the lucky one."

I leaned into him for a long moment, soaking up the heat and solace his large body offered. His touch was like a balm to my soul. Sometimes in the still darkness of night, when I found myself feeling lost and adrift, I would reach for him. The second my skin touched his, my heart calmed, and my mind relaxed, the connection between us potent and undeniable.

I'd never before believed people who said their partner completed them; now I knew what they meant. It was the physical closeness, that deep level of trust I'd never found with another person. Eric was everything to me, literally the other half I hadn't known I was missing.

Peeling myself away, I peered up at him. "I should get going."

"I know." He framed my face with his large hands and dropped another soft kiss on my lips. "Have fun. And don't forget about dinner tonight."

A grin spread over my face. It was our first real date, and I was more excited than I should be. Though we'd been dating for almost two months, things had been hectic and I was glad the holidays were over so we could focus more on our relationship. There was a restaurant at the resort, but Eric had decided we deserved something special, so tonight we were headed down to a steakhouse in Kalispell to relax and unwind.

"I can't wait."

I stretched up on my toes and stole one more kiss before pulling away and grabbing my keys from the small table near the front door. Eric's searing gaze watched me the entire way, sending tendrils of heat curling through me.

God, I loved that man more than anything.

A smile on my face, I hopped down the two wide porch steps and bounded through the powdery layer of snow to my car. The little Cavalier had served me well, but I'd recently considered upgrading to an SUV. Eric had tried to buy something for me a few weeks back, but I'd turned him down. It wasn't that I didn't appreciate the gesture—I did. But he'd already done so much for me, and I didn't want to feel indebted to him more than I already did. I wanted him to know that I was with him because I loved him, not because of what he could offer me. More than that, I wanted to prove to myself that I could do it on my own. For the first time in my life, I had a job—one that I loved and that paid well—and I was determined to forge my own path through life.

I hummed a happy little tune as I navigated the short drive down to the lodge, then pulled into the employee lot and put the car in park. For the past couple of months, ever since the incident at Eric's house, we'd been staying in a cabin that had once belonged to Mia's late father, Bruce. It was empty and they had offered it up, not wanting to part with it. It was one of only a handful of homes high up on the mountain, and Jack and Mia's place was only a few miles away. It was private and peaceful, and an added bonus was that it was only a few minutes' drive to the resort.

My gaze lifted and I froze in place as an Escalade slowly drove down the narrow lane of parked cars. The sight hit me with the force of a freight train, bringing with it a thousand memories I thought I'd buried. Horror replaced my earlier joy, turning my blood to ice in my veins. I grabbed the steering wheel, holding on for dear life, ready to throw the car in drive and race away. All black with tinted windows, the huge SUV was the same high-end vehicle my uncle had chosen for himself and his men.

Heart banging against my ribcage, the sound echoing in my ears, I resisted the urge to slump down in my seat and hide away. Had Uncle Massimo finally found me? I held my breath as I studied the driver through the darkened side window. Dressed in what appeared to be a casual long-sleeved shirt, it wasn't the pristine suit I was expecting of the soldiers who worked for my uncle. Sunglasses and a ballcap obscured most of his face, but he didn't look familiar.

Thank God.

The Escalade rolled past, and my eyes darted to the license plate affixed to the back of the vehicle. South Dakota. I relaxed my hold on the steering wheel and slowly let out a relieved sigh. I'd half expected to see an Illinois plate on the bumper, some indication that the man had come all the way from Chicago to find me.

I watched as the Escalade stopped at the end of the row. The driver hesitated for several interminable seconds, then turned left toward the visitor parking lot. He was just lost, then.

My lungs deflated as I let out the breath I'd been holding and I pressed one hand to my chest, willing my heart to slow its rapid pace. I briefly closed my eyes and swallowed down the last of my fear. Uncle hadn't found me yet; he wouldn't. I'd left literally everything behind—clothes, cell phone, credit cards. I was untraceable and living in a remote mountain town. My fear was unfounded; I was safe.

Shaking off the lingering chill that clung to my spine, I slipped the keys from the ignition then climbed from the car and headed inside. A glance at my watch told me I had approximately forty minutes until our meeting with the supervisor. I jingled the keys as I walked, and I opened the pro shop first.

The manager Jack and Mia had hired would be here shortly, but I enjoyed opening each morning, getting everything ready in the peace and quiet before the bustle of the day began. Once it started, it wouldn't stop again until after midnight when the restaurant bar closed down.

I booted up the computer and glanced through yesterday's sales, making quick note of anything that needed to be restocked or reordered.

"Good morning!"

Jenn's happy voice cut through the still air, and I smiled at her as she approached the desk. "Morning."

I moved out of the way so she could use the computer to clock in, then she turned to me. "How was it yesterday?"

I handed her the papers. "Pretty decent for a Tuesday." I checked the clock on the computer. "All right. I'm off."

With a smile and a little wave, I headed down the long hallway toward the spa. Tony, the supervisor for the addition, stood outside the large oak doors, and he threw a smile my way. Somewhere in his late sixties, he was still handsome, salt and pepper flecking his dark hair. I wasn't terribly comfortable around most men, but Tony put off a fatherly vibe that had immediately set me at ease.

Mia joined us and for the next two hours, we discussed the progress of the spa. Each room of the facility had been framed in and plumbing and electricity had already been run. They planned to start the drywall next week, then the flooring would go in. The tile we'd chosen for the salon was backordered, but it wasn't a huge concern, according to Tony. All of the other materials were in the back waiting to be installed, so they could finish the salon once everything else was done.

We thanked Tony, then Mia turned to me, her eyes bright. "I have a surprise for you."

"Okay…" I drew out the word, confused.

"Close your eyes." I did as she asked, then her hands landed on my shoulders. "Now turn around three times."

"What? Why?"

"So you won't know where we're going." Her tone was tinged with exasperation, and I let out a little laugh.

"How will that help? I could just open my eyes if I really wanted to know."

Mia paused, and her hands lifted away from me. I could just imagine her gesticulating wildly as she spoke. "Whatever. You know what I mean. Baby brain."

A low chuckle met my ears, and my eyes popped open as Jack approached. "Don't let her fool you. That started long before she got pregnant."

I pressed my lips together to hide my smile as Mia leveled a haughty glare at her husband. "Are you intentionally trying to pick a fight?"

"Never." His expression never changed, but I could see the teasing glint in his eyes as he stared at her.

Mia lifted one brow at him. "Mhmm."

He stepped close as if to pass us by, then dipped his head and spoke low in her ear. Mia's cheeks turned pink, and she licked her lips as Jack straightened. He took her chin between his thumb and forefinger, then looked deep into her eyes for several long seconds. Finally, he released her and nodded toward me.

"Try to keep her in line."

I shrugged helplessly, a smile pulling at the corners of my mouth. "No promises."

"You're telling me," he murmured. With one more meaningful look at Mia, he turned and strode down the hall. My gaze drifted toward Mia as she watched her husband, a hungry look of longing etched on her face.

It was always interesting watching those two interact. Mia was perpetually bubbly while Jack was so intense. And yet it just… worked. I could feel the desire, the love crackling between the two of them, despite the fact that they were rarely—if ever— affectionate in public. I knew part of that was Mia's choice. Since she was partial owner of her late father's company, Hamilton Construction, I knew she felt she had to try twice as hard to be taken seriously in what people still considered a man's role.

"If you'd rather wait…"

Mia's head snapped toward me, and her eyes cleared. "No! I've been waiting all day for this."

I barely suppressed a smile. "It's barely eleven o'clock."

Pretty blue eyes rife with mock condescension glared at me. "You know what I mean."

I laughed, and she cracked a smile. "Seriously, this kid's killing me. I'm tired and hungry all the time, and I swear I'd forget my head if it wasn't attached."

"I'm sure that's normal," I assured her. Playing along with whatever scheme she'd concocted, I turned around and closed my eyes. "All right. I'm game."

Her hands fell to my shoulders once more, and she guided me forward. "No peeking."

"Okay, okay." Curiosity tugged at me as we passed the kitchen, the sounds of clanging pans giving away our location. Another minute later, Mia pulled me to a stop. "Okay… Open!"

I blinked my eyes open and came face-to-face with… A door? "Ummm…"

Mia moved to my right side and tipped her head toward the plaque hanging on the wall which read "Special Events Coordinator."

I whirled toward her. "What is this?"

A huge smile lit her face. "Your new office."

I turned back toward the oak door, emotion clogging my throat.

"I know we haven't talked about it," Mia spoke up, "but I wanted it to be a surprise. Even if you don't want the position, the office is still yours."

I swallowed hard and blinked away the tears of gratitude

that had formed while she spoke. "Mia, I... I don't know what to say."

She lifted her hands and spread her fingers wide. "I'm not an expert, but "yes" seems as good a response as any."

I covered my face with my hands, grinning like a fool. "Yes!"

"Yay!" Mia's arms came around me in a huge hug, and I held on tight.

Never in my life had I felt happier, more accepted than I did here. Months ago I'd arrived in Pine Ridge alone and scared, and badly in need of funds to keep me going. Eric found me on the side of the road when my car ran out of gas, and he'd called in a favor to Jack to hire me on. Now I had a man who loved me and friends and coworkers whom I adored.

Life truly didn't get any better than this.

Don't miss <u>Beautiful Deception, now available everywhere</u>!

ALSO BY MORGAN JAMES

QUENTIN SECURITY SERIES

Twisted Devil – Jason and Chloe

The Devil You Know – Blake and Victoria

Devil in the Details – Xander and Lydia

Devil in Disguise – Gavin and Kate

Heart of a Devil – Vince and Jana

Tempting the Devil – Clay and Abby

Devilish Intent – Con and Grace

Quentin Security Box Set One (Books 1-3)

Quentin Security Box Set Two (Books 4-6)

*Each book is a standalone within the series

RESCUE & REDEMPTION SERIES

Friendly Fire – Grayson and Claire

Cruel Vendetta – Drew and Emery

Silent Treatment – Finn and Harper

Reckless Pursuit – Aiden and Izzy

Dangerous Desires – Vaughn and Sienna

Cold Justice – Nick and Eden

Rescue & Redemption Box Set One (books 1-3)

RETRIBUTION SERIES

Unrequited Love – Jack and Mia, Book One

Unbreakable Love – Jack and Mia, Book Two

Pretty Little Lies – Eric and Jules, Book One

Beautiful Deception – Eric and Jules, Book Two

Hidden Truth – John and Josi

Sinful Illusions – Fox and Eva, Book One

Sinful Sacrament – Fox and Eva, Book Two

Retribution Series Box Set 1

Retribution Series Box Set 2

Retribution Series Box Set 3

The Complete Retribution Series

Thrillers and Mysteries

SECRETS OF BROOKHAVEN

Out of Sight

Out of Breath

Out of Time

STANDALONES

Dead of Winter

ABOUT THE AUTHOR

Morgan James is a USA Today bestselling author of contemporary and romantic suspense novels. She spent most of her childhood with her nose buried in a book, and she loves all things romantic, dark, and dirty. She currently resides in Ohio and is living happily ever after with her own alpha hero and their two kids.

Keep up with Morgan and stay up to date on sales, giveaways, and new releases:

Website | Facebook | Instagram | BookBub | Goodreads

www.ingramcontent.com/pod-product-compliance
Lightning Source LLC
Chambersburg PA
CBHW050835190726
48286CB00007B/2095